THE GHOST YOU CAN'T SEE

BOOK THREE OF
THE ISSACHAR GATEKEEPER

L. G. Nixon

Fitting Words

The Ghost You Can't See

Copyright © 2022 by L. G. Nixon

Published by Fitting Words—www.fittingwords.net

Library of Congress Cataloging-in-Publication Data
ISBN: 978-1-7379244-0-1

Don't miss any of the adventures!

THE ISSACHAR GATEKEEPER

To those whom I have loved:

You have left behind a legacy of kindness and a faith-filled journey.

May I be as bold as you.

And from the children of Issachar came men and women of honor who were strong and valiant.

They had understanding to know what to do; to do justice, to love kindness, and to walk humbly with their High King.

—The Chronicles of Ascalon

Table of Contents

Prologue

Bohemia, early thirteenth century

The scriptorium was a hive of activity. Candlelight flickered over the domed frescoed ceiling with scenes of prophets and scholars engaged in intellectual activities or sharing a cup of wine. The floor-to-ceiling bookcases were filled with books, manuscripts, and scrolls containing a vast amount of knowledge acquired and maintained over thousands of years. Chairs and pews usually lined the large hallway-like room, providing a comfortable resting place where the monks could sit and read. The scriptorium was one of the most beloved rooms in the old monastery.

But not tonight.

Tonight, rows of hooded monks huddled over wood tables, heads bowed, their quills scratching at huge vellum pages. They dipped their quills into the thick and pungent ink in small pewter pots, which magically refilled. They covered each page with details of a hideous, vile, and mysterious knowledge of ancient magic. They also documented spells, forbidden languages, and good and evil images. The information punctured and invaded their minds. Their handwriting, identical in every detail, was not their own. It belonged to the Dark Prince who had uttered the curse. Now, even the knowledge contained in all their books could not help the black-robed monks break the spell.

Somewhere in the ancient church, a clock tolled the hour, the deep tones echoing unnaturally along the corridors in the oppressive darkness. Tonight, the tones were discordant and jarring, symbolic of the terrors inside the old monastery. The windows were a dark backdrop reflecting the room's abnormal activity, the candlelight quivering in the panes.

The Dark Prince meandered among the writing tables, his hand elegantly floating up and down as though he were conducting a symphony orchestra. His footsteps were loud in the relative silence of the room, his boot heels thudding against the flagstones. He stopped and lazily considered the monk before him as a devious smile creased his face. The Dark Prince leaned over the desk and pushed the monk's hood back to reveal the man's face. The monk was sweating.

"Herman, what's this?" Darnathian asked innocently. He pulled a chair close and sat, leaning toward the monk. "You're sweating profusely. Is the temperature in the room too warm for you? I can remove a few of the fires in the grates if that would make you more comfortable." He made a pretense of glancing about the room. Evenly spaced along the inner walls, recessed stone fireplaces danced with low, glowing fires, which kept the scriptorium dry and comfortable. The room's stone construction meant it was warm in the winter months and cooler in the summer. The green flames danced with grotesque images and tickled the cursed logs without consuming them, emitting an even heat.

"No, my lord, it's quite all right. It's very comfortable, really it is," Herman the Recluse said. "No need to put the fires out." Herman shook uncontrollably under Darnathian's scrutiny.

"Do be careful, Herman. It would be a shame if your nervousness caused you to make any mistakes in my Codex," Darnathian whispered. "I would have to punish one of your brothers for your indiscretion. I'm sure you wouldn't want that to happen, would you?" He stared steadily at the monk, his eyes glowing like liquid amber. Darnathian leaned back in the chair and stretched his long legs, then pulled the tails of his riding cape over the tops of his thigh-high boots.

"No, no, my lord, please don't hurt them. The fault is all my own! I'll be cautious. You have my word," Herman whimpered. His hand shook as he dipped his quill into the ink again. A drop of bloodred ink hung suspended on the tip. He quickly laid it to the vellum and continued scribing, detailing the images in the page's margin as they appeared in his mind.

"There's a good man," Darnathian quipped, leaning forward to pat the monk on the shoulder. "My Codex will be an invaluable source to human-kind one day. You mustn't make any mistakes in the scribing. Do you understand, Herman?"

Herman's head bobbed violently up and down. His eyes darted quickly to the Dark Prince before returning to the vellum in front of him. Even the flame of the cursed candle shook in Darnathian's presence. Herman swallowed hard.

"Whatever did a sniveling little snippet of a man like you do wrong to be sentenced to death, I wonder?" Darnathian mused. "Such a magnificent punishment it was going to be too. You were to be ensconced permanently into the walls of your beloved monastery. It's something I would have thought of." He held up a hand and smirked. "Wait! I have done that before! Has one of your brothers been reading from my book?" Darnathian threw his head back and laughed heartily. He stood, straightened his cape, and strode to the next desk to inspect the monk's work.

Herman shuddered in his chair. His hand, compelled to keep writing, ached from the effort. He had been scribing for several long hours already, and he was exhausted, not only physically but emotionally and spiritually. Although Darnathian had saved him from a heinous punishment, the cost had been his soul. Herman was regretting the deal he had made with the

Dark Prince. His poor, selfish choices were responsible for his predicament, and now those same actions were bringing repercussions on his brethren. The brethren would survive, but they would suffer lifelong trauma from their touch of evil, and it was his fault. If he had taken his punishment, then none of this would be happening.

While Herman considered his nearly empty inkpot, the well was refilled with the bloodred ink, bubbling to the brim, and threatening to overflow. *What evil magic is this?* Herman wondered, his quill shaking in his hand. He glanced around the room at his brethren as they furiously dipped and scribed, filling the pages before them. As each page was completed, it levitated and floated to a long table in the middle of the room and fluttered down on top of the preceding pages.

Curious, Herman rose, stretched his aching limbs, and quietly approached the table. The number of pages was staggering. He leaned cautiously over the last page as it nestled into the stack. He couldn't believe his eyes. Every page was filled with identical penmanship, as though one person had scribed the entire manuscript. He read the inscriptions, and his mouth dropped open in awe and wonder. It was a complete section of the Ascalonian text, and each word was recorded truthfully from the Chronicles of Ascalon.

His hands shook as he carefully turned the last page over. The text was undeniably from the Chronicles. *What is this monstrosity?* Herman thought. *A compilation of all knowledge? How can this be?* Turning over several more pages, he discovered a shocking inscription called Darnathian's Prayer. The blasphemous text sent terror rumbling through his core. *Oh no!* He thought. *It cannot be allowed to happen. I am doomed already, but this must never see the light of day!*

Glancing at Darnathian inspecting yet another brethren's scribing, then to the corner where the daemons lurked, Herman turned aside and surreptitiously rolled up the pages containing the prayer. He stuffed them in his robe, tucking them securely beneath the rope he wore as a belt around his waist. Then he slowly walked toward the large double library doors and reached for the latch.

"You there!" Darnathian's voice boomed through the room. "Where are you going?" His footfalls echoed on the stone floor as he strode quickly toward the quivering monk whose hand tensed on the door latch.

"It's just me, my lord. I need to stretch my legs a bit—if I may? I get quite stiff after sitting for so long. Not as young as I used to be, you know," Herman squeaked. His entire body shook, his robe quivering as if in a breeze. "I won't be long, my lord, I promise. Just a turn or two around the courtyard will do." He held his breath, willing himself to maintain eye contact with the Dark Prince, and prayed Darnathian wouldn't discover his actions before he hid the documents.

The Dark Prince considered him carefully. He casually flipped a hand, waving the monk aside. "Be quick with it then. Just make sure you don't get lost on the way back." He returned to his inspection and forgot about the monk named Herman the Recluse.

Something Peeking

Lucy grimaced as the enormous grandfather clock tilted precariously, slid to one side, and nearly flipped the wheeled hand truck it balanced on. There was a collective gasp from the three women in the foyer who awaited its arrival.

Standing with Schuyler in the archway of the formal dining room, she watched the scene unfold. Lucy glanced at each of the women. Her mom, Jeannie, was wide-eyed and anxious, while her grandmother, Leona Elliot, had a hand clasped over her mouth. Mrs. McGoo, their neighbor and bene-factress, was glaring at the three workmen in grubby overalls.

Lucy held her breath, brows raised and eyes wide, as the workmen pushed and tugged the behemoth through threshold of the double door-way. The cart's wheels squealed in protest of the extreme weight it carried. The men, their feet slipping, dragged the clock into the foyer across the restored wood flooring of the recently established Carriage House Bed-and-Breakfast. They set it upright with a thump and a precarious wobble before it came to a standstill. A piercing shriek emanated from somewhere near the clock. Startled, Lucy leaned backward.

"Good heavens!" Grandma Elliot gasped. "What was that sound?" She glanced from Jeannie to Mrs. McGoo. Jeannie stood open-mouthed and speechless while Mrs. McGoo eyed the clock suspiciously.

The three men glanced at each other. The one who'd introduced himself as Fergus inspected the wheels before turning toward the women. He shrugged his shoulders nearly to his ears, then unstrapped the clock from the cart.

George, the second man, whose face was as red as his damp hair, pulled a hanky from his pocket and mopped his forehead while casting his gaze at the clock. "Och, but tha' there's a beast of a clock, it is," he said in a thick brogue. "Tha's gotta be the biggest ol' longcase I ever seen. It's surely the heaviest." He dabbed at the sweat beading on his cheeks.

"Ay, that it is," Fergus drawled. "And the strangest-looking clock to be sure." He nodded sagely and swiped his sleeve across the perspiration on his brow, causing his own bushy red eyebrows to stand up at odd angles. "Dun't rightly know what the man tha' made it was thinkin'. It's old, tha's for sure." After a beat, he added, "Well, guess we shouldn'a dawdle. I'll go fetch dat brass." He went down the porch steps toward the clock smith's truck parked on the side street.

The third man said nothing but turned and followed Fergus to the truck. George picked up the straps and blankets, tossed them on the cart, and wheeled it out the door, leaving the ladies to gawk at the strange clock.

It had stopped working centuries before, and no one could seem to figure out why. But the old clock's uniqueness surpassed its need to be functional.

The hardwood casing was dark with age and had been polished until it was silky smooth and gleamed with vitality. It featured a cobble of styles and wood species that had been masterfully joined. Its rather large, round, and simple face was scratched and yellowed with age, and its reddish-brown wood bonnet had a fancy, pointed finial on top.

The neck and huge circular center section contained the access door and porthole window for viewing the pendulum and comprised yet another wood species that, while lighter, was stained with inky blue blotches, like measles. A round circle section balanced on an elongated stretch of dark wood that flared slightly before settling on a squashed base that fairly oozed to the floor, like a blob of melted brown candle wax. Carved feet, like lion paws, peeked from under the bottom.

"What's up with the weird antiques?" Lucy scrunched her face as if she'd swallowed a lemon and clenched her jaw in a grimace. She stepped closer to the enormous clock, the top of which reached almost to the bottom of the chandelier suspended from the high ceiling. The behemoth clock stood at nearly ten feet tall and was at least four feet wide and two-and-a-half-feet deep, large enough for a man to stand in.

"I'm gonna need a ladder to dust this thing! What's it doing here?" Lucy said, taking in all the details of the monstrosity. She tucked her shoulder-length nut-brown hair behind her ears and stared at the clock face. Her mouth dropped open, then clamped shut with a pop.

Its tarnished hour hand was like a short, stubby human arm, the bent elbow included. It ended with a hand, three fingers of which were folded into the palm while the thumb and index finger pointed at the numbers. The minute hand, in contrast, was painfully long, thin, and tarnished. Its swordlike point was needle sharp, with a curved grim-reaper sickle beneath the point.

Lucy waggled her head in disbelief, then peered into the portal and flinched. Two beady red eyes in a humanlike face blinked back at her. She peered closer, but the anomaly was gone. While it might be her distorted reflection in the glass or her overactive imagination causing her to see things, it was more likely her distrust of antiques. The house had received a blessing, so no entities could sneak in. She turned, blocking the portal with her body—just in case.

"Where on earth did this thing come from, anyway?" she asked, thumbing at the strange structure behind her. "And what are we gonna do with it?" She folded her arms in a defiant stance. "I vote we move it out to the barn."

"It's the last of the antiques from your great-aunt Isabel," Mom said, "and it's not going to the barn! I thought about selling it, but I can't. The clock is so unique, and Aunt Isabel loved it. Besides, it doesn't work; it never has." She lovingly patted the old wood as she gazed up at the insipid clock face. "I guess that's what makes it special. It's supposed to have come from a thirteenth-century monastery, you know."

"You mean one of those places where the men wear robes and sit around all day chanting? Well, its weirdness does kind of go with the giant bat-eating-an-octopus chandelier."

Mom harrumphed and pursed her lips.

"I'm just stating the obvious." Lucy pointed at the light. The chandelier was original to the old Victorian house. After a thorough cleaning, polishing, and rewiring, the details were still unfortunate. It really was an octopus being engulfed by a large bat, the bulbous head hanging upside down on the bottom. At least it was shiny, with new replica glass globes on each of the eight spindly arms.

"I stand by my original statement," Mrs. McGoo said. "Whoever thought that thing would be nice to look at? For goodness' sake." She crossed her arms, her lips pursed in a lopsided pucker. Lucy snorted. Mrs. McGoo was a kindred spirit. Schuyler snickered behind her hand.

"Well, I like both, so they stay. And that's that," Mom said, stomping down the hall toward the kitchen. "I'll get the workmen some cold water. They seem to need it."

"I brought sandwiches for lunch, so I'll come help you, Jeannie," Mrs. McGoo said, following Lucy's mom. Grandma Elliot winked at the girls and joined the ladies in the kitchen.

"Schuyler, quick." Lucy jerked her head toward the clock, then glanced down the hall. The ladies were chatting, and the men hadn't returned yet. Schuyler peeked through the round glass portal. The dark interior appeared to be empty.

"You saw that thing, didn't you? It was like a weird, scrunched-up human face," Lucy whispered.

Schuyler nodded. "Do you think it's haunted?" She twirled her magical bracelet nervously around her wrist.

"Dunno, but I know this—the house is blessed, so nothing can attack us. If there is a spirit in there, it can't get out. The blessing covers everything and everyone within the house. I'll scope it while no one is around."

"But where would it go? It's not there now." Schuyler went to the foyer door and peeked out. "All clear—the workers are chatting by their truck."

Lucy grabbed her backpack from behind the guest check-in desk. The desk was reminiscent of an eighteen-hundreds-era hotel registry counter. Painted white and topped with a gray granite top, its curved design was elegant but simple. She unzipped the bag and pulled out the artifact.

The Spectrescope appeared to be a large magnifying scope, but it allowed her to see and track ghosts. It was one of several magical artifacts that had been in the carved wood trunk she purchased one day from a vendor at the flea market. Made of an unknown metal, the runes around the handle could morph into different shapes to transmit messages, and removing the big lens allowed the Spirit Sword to emerge from the handle with an ethereal blue light.

Lucy chanced another glance toward the kitchen where the women were talking, then quietly unlatched the clock door and swung it open, peering inside. The Spectrescope hung limp in her hand as she stood, too dumbfounded for words.

While the exterior was unadorned and utilitarian, the interior of the clock was unlike anything she could have imagined.

The clock was inside out.

One interior wall of the cabinet held a carving of a woman's face. The caricature's eyes were closed, her face contorted in a grimace with brows scrunched and mouth downturned at the corners. A frame with vines and leaves, each tendril ending in a serpent's head with its mouth open, surrounded the woman's head. Below her was a carving of a basket carried by two women with scruffy wings.

On the back panel, two carved tree-like columns reached from the floor to the top, each with an effigy, a man on the left and a woman on the right. The woman clutched her garment at the throat with one hand, the other arm and hand reached forward. Both intricately carved forms were captured in flowing detail as they burst from the tree trunks, as though fleeing some unseen terror. The roots of the tree crawled along the sides of the cabinet and wound their way through carvings of animals with human faces. The floor itself was stone.

More carvings adorned the other sidewall. The hideous creatures were beyond imagination. Lucy glimpsed several gargoyles among the carvings of wood nymphs, their tongues scrolling amid wild hair and eyes. In the middle was a sculpture of a man's face, angry and menacing, with a flowing mustache and beard. Since it was directly opposite the panel of the woman, it appeared to be scowling at her. Leaves sprouted around his head and tangled his hair. The detail was amazing.

"Lucy," Schuyler whispered, nudging her in the shoulder. Lucy finally clamped her mouth shut, raised the Spectrescope, and searched the interior.

"Did you find the spirit? Is the clock haunted?" It was warm in the old Victorian; the air-conditioning was yet to be installed. Lucy could hear Schuyler fidgeting, probably trying to tuck her frizzing curls behind her ears.

Lucy stepped aside and pointed. "See for yourself."

Schuyler leaned in and gasped. "Are you kidding me? It's like the clock-maker assembled this thing inside out!" She stepped back and turned a bewildered face to Lucy. "Who does that? But—is it haunted? This is so creepy; it must be haunted."

"I don't think so. The Spectrescope didn't reveal any ghosts or spirits hiding inside, and there was no purple residue from spirit activity. But I think something else is there." Lucy examined the woman's face and ran her hand over the vines. They felt rubbery to the touch. "This reminds me of a door knocker but without the iron ring. There must be a secret compartment behind this panel."

"Why would there be a door knocker on a panel on the inside of a clock cabinet?" Schuyler waggled her head. "This gets stranger by the minute."

"You didn't see or feel anything rush past you when I opened the door, did you?" Lucy asked, slipping the scope in her jean's waistband and pulling her T-shirt over it.

"No." Schuyler shrugged. "But where would it go? If the blessing prevents it from getting out, then—"

"It's still in there." Retrieving a small flashlight from the backpack, Lucy moved the beam over the interior walls, searching for a place the entity could hide. "I still don't see where it could have gone." The beam flashed over the face of the angry man. Lucy flinched, sure that she'd seen the eyes move. But when she looked again, it was only a carving. *It was probably just the play of light over its features*, she thought. *At least, I hope so.*

"This is major weirdness, and knowing what we do about magical antiques, it's truly disturbing," Schuyler said. She pointed at the clock face. "Those clock hands are so macabre. What's up with that?"

"No clue," Lucy said, grabbing the carved heads of the man and the woman and giving them a swift tug. They didn't move. "It probably means, 'Your time is up.' I bet some old dude thought it was a clever idea to scare little kids. Sheesh." The cabinet muffled her voice. She wiggled farther in as she probed the bottom panel for any sign of a compartment.

"Lucy Hornberger! What are you doing inside my clock?" Mom bellowed. She grabbed Lucy by the shirt and pulled her out of the clock.

"I'm not hurting anything!" Lucy stood and flicked off the flashlight beam. "I was just inspecting the carvings!"

"Well, inspect something else besides my clock! This is a priceless antique, and I don't want you messing around with it," Mom groused.

"Fine! I'll look elsewhere. When's lunch?"

"Lucy, sometimes you can be so—what carvings?" Mom said, her brows scrunching.

"The carvings on the inside of the cabinet." Lucy rolled her eyes. "Some old dude assembled the clock inside out."

Mom pursed her lips, snatched the flashlight, and flicked it on. Passing the light over the old wood, she studied the inside of the cabinet. "It's just a bunch of old scratches. Maybe it's the clockmaker's signature and date. It's hard to tell." She handed the flashlight back, folded her arms, and harrumphed. "Carvings indeed."

"See? I didn't hurt anything," Lucy said, tossing the flashlight into her bag and crossing her arms too.

The workmen entered the foyer and paused, glancing from Lucy to her mom. Jeannie waved an impatient hand at them, urging them to continue.

"Lunch is happening now, girls, if you're hungry," Grandma Elliot called, standing in the kitchen doorway. Her bouncing finger urged them toward the kitchen and away from Jeannie.

"C'mon, let's get some lunch," Lucy said, leaving her mom to direct the workmen where to place the clock.

"Ooh! Good idea," Schuyler said. "I'm hungry."

Lucy snorted. "When are you ever not hungry?" She ducked as Schuyler swiped a hand at her head. "You're always hungry, girlfriend." Schuyler lifted her chin as if she were ignoring Lucy.

"Sandwiches and snacks are on the counter, and sparkling water is in the refrigerator," Grandma said, placing a soft hand on Lucy's arm and halting her. "Give your mom a little space, okay?" she whispered. "It's more complicated than you know, with all the renovations, the move-in, and the licensing to set up a hospitality business and an antique shop. Jeannie is stressed, so put a sock in it." Grandma Elliot raised one eyebrow as she scrutinized Lucy over the rim of her eyeglasses.

"Uh, yeah, okay," Lucy said. "You're right, Grandma. I'm sorry." A smirk dimpled her cheeks. "If I have to put a sock in it, can I at least use a clean sock?"

Grandma burst out laughing. "Oh, go on, you." She gently steered her granddaughter through the doorway into the kitchen. "Are you staying for dinner tonight, Schuyler?" she asked.

Schuyler nodded. "Yes, please, and overnight too. My mom and dad have dinner plans tonight, so they will be home late." She joined Lucy at the counter and pulled out an upholstered chair.

"Well, we are grateful for your help. It's a big job getting everything unpacked, settled, and placed." Grandma Elliot placed a platter of sandwiches on the counter.

"I guess that makes Schuyler the first official guest of the Carriage House Bed-and-Breakfast!" Mrs. McGoo said with a laugh and a wink at Schuyler, then she returned to her search for the plates and cutlery. There were numerous cupboards and drawers.

"Hmm," Lucy said with a smile. "You're not a guest. You're family."

"This is kind of fun, don't you think?" Schuyler settled into the chair and placed a napkin across her lap. "I love this place. It feels like a new house after all the renovations. Mrs. Walters would never recognize it, but I bet she would love it." She took a piece of fruit from a woven basket on the counter. "The white cabinets with the gray marble countertops are so chic. I never would have thought of eliminating the upper cabinets and replacing them with all the windows. It makes the room feel big and bright. It's brilliant. And I love the patterned tile backsplash."

"It's only brilliant until someone has to wash all those windows, which will probably be me," Lucy grumbled. "Or maybe I'll get lucky and Mom will hire a window-cleaning service."

"Don't count on it," Mom hollered from the breakfast room. Lucy grimaced.

"B and Bs are better than a hotel. It's like coming home." Schuyler peeled the banana and took a bite. "My mom is excited to make the pastries for your guests. She's been planning the breakfast menus for weeks now and loving it."

"Hey, if I see your mom's chocolate triple-berry torte on the menu, I'll be excited too!" Lucy laughed. "It would be a staple in my diet if I knew how to bake like your mom. Maybe we can get her to make it more often. We can say it's for the guests."

"Trust me," Schuyler said, rolling her eyes, "I've tried, and she won't. She says it's time consuming to make and only for special occasions." She neatly folded the empty banana peel and laid it next to her plate. "So, what are we going to do about the thing inside the clock?" she whispered. "There was definitely something peeking."

"You know, it kind of reminds me of the vanishing staircase when we were hunting Darwin Stewart. So, maybe it's—"

"It's a portal!" Schuyler placed a hand on her cheek. "So, what should we do?"

"After everyone goes to bed tonight, we'll investigate it." Lucy waggled her eyebrows. "Got armor?"

"Oh boy," Schuyler replied, looking heavenward. "I've got a bad feeling about this."

The small Georgian mantle clock in the parlor played a series of chimes before it made three distinct bongs, its mournful sound barely registering in the rest of the large house. The moonlight waning through the windows on either side of the front door cast feeble shadows across the foyer, which added to the girls' apprehension. They stole quietly down the stairs.

Lucy sat on the bottom stairstep, the Spectrescope in her lap, and stared at the huge monastery clock. Schuyler sat beside her with her knees folded to her chest, her arms wrapped around them.

The foyer was clear of moving cartons at last. Lucy and her family were now settled into their new home, and while she knew she should be excited, she wasn't. Her mom had used the inheritance from Great-Aunt Isabel to purchase the old Victorian home from Mrs. Walters. After their home had burned in a mysterious fire, they'd lived with the McGoos until the renovations were done and the house was ready to move in.

Built in the late eighteen hundreds, the Walters house once served as a carriage stop along the Michigan and Indiana stagecoach route. The newly renovated Victorian home was now called the Carriage House Bed-and-Breakfast. It was farmhouse chic, blending antiques with modern amenities. The result was casual, classy, and comfortable—everything a bed-and-breakfast establishment should be. Mom's dream was to own a bed-and-breakfast. Lucy didn't see the appeal.

Balancing her elbows on her knees, Lucy dropped her head in her hands, wondering how the old clock had survived for centuries when she barely felt able to survive until the end of the week.

The move to their new home was bittersweet. Lucy missed the creaky old house that had always been home, but the house was gone, and the lot was empty. Darnathian, the Dark Prince, had tried to destroy Lucy and her magical artifacts, but instead he'd burned down her house and killed her cat. The Hornbergers would have been homeless if not for the generosity of their neighbors, Bill and Vivian McGoo, whom Lucy loved. They were her guardian angels sent by the High King to guide her. They also worked at the school where Lucy and Schuyler attended. It was good to know help was so near.

Once the barn renovations were complete, the McGoos and Grandma Elliot would move into the new loft apartments, and the converted horse stalls would become a shop called the Carriage House Gifts and Antiques. Grandma Elliot would return to Grand Traverse Bay tomorrow to sell the home she'd shared with Great-Aunt Isabel.

Lucy sighed. Her mind was a jumble of thoughts—so many changes in such a short time. She was finding it difficult to adjust to the new house, and now she had an anomaly inside the monastery clock to vanquish too. And where was Iam in all of this? She hadn't seen him in days.

Schuyler bumped her shoulder.

"Penny for your thoughts?" Schuyler yawned and twirled her bracelet. She wore her magical vest with her pajamas and sneakers, and her blond curls stuck out from under the beret. "You've been restless since we started unpacking and setting up the house. Aren't you excited about the move? Or are you worried about the haunted monstrosity over there?"

Schuyler shuddered. The shadowy form across the room was bigger than the Grigori—or the watchers, as they called themselves—that they had vanquished at the school and, later, at Lucy's house. She pulled the vest closer to her chest.

"No, yeah, maybe," Lucy mumbled. "I dunno. This past year and a half has been crazy, don't you think? Finding out there's a spiritual realm coexisting along with our reality, filled with good spirits and evil spirits. I never believed in the supernatural before. It's a little overwhelming to find out it's very real." She caressed the Spectrescope in her lap. "I'm glad though. I might never have met Iam, the High King." She turned to face her friend. "What if we had never gone to the flea market that day? I mean, would we even have met him? Now that I know him, I can't imagine not having him in my life! I love him so much."

"I know what you mean." Schuyler smiled and twirled a lock of hair. "I find it amazing he was there that day to meet you. The Spectrescope chose you, but you didn't have to keep it or choose to believe. But you did. Then we went to the flea market together, and we both met him. Think about it—the High King chose *us*." She bumped shoulders with Lucy again. "So, cheer up grumpy pants."

"Look at you, getting philosophical and all. You're right though. It's amazing. It's scary, too, how close we came to missing him, to missing all of this," Lucy said, waggling the Spectrescope. "Now it makes so much sense. You and I, and everyone we love, are eternal spirits, endowed with knowledge and a need to know—"

Click! The clock door unlatched. Lucy raised the Spectrescope, her hand on the lens head, ready to remove it to reveal the Spirit Sword.

The door eased opened a crack.

The girls shrank into the shadows along the stairs to watch and wait.

The door moved, the hinges moaning as it swung open, exposing the pitch-black interior. Soon, a pale face with a long nose appeared in the opening, tufts of sparse hair sprouting erratically about his mostly bald head.

Lucy's lips pressed together with a scowl. A quick glance told her Schuyler was feeling the same emotion at the unexpected appearance of the toady little daemon. Their previous failed encounter with the creature still rankled Lucy. He was the one daemon they hadn't gotten to vanquish, but at least he hadn't returned before now.

"Ooh, Master will be so pleased with Grehssil, he will," the daemon said, his head bobbing like a pigeon. "Finally, the door is open, it is, and

Grehssil figured out the spell to do it." The creature giggled quietly and gleefully rubbed his hands together, his head rubbernecking as he prepared to step out of the clock portal. He lifted his scrawny foot and placed one leg over the threshold.

And promptly got *zapped.*

His legs went stiff, and his arms clamped to his sides, his body thrashing and convulsing uncontrollably, as though several thousand millijoules coursed through his muscles.

Lucy and Schuyler smothered their mouths and doubled over, giggling, tears streaming down their faces. It couldn't have happened to a more annoying creature.

The daemon finally collapsed backward, disappearing into the dark interior. The clock door swung on its hinges and closed with a thump.

The girls did an exploding fist bump.

Grehssil had been Tasered.

A Hair-Raising Event

Grehssil sat whimpering and quivering in Darnathian's office. Cradling his broken arm, he rocked back and forth in the strange chair as it conformed to his body, shrinking to fit the contours of his bony frame. The chair, with menacing ram-like horns on the backrest and pointed oxbow horns on the arms, made whoever sat in it appear to be sprouting pointy appendages.

Although Grehssil found the chair comfortable, it was altogether disconcerting, knowing, as he did, dark magic had made it. He fully expected the rocking chair to wallop him with a bowling ball. He shuddered, surreptitiously glancing about for the heavy balls.

Early on, the master had been fond of the odd game of bowling and had a bowling lane installed with an automatic ball return in the entertainment wing of the middle dungeons, where the supersized swimming pool, indoor tennis court, and the torture chambers were located. But after he botched several games in a row, Darnathian had become enraged; he was not used to losing. The Master abandoned the game, and the wood lane reconfigured into the chair with the bowling pins styled into grips on the end of the arms and the tips of the rockers.

The Master fumed now over Grehssil's failed attempt to access the Hornberger's new house. He paced the length of the vast chamber. The bookcases overflowed with tomes, books, and ancient manuscripts, lining the walls from floor to high ceiling. An iron spiral staircase in the corner provided access to the upper bookcases on the balcony that circled the room. The massive fireplace in the center of one wall belched heat into an already too-warm room. A large, gilded cage hung under the mezzanine.

The only spaces not filled with books held tall, mullioned windows showcasing the rolling mountains that surrounded the castle. More manuscripts covered the large carved desk in the center of the room.

"What the blazes were you thinking, you fool?" Darnathian slammed a fist on the desk, startling the daemon. "It has taken centuries for that portal to open, and now you may have alerted someone to its existence!"

"Grehssil is sorry, he is," the daemon said, his drooping head wobbling side to side. "I was excited, I was, to see the portal open. I thought if I found the Spectrescope, Master would be happy with Grehssil. And now my arm is broken, hurt it does. Can you fix it, Master?" Grehssil moaned with pain. He watched Darnathian expectantly, not comprehending how close he was to annihilation. This was another in a long line of foolhardy endeavors by the scrawny daemon.

"Did anyone see you?" Darnathian quit pacing and observed Grehssil with angry eyes, the color of glowing embers. "Where was that dratted Lucy Hornberger?"

"No, Master, no one saw, they didn't. The Hornberger girl wasn't there. No, no. They placed the old monastery clock in the foyer. It was late, and everyone was sleeping." He held his arm up, waiting for the master to fix it. The daemon's bulbous eyes implored the dark prince to be magnanimous.

"How did you break your arm?"

"I fell," Grehssil murmured. Darnathian shook his head.

"Why didn't you get through the portal into the house?"

"The house must have a powerful, strong blessing on it. Grehssil could not leave the clock. As soon as I stepped over the threshold, I got zapped, then I fainted and fell down the stairs."

"Zapped?"

"Yes, Master. Zapped, electrocuted, fried. Hurt bad, it did. Grehssil's hair is curly now." He pointed at a curly tuft.

"At least that's something," Darnathian growled, leaning over his desk. He took a small glass vial from the drawer and held it up. The golden-blond strands of hair shimmered in the light from the windows. A smile crept across his face, evil and cunning. He turned and tossed the vial to the daemon. Grehssil fumbled it and almost dropped it on the floor.

"Be careful, fool!"

"I didn't drop it, I didn't. What would you be wanting Grehssil to do with it?" He rolled the vial about in his hand, admiring the lustrous strands of hair.

"Take it to Stolas. He'll know what to do."

Grehssil's arm still tingled painfully. The Master had waved his hand over the bones and whispered an incantation. The bones had crawled like worms under the skin. Grehssil was still ill, his stomach churning inside his belly. But it was over, and the bones were knit back together.

The torches in the charred wall sconces flickered a feeble light over the stone corridor as Grehssil's shuffling feet carried him further into the recesses beneath the castle. Beyond lay the lab where Stolas experimented with herbs and plants and concocted his special remedies. His lab door was closed, and the painted wood Do Not Disturb sign hung there on a peg. Grehssil knocked.

The Ghost You Can't See

"What is it?" Stolas's muffled voice demanded. Grehssil heard a whir-ring sound coming from behind the door as some infernal machine blended a new concoction.

"It's Grehssil! Master has a project for you." The daemon waited as Stolas scurried to the door, his talons clacking against the rough stone floor on this level. The door whipped open, and a very impatient owl with impossibly long, skinny legs stood in the doorway.

"Oh, very well. Come in if you must, and make it quick. I have an experiment running, and I can't be bothered. What is it this time?" If not for his demeanor, and the fact he was a daemon, Stolas would almost be enchanting. His large black pupils were startling against brilliant gold irises surrounded by dark leathery skin, all set in a soft, fuzzy circle of brown and ivory feathers.

The overall effect was a permanently startled expression, which alone was humorous but became hilariously funny because of the tiny, jew-eled crown he wore on top of his head. But Grehssil knew that if he ever laughed, the owl would melt his skin off his brittle bones. Laughter was not tolerated in the lower dungeons of the castle. And certainly not by the divo herbologist.

"Master said to give this to you," Grehssil said, holding the glass vial. "What will you do with it?" Behind Stolas, Grehssil could see glass beakers filled with glowing substances that wafted tendrils of smoke into the air. He stood in the corridor. Entering the dark, stinky lab was always a risk.

"Oh, yes, yes. I remember seeing this before. I know exactly what to do with it. It will be my best creation yet." Stolas snatched the vial and slammed the door.

The Message in the Window

After Grehssil was gone, Lucy probed the clock's interior with the Spectrescope. The portal was closed, and the carvings were gone. She and Schuyler went back to bed but giggled into their pillows for the rest of the night. They finally fell asleep just before dawn.

When Lucy's mom knocked and opened the door to wake them for breakfast, Lucy awoke slumped over the edge of the bed, mouth hanging open, and an arm and a leg suspended in midair. Schuyler giggled in her sleep where she slept on the built-in daybed under the slanted ceiling at the end of the room.

"Wake up, girls. Breakfast is almost ready," Mom said. Lucy's eyes were blurry from a lack of sleep. She and Schuyler watched each other, struggling to stay awake. Mom shook her head, pinched her lips in a lopsided pucker, and closed the door.

They tumbled from the sheets and slowly made their beds, showered, and dressed. Lucy stopped in the viewing room on the guest level as she made her way downstairs.

It was a small room at the top of the stairs on the second floor. After they had defeated the ghost called Darwin Stewart, they had come to the house to close the portal to the dark side and discovered this room right before they encountered a wart-faced daemon. Everything was fine now; the daemon vanquished, the portal sealed, and the house blessed forever.

Lucy called it the viewing room because it held a beautiful stained glass window that filled one entire wall and a single bench seat like the ones found at an art gallery. The room was too small to be a bedroom or even a home office.

During the renovations, the designer, who called it outdated and childish, wanted to remove the window and turn it into a half-bath. Lucy's numerous entreaties had made the carpenters furious, put the designer in a huff, and frustrated Mom. However, Lucy prevailed, and the little sitting room remained safely unharmed.

"I love this room," Lucy said softly, almost to herself. She set the laundry basket she carried on the floor and stepped into the room.

"I'm so glad the designer came to her senses," Schuyler said. "I can't believe someone would want to turn this into a bathroom. It seems so disrespectful to the beautiful creatures in the glass." She sat next to Lucy on the little bench and gazed at the window, snickering. "Plus, two rolls of duct tape over the door and a sit-in probably helped too." Lucy snorted.

Today, the windowpanes were backlit by the morning sun, the colors illuminated and glowing. The lovely scene depicted dryads and fauns under a bountiful tree in the center of a meadow. The tree had a flame at its core. It was captivating and hauntingly mystical. The lifelike creatures were meticulously detailed. Knowing a little about the spiritual realms, Lucy hoped they were real and lived somewhere in the universe.

"Ooh! I smell bacon!" Schuyler said. "C'mon, let's go get breakfast. I need sustenance before your mom puts us to work again." She bounded through the door and down the stairs.

"Food and Schuyler. They're inseparable," Lucy said. She started closing the door behind her, then heard a giggle. Her head whipped around as she gaped at the mystical scene.

A dryad was giggling and waggling her fingers.

"Oh. My. Gosh!" Lucy exclaimed. Stepping back into the room she quickly shut the door and leaned against it. "You can hear me?" The dryad nodded, smiling.

"I can," she said, locks of her blond hair wavering as though lifted by a breeze. Near to her, a faun played a lively tune on his wooden flute and winked. Lucy laughed.

"Is this a portal?" She hurried to the window and placed a hand against the pane. The dryad shook her head, her smile faltering a little.

"How is this even possible?" Lucy grinned, gazing wondrously at the scene. The dryad's emerald dress rustled as she moved. Although she was one dimensional, she was beautiful. The faun pranced about the meadow with his instrument, his fingers dancing over the pipes. The melody was otherworldly.

"The High King has given us powers to use only for good," the dryad replied. "You are hearing this in your mind. This is how we can communicate."

"May I ask—who are you?"

"I am Haniel," she said with a laugh. "It means 'one who guards.' And this charming young faun is Pheman. His name means 'trust.' He keeps me company here in the meadow. He plays the most wonderful music."

"I don't want to seem unkind, but are you real?"

"Oh yes, dear Sho-are. We are quite real and alive. The window is only a facsimile to give you a glimpse of what is and to give you hope."

"I'm sorry. What's a Sho-are? I've heard the name before, but I don't remember what it means."

"It means Gatekeeper."

"Oh, yeah. Anyway, where are you?"

"I cannot tell you, only that we are here to protect the Life Tree. The imagery of the glass hides our location. It would be very dangerous for you, and for us, if our location should be discovered. The High King has placed a great a gulf between us that cannot be crossed. I'm sorry, Lucy."

"Because of Darnathian, the Dark Prince," Lucy growled, the joy dropping from her face.

"Yes. His Irredaemon and Ormarrs are everywhere, and they are always listening, gathering information to use against the High King's chosen. You must be careful, Lucy. You are protected, as is everyone who is with you within the walls of this house and its property. The High King has blessed it forever. Outside these boundaries, however, it is a different matter."

"Are you safe, Haniel?" Lucy reached her hand up and placed it over the glass depiction of the dryad's hand. It was still glass and cool to the touch. The dryad smiled at the gesture.

"Yes, Sho-are, we are quite safe here. The High King has protected the meadow by fire and by sword. You have the protection of the Triune seal. Yet, you must be vigilant. Your adversary, Darnathian, is always prowling about. You are not only the Issachar Gatekeeper but also the keeper of many secrets."

"So I've been told," Lucy said, plunking down on the bench again. "I don't even know where the Issachar Gate is, let alone know how I can protect it."

"I cannot tell you where the gate is. Its location is hidden and will be revealed to you only when you need to know. As for protection, you have your armor and your special tools. The guardians, Bill and Vivian, will also protect you. But you must wear all your armor to be effective," the dryad said. The music from the pipes was making Lucy's head spin. Or maybe it was the lack of sleep.

"Daphne from Ascalon once told us the same thing, but what does it mean? Lucy asked, clearly perplexed. "Our bracelets contain our shields and swords, and the vests and hats morph into our breastplates and helmets. What else is there?"

"Your shoes."

"My shoes?" Bewildered, Lucy looked at her sneakers. "I don't understand."

"You must wear your shoes so you can firmly stand in the presence of evil. They will give you a firm foundation," the dryad said with another little giggle. "But only if you are wearing them, silly girl."

"But we always—"

"Lucy! Get down here! Breakfast is getting cold!" Mom bellowed at the bottom of the stairs. She pounded her knuckles on the wall for emphasis. "Now!"

Lucy opened the door and yelled, "Be right there!" Easing the door shut, she turned around, but the window was just a pretty window again.

"Drat!" Lucy picked up the laundry basket and went downstairs.

After breakfast, Lucy retrieved the laundry from behind the check-in desk in the hallway where she had stashed it and hefted the basket onto her hip. Schuyler went back upstairs to Lucy's room to get her phone.

"Mom!" Lucy carried the basket to the kitchen. "What should I do with the laundry? I brought it down, but we don't have a washer and dryer. Should we take it to a Laundromat?"

"Lucy, for goodness' sake! Use the guest laundry on the second floor," Mom grumbled, stacking the clean breakfast dishes in the drying rack on the counter and wiping her hands on a towel.

"I didn't know the guest laundry was operational. When did that happen?"

"A couple of days ago. Now that I think of it, you were probably running errands with Grandma when the plumbers arrived," Mom said, laying the towel on the gray marble counter. "I'm sorry, honey, I don't mean to snap at you. Our first guests are due to arrive in a few days, and I need to be sure we're ready for them."

"It's okay, Mom. But who are they, and how long are they going to stay?" Lucy said, plunking the basket on the snack counter. Maybe in time she could get used to the idea, but living with strangers was still an odd concept to wrap her mind around.

Mom paused and stepped around the island to stand next to Lucy. She spoke slowly, as if choosing her words cautiously so as not to make Lucy feel more anxious. "I'm sure it will only be for a couple of weeks. Mr. Sasson's company transferred him to Grand River Valley, and his wife is currently unemployed. I offered to help them find a house while she searches for a job." Mom pulled out a counter chair and sat.

"That long? It's like—forever!" Lucy said, crossing her arms. "I thought we would ease into this new way of living with strangers, not jump in with both feet! And even if they find a house right away, it will still take weeks."

"Lucy, I know you're—" Mom flinched as her cell phone rang, and she grabbed it off the counter. She held up a finger, checked the incoming call, and swiped the screen. "Yes, good morning, Mr. Sasson. I was just checking . . ."

Lucy wandered into the breakfast room and tuned out the conversation. The soft, creamy yellow walls with white beadboard trim and a chair rail did little to cheer her. Neither did the fun, colorful print curtains at the windows. She plopped into a chair at one of the small dinette tables and slapped the fake flowers back and forth in the vase. Her emotions were jumping all over the place.

She liked her new bedroom, even if she wasn't all that excited about the house or living in a B and B establishment. It would take some getting used to. While it was her mother's dream, it wasn't hers. School was starting soon, Dale was off to college, and now she was going to be living with people she didn't know. She wasn't sure what to do about the clock portal.

Everything was changing. Again.

"Thanks for letting me know," Mom said, ending the call and pasting on a smile as she entered the room. "Well, that was unexpected. It was Mr. Sasson. They had a change of plans."

"So I gathered," Lucy mumbled, then sat up, her demeanor brighter. "Wait—they're not coming?" she said hopefully.

"Uh, no. They are still coming, but the change of plan means they will be here sooner than expected. Much sooner." Mom sat in the other dinette chair, placed an elbow on the table, and dropped her head into her cupped hand. She sighed heavily. "They will be here today."

"But they can't! We're not officially open. We have tons of things that need to be done before people just start showing up whenever they want." Lucy grabbed her mom's cell and swiped through the recent calls. "Here, call Mr. What's-His-Name and tell him they can't come today. We're not ready!"

"Lucy, we will have to adjust and do the best we can. There's no other option. They sold their house, and the new owners took possession. So basically, they're homeless." She looked knowingly at her daughter before dropping her gaze.

"What else aren't you telling me?" Lucy squinted her eyes and waited. Mom's expression implied she was hiding something. "I have a feeling there's more to this story. So spill it." The grumbly demeanor was back in force. She slumped in the chair.

"Their son, Mathias, starts school next week with you and Schuyler. Maybe you can take him under your wing and help him navigate being the new kid in town?"

"Oh, great!" Lucy complained, crossing her arms with a huff. "I get to live with the new kid and help him in school. This keeps getting better and better. How old is he, anyway?" Her lips clamped tight, her foot tapping a staccato on the pinewood floor.

"I don't know," Mom said, a feeble smile hovering on her lips. "They only asked if he could catch the school bus nearby, so his age never really came up."

"If I have to babysit him while they are here, I'll have to triple my rates for invading my space."

"Lucy. . ." a voice drawled in her ear. Her eyes popped open wide as her glance darted around the room, her face flushing pink. She knew that voice. Iam, the High King, wasn't happy with her.

"Are you all right?" Mom reached across the table, cupped Lucy's cheek with her hand, and then felt her forehead, checking for a temperature. "Your face got hot pink suddenly."

Lucy flinched and pulled away. "Uh, yeah. I'm fine; probably just a little heartburn from eating too fast." *And Iam giving me a guilty conscience for my careless attitude*, she thought.

"Well, since our guests will be here sometime this afternoon, I need you and Schuyler to check the guest bedrooms and bathrooms. They need to be perfect for our first guests. Can you please do that for me?" Mom placed her hand on Lucy's arm. "It would be a big help. Towels and soaps are in the bathroom cabinets."

Lucy pursed her lips, dimpling her cheeks, then nodded. "Yeah, we can help," she said contritely. Her mom shouldn't have to do everything.

"Good," Mom said, giving her arm a little squeeze. "While you're doing that, I'll run to the grocery. I'll call Becca Williams on the way and let her know about the change in plans."

"I'll tell Schuyler, and we'll get started." Lucy grabbed the laundry basket from the kitchen counter. "I'll do the wash too," she called over her shoulder and hurried to the second floor. Schuyler was coming down the stairs from the third floor, her quilted bag slung over a shoulder.

"Your face is red. What's up with that?" Schuyler asked, setting the bag on the floor. Her phone dinged, so she skimmed the text. "Mom is running late. She'll pick me up later this afternoon. I have some extra time, so what do you want to do?"

"Let me get the laundry going, and we can go up to the sitting room and talk. I need to tell you something," Lucy said, sliding open the bifold doors in the hallway under the stylized sign that read Guest Laundry. Once the washer was going, she led the way up the small back stairway to the sitting room on the third floor, where the family quarters were located.

The room was small but efficiently appointed, with floor-to-ceiling bookcases at one end of the long, narrow room, a built-in workspace and shelving at the other, and a comfortable leather couch and rug against the wall facing the windows. The cozy room had been an afterthought when the designer was reclaiming the attic space. A bump-out addition over the kitchen created the small room. Other than the viewing room, it was one of Lucy's favorite spots in the house. Lucy plopped into the desk chair.

"Okay, girlfriend, what's up? You've been acting weird since breakfast, and your face was neon just now, not to mention droopy." Schuyler curled her feet under her as she settled into the couch and looked intently into Lucy's face.

"It's nothing—only another major change of plans. Our guests are arriving this afternoon. Big whoop." She rolled her eyes, her nose scrunched. "They weren't due to arrive for several days, but their house sold and they were 'homeless,'" she said with finger quotes. "Mom gave me a guilt trip about it since we were homeless recently too. And I'm supposed to help their son at school."

"How old is the son?"

"Dunno. Mom only knew that Mathias will go to school with us." Her finger randomly traced the fabric's pattern on the chair arm. "I guess it's convenient having elementary through high school in the same building. At least we're freshmen this year. If he's younger, he will be in a different wing. You know, I never thought about people with kids staying here. It could get complicated with the ghost hunting thing."

"How? The house has a blessing, so it's not like anything can happen here or on the property. Don't you think it should be safe for children?"

"I guess. But kids? I'll become the built-in babysitter. How's that fair?" She slouched in the stylish desk chair. The fabric colors mimicked the paint colors of the cabinetry. "And the clock portal isn't the only portal in the house," she said, rocking the desk chair back and forth on the wide plank pine flooring. "The stained glass mural is a portal of sorts too."

"What?" Schuyler's eyes bulged as she sat up and leaned toward Lucy. Her eyebrows were hiking into her hairline. "Can we go through it? Where does it go?" She nearly vibrated off the couch.

"Remember the mirror on the dresser in the master bedroom?" Schuyler nodded. "When the mirror portal activated, we could talk to Daphne, but no one could pass through from either side. The window is the same. A dryad spoke to me, and a Mr. Tumnus–like faun was playing his pipes and dancing."

"Holy cowabunga, girlfriend! Let's go talk to them!" Schuyler made to get up, but Lucy put a hand on her arm.

"I don't think it will activate just because we want it to. Like Daphne, the dryad wanted to give us a message. I'm not sure what it's supposed to mean. You know how fond these spirits are of riddles."

"Oh no. Seriously—more riddles?"

"Let's see if you get this one—the dryad said we must wear our shoes." Lucy stretched out her legs and wiggled her sneakered feet.

"Our shoes? I don't get it. Of course we wear shoes." Schuyler slumped back into the couch and hugged a checkered pillow. As she ruminated, her expression went from bewilderment to realization. "I know what she means! We must check the trunk!" She tossed the pillow aside and hurried from the room. Lucy's bedroom was across the hall.

"I am so daft!" Lucy entered and slid to the floor in front of the carved wood trunk. The sunlight, cascading through the windows, caressed the runes etched in the wood, the symbols iridescent in the beam. She opened the trunk and carefully removed the artifacts inside. There was the Crystalline mirror, the Augur Sphere, the little velvet box containing the Belt of Truth, the vest and hat, and her backpack, which held the Spectrescope. The spare brass doorknob was there, too, still firmly attached to the base. But nestled in the bottom corner of the dark lining was an item she didn't remember seeing before. It was the strangest pair of eyeglasses she could imagine.

The Spectacles, being of the same odd metal as the Spectrescope and the other magical artifacts, gleamed with a satiny finish. Elongated hoods surrounded the lenses and were decorated with tiny, delicate leaves and vines; they blocked the peripheral vision of the wearer. The bridge, comprised of more diminutive leaves, held a tiny replica of her shield, and attached to the bow were two articulating arms with small lenses, one etched with a cross and crown.

"Wowza." Lucy held the Spectacles to the light. The small lenses had vivid color. While the articulating arms appeared fragile, their poles were extremely rigid. "I wonder what they do." She handed them to Schuyler, who took the Spectacles and scrutinized them.

"You've never seen these before?" Schuyler asked, incredulous. "I remember Mrs. McGoo retrieving them from the floor during the house fire. The artifacts tumbled from the trunk when I dropped my end and it toppled over. I'd forgotten about them until now." She settled them on her nose and glanced about the bedroom. She hunched her shoulders, her palms raised in bewilderment.

"I was a little frantic if you remember. I couldn't find Metrocom," Lucy whispered. "He would've had such a blast in this house, with new people to greet and so many sneaky places for a cat to hide. I miss him. He was my best bud." She sniffled and placed the artifacts back in the trunk. Her hand brushed against something rubbery. She snickered and held up a pair of leather sandals with rubber soles.

"Well, what do you know? Magical shoes!"

Just Another Day for Lucy

A car rumbled into the driveway behind the Carriage House Bed-and-Breakfast. It backfired, coughed, and knocked before its engine fell silent. A series of squeaks and slamming doors announced the Sasson family's arrival. Lucy pulled the curtain aside and peeked out the window at the wearied family below, trudging along the stone pathway leading to the front of the house.

"Oh no! They're here," she grumbled, dropping the curtain. "We're not ready for guests yet. What was Mom thinking?" She plopped into the chair by the window and scowled.

"I think you mean *you* aren't ready for them." Schuyler nudged past her and spied on the family, who appeared foreshortened from the third floor of the old house. It was difficult to tell how old the son was as he followed behind with his head bowed.

"There's only three of them," Schuyler said, smirking. "You make it sound like an invasion of sorts. How bad can it be?"

"Drat!" Lucy jumped to her feet. "I was supposed to check the bedrooms and bathrooms. I still need to hang the towels and put the soaps and shampoos in their baskets. Mom left for the grocery store. We're gonna need to handle this ourselves." She hurried into the hall and hesitated, confused.

"Uh, Schuyler, you go check the rooms—towels and soaps are in the bathroom cabinets. I'll go stall them." She shooed Schuyler down the hall. "Oh, could you fluff the new decorative pillows on the beds? I unpacked them yesterday, and they're probably still flat."

"Okay, but which rooms should I check?" Schuyler flung her hands in the air.

Lucy thought for a moment. The original master bedroom, with the round sitting area that formed the turret, was now guest suite one. The newly redesigned bedrooms each had an ensuite bathroom. Bedroom two was the next largest bedroom, but she decided guest suite four, across the hall and the smallest suite, would be fine for the son.

"Uh, put them in guest suites one and four so they will be across the hall from each other." Lucy dashed down the stairs, skidding to a halt in the foyer.

Taking slow, deep breaths to calm herself, she smoothed her hair and tugged her shirt into place, then opened the door and stepped to the porch railing to wait. She pasted on a smile. At least she hoped it was a smile and not a maniac grin.

Of medium height, with dark-brown hair and deep-set eyes, Mr. Sasson looked exhausted despite the healthy glow of his honeyed skin as he climbed the steps, dragging a large suitcase. His wife was of the same heritage, but fatigue lay in circles under her almond-shaped eyes. Though neatly dressed, her slacks had wrinkled, and a drooping barrette held her long, dark hair back on one side. The son traipsed along the pathway and pulled his own suitcase. He was much older than Lucy expected. She noted, with consternation, that Mathias was a surly teenager about her own age.

"Uh, welcome," Lucy said, stepping aside as they mounted the steps. "Um, to the Carriage House Bed-and-Breakfast, I mean. We've been expecting you. Could I help you with your suitcase, Mr. Sasson?" She opened the door and ushered them into the foyer.

"And who are you, young lady?" Mr. Sasson asked. "I assume you are not Mrs. Hornberger. And, no, you cannot help. The suitcase is much too heavy for you." He wheeled it through the foyer and set it next to the check-in desk. His wife quietly observed, while the son, Mathias, who clearly wanted to be anywhere else but here, shuffled from one foot to the other and stuffed his hands into his jeans pockets. He stared wide-eyed at the chandelier.

"Um, my name is Lucy Hornberger, and my mother, who isn't here just now, is the owner and proprietor. She will be back shortly. Your rooms are nearly ready, so if you would—"

"What do you mean, 'nearly ready?' We phoned ahead to let you know of our change of plans," Mr. Sasson said heatedly, his thick brows surging together. "This is unacceptable. It's been a long, exhausting drive, and we would like to go to our rooms now, if you don't mind." He defiantly raised his chin.

Lucy pulled in a breath to retaliate, but clamped her mouth shut instead. Her mom didn't need added stress caused by Lucy being disrespectful to their first clients. Iam would not be pleased either. Instead, she stretched her pinched lips into a thin, tight smile, and carefully chose her next words.

"Yes, well, about that." Lucy squared her shoulders and hoped she projected an air of confidence she didn't feel. "We haven't officially opened, and we are just settling in ourselves after the renovations. Unfortunately, your change of plans ricocheted into our plans. If you will please be patient, we will accommodate you and your family as best we can."

Lucy stepped behind the check-in desk, opened the guest registry book, and retrieved a pen from the drawer. "Now, if you would, please sign in. Mrs. Hornberger will go over the details with you when she returns.

In the meantime, you may leave your bags here while I give you a quick tour of the house and answer any questions you may have. By then, your rooms should be ready." She maintained a tight smile, handed the pen to Mr. Sasson, and pushed the registry book toward him. "Agreed?"

Mr. Sasson studied Lucy for a moment. Then he signed the book.

"I am sorry, young lady, for my rudeness. Please forgive me," Mr. Sasson said, his features softening. "It has been a rather unsettling time for my family, so many changes in such a short time." His faltering smile touched Lucy, empathy nudging her heart.

"Trust me, Mr. Sasson," Lucy said quietly, "I know how it feels when your life implodes. Been there, done that." Noticing the fatigue in his eyes, she smiled at him. "Why don't you follow me to the breakfast salon," she said, ushering them into the cozy room. "You can all relax for a few minutes while I make some coffee and fix some refreshments."

"A cup of coffee would be wonderful, thank you," Mrs. Sasson said, speaking for the first time as she settled into an overstuffed chair. "Oh, this is heavenly." She sighed, relaxing into the plump chair. Mr. Sasson sank into the matching chair, his legs stretched out and arms hanging limp over the sides, a contented smile on his face.

"Coffee, Mr. Sasson?"

"Oh, yes, please. Thank you, Miss—"

"Lucy." She smiled, went to the kitchen to start the coffee, and glanced into the foyer as she passed the open archway. The teenager was sitting on the steps, sulking, and staring at the chandelier. Lucy left him to his musings and set the coffee to brew, then placed some of Mrs. McGoo's chocolate chip cookies on a decorative plate. She quickly cut an apple and some cheese and arranged them on the plate next to the cookies.

With that done, she put the plate on the sideboard in the breakfast room next to the waiting cups and saucers. Mr. and Mrs. Sasson had fallen asleep. She tiptoed from the room, leaving them to nap. She would wake them when the coffee was ready if the aroma didn't wake them first. Mathias was still sitting on the steps when she entered the foyer.

"Hi, I'm Lucy," she said, sitting on the steps and offering her hand. He ignored it, and she folded her arms, tucking her hands under and pretending she hadn't just been snubbed. "You must be Mathias. It's nice to meet you."

"Whatever," came the bad-tempered reply. He moved away from her and leaned against the wall, his arms crossed like a police barricade, and his face like a stone statue. His brown eyes with warm golden flecks warily studied the monastery clock against the opposite wall.

"Okay, then. Wonderful talk," Lucy said, getting to her feet again. "Since you obviously want to be left alone, I won't bother asking if you would like a snack or something to drink. You can figure it out for yourself later." She whipped around, flicking her hand. "Uh, buh-bye." She stepped to the check-in desk and slammed the book shut, then dropped into the desk chair.

"What's up with the creepy light?"

"I'm sorry. Did someone say something?" She stretched her eyebrows upward in an exaggerated expression of bewilderment as she pretended to search the foyer. "Oh, were you speaking to me?" she said, addressing Mathias and pointing to herself.

"Ha ha, you are so funny." Mathias stood and walked over to the desk, his hands stuffed in his pockets again. "I'd be stark raving mad if I had to live with that bat-eating-an-octopus thing. And what is that monstrosity supposed to be? It looks like petrified brown ooze." he said, staring at the clock. "All these weird antiques must make you snarky and disagreeable."

"Excuse me? I'm disagreeable? You've got to be kidding," she retorted. "And it's not a monstrosity—it's my mother's *monastery* clock."

"See what I mean? You're disagreeable. Your terrifying chandelier and scary clock are the things you find in nightmares," he said, pointing at the light again.

"Well, we need the disturbing antiques to go with the menacing light, don't we? That way, our guests won't overstay their welcome." Her brows jettisoned skyward again, emphasizing her stink-eyed stare. "Just wait till you see the lamp in your room—the shade has eyes that blink at you if you stare at it long enough."

"What? You're weird. Living here is going to be impossible. I do not know why my parents wanted to stay in a stupid bed-and-breakfast, anyway. I wish we could leave right now," he said, glaring at her. He turned, leaned his back against the counter, arms folded again.

"There's the door," she said, pointing. "Or would you prefer to stay in an old barn? We have an ancient stable out back, filled with decades of old horse poop and hay, or what's left of it. You can be helpful by mucking it out."

His mouth compressed into a tight line. "There is going to be no living with you! Hopefully, it won't be for long."

"Oh, it gets even better. You and I will go to the same school and ride the bus together! How fun is that?" Lucy stood, leaned over the desk, and poked him with a finger, punctuating her next words. "So. Get. Over. Yourself!"

Mathias snorted, and traces of a smile dimpled his cheeks.

"Lucy!" Schuyler yelled, rushing down the stairs. She skidded to a halt in front of the desk. "I made all the—" Her mouth fell open when she saw Mathias. "I, uh, put the soap and towels on the beds, and, uh, flushed the pillows in the bathroom like you said. Okay?" she said, twirling a blond lock around a finger and gazing at Mathias, who looked gobsmacked by everything she had said.

Lucy struggled to keep a straight face but snorted instead. "By which, I think you mean you put towels and soap in the bathrooms and fluffed the pillows on the beds?"

"Duh, I just said that. Weren't you listening?" Schuyler asked. Mathias gaped at her.

Lucy dipped her head, covering her face with a hand. Yup. School was going to be interesting this year.

A Fickle Friend

The girls were sitting at the table in the back corner, and Schuyler was doodling in her workbook, the initials M. S. hidden among the doodles. Lucy couldn't stop snickering. The teacher was glancing around the classroom, hoping to catch whoever was committing the infraction. Each time he turned in their direction, Lucy wiped the smile from her face and pretended to contemplate the math problem in the open book in front of her.

Nearby students glanced her way, knowing Lucy's penchant for causing distractions. They were clearly enjoying the teacher's frustration. At least it was a break in the monotonous drone of his discussion about math equations.

"Let it go, girlfriend." Schuyler jabbed a finger into Lucy's shoulder. "Or I'll squeal on you to the teacher myself. We've been over this. It happened weeks ago, and you're still laughing."

"I flushed the pillows," Lucy whispered and was immediately head slapped by Schuyler. "Oh, c'mon. It was hilarious. Mathias had no clue what you were talking about." Lucy's head bobbed as she smothered another round of giggles. "It's payback for the way you tease me about Paul." Lucy wiggled a finger at the doodles on her friend's notepaper.

"It's not funny." Schuyler's face pinched, her eyes squinting. "He probably thinks I'm derpy."

"Are you having a problem, Miss Williams?" the teacher asked, turning from the whiteboard, marker still in hand, a peeved expression puckering his mouth at the interruption.

"Sorry, sir. Uh, no problem. Um, just thinking out loud." Schuyler sighed, erased an answer in her textbook, and plopped her chin in her hand. She turned away from Lucy, pouting.

"I'm only teasing you," Lucy said. "If I don't do it, who will?" She pulled a toaster pastry from her backpack and offered it to Schuyler. "Peach offering?" She smirked, batting her eyelashes.

Suspicious, Schuyler squinted, then snatched the pastry from her and opened it, the cellophane wrapper crinkling loudly. She hid it under the textbook and broke off a piece of the frosted, flaky treat. Her lips curled in contentment as the peach jam and sugar melted in her mouth. "Thanks." She popped another bite in her mouth.

"Food—it works every time."

Schuyler turned a wrinkled nose toward Lucy and finished the pastry. She swiped the crumbs into a pile on the side of the desk to dispose of later. "Where is Mathias? I haven't seen him yet today."

"He has science lab with Paul. We'll probably see them at lunch." Lucy flipped a page in her textbook and studied the next set of equations. "You know, sometimes I feel like we're part of a silly sitcom about living with strangers. It's weird, not entirely unenjoyable, but mostly weird." Her pencil tapped a rhythm on the table.

"Hmm, how so?" Schuyler erased another answer. It was unusual for her to be having so much trouble with math.

"Mr. and Mrs. Sasson seem nice, but we're just getting to know them. Mathias, however, is grumpy, like all-the-time grumpy and obnoxious.

Unless he's at the Carriage House, then he's kind of normal acting. I don't get it. It's like I'm living with Dr. Jekyll and Mr. Hyde."

"He's a teenage boy. Or maybe because his parents are there, he feels he should maintain a certain demeanor. You know how it is being displaced from your own home. You love the McGoos and enjoyed living with them, but it's not the same freedom as being in your own space." Schuyler made a squeak. "Ooh! I think we need to do a group study time together at your house. The library room would be perfect. Let's ask Paul and Mathias to study with us."

Lucy eyed her friend suspiciously at the abrupt change in topic. "Yeah, we could probably do study time. Then maybe you can see what I mean about Mathias." Lucy glanced at the sample equations on the whiteboard, then flipped to the next page in her workbook. "I don't know what's going on with him. When we're eating breakfast, he's pleasant and even amusing. We get to school, and he's biting my head off or bumping me out of the way. He nearly ejected me from of the bus this morning. He's so bad tempered sometimes. Sheesh."

The bell rang for the lunch break, and students began filling the aisles, pushing toward the door. Their teacher yelled the instructions for the homework assignment over the din of shuffling feet and murmuring voices. Lucy crammed her books into her backpack as she joined the throng.

Schuyler stretched to find Paul and Mathias amid the students swarming the hallway. She waved at Paul, who was the taller of the two boys, when he turned her way. He smiled and whipped a couple of fingers back and forth, showing they would join the girls for lunch. Schuyler nodded enthusiastically when he indicated he would save four seats.

"Oh, good! Paul's gonna save seats for us. I'll be right back!"

Schuyler hurried down the corridor among the throng of students. Lucy shook her head, then headed for the cafeteria. Paul and Mathias sat at a table; their backpacks slung over two of the seats. Lucy slid into one and placed her backpack on the floor with Paul's. Paul grinned at her, took a bite of his ham-and-cheese sandwich, and chewed. The aroma of tacos filled the space. It was the first Taco Tuesday of the year, and students were busily munching the spicy entrée. Mrs. McGoo volunteered in the cafeteria, but not on Taco Tuesday.

"Where's Schuyler?" Mathias asked, a scowl rumpling his forehead while he munched on a carrot. Apparently, his mother was as health conscience as Lucy's. "Wasn't she just with you? Or did she finally find some new friends?"

"Hello to you too. I'm fine, thanks for asking." Lucy rolled her eyes. "I guess Schuyler had something to take care of, but trust me, she never misses lunch." She unpacked her lunch. It was Lucy's turn to scowl when she saw the contents: celery sticks, peanut butter, and applesauce. She pouted while Paul happily chomped away. She could almost taste the chocolate chip cookie he was eating. Resigned, she bit into a celery stick and grimaced. It was tough and stringy.

Schuyler entered the cafeteria. She passed their table, unnoticed by the boys, and sat at another table with Madison, who had always been rude to Lucy and Schuyler. Lucy's mouth dropped open. She couldn't believe it.

The celery stick drooped in her hand as she watched Schuyler laughing and chatting with the enemy like they were best friends forever. Schuyler leaned close and whispered in the other girl's ear. Madison raised a hand and rubbed her ear. She turned toward Lucy as though she knew they were being watched and waggled her fingers. Grinning, Schuyler rose, twirled a lock of hair around her finger, and sauntered out the door.

"Earth to Lucy!" Paul had a bewildered expression on his face. "Are you listening? I asked if you were available to tutor me in history again?"

"What? I'm sorry, Paul. I didn't hear what you said. Did you need something?" Lucy stuck her celery in the applesauce and ate a spoonful of peanut butter. It was gooey and nearly glued her tongue to the roof of her mouth. She quickly uncapped a water and took a swig.

"Are you all right?" Paul asked. "You're behaving a little strange, even for you. What's up with the odd eating habits?" He offered her a cookie, but she shook her head, refusing the treat she'd been longing for.

"Uh, just a little distracted, I guess. It's been a busy time settling into the new house and everything." She picked at her lunch. Suddenly, she wasn't feeling hungry. Betrayed, but not hungry.

"What's new?" Mathias said, his scowl firmly in place. "You're always distracted. It's probably the aftereffects of living with those weird antiques. They've infected your mind with their strangeness." He waggled his head and twirled a finger in circles by his temples, indicating she was a little crazy. Paul, who was engrossed in the novel he'd brought, didn't interject. Lucy sucked in a breath, about to retaliate, when someone approached.

"Hey, guys!" Schuyler dropped into the seat next to Lucy and pulled her lunch from her quilted bag. She received a new bag every school year from her grandmother. This year it was turquoise with a paisley pattern. "So, are we on for group study at the Carriage House?" She frowned at the bewildered expressions on the boys' faces. "Didn't Lucy ask you about it yet?" She glanced from one to the other, then at Lucy.

Lucy removed the celery stick and shoveled applesauce into her mouth. She didn't quite know how to respond to Schuyler's new Benedict Arnold persona. "Are you sure you don't want to ask your friend Madison to join us too?" She flicked her spoon in Madison's direction. Paul's gaze remained fixed on his book as he nibbled at his lunch. Mathias chewed his carrots with a smirk.

"Why would we ask her to join us? You're acting weird. What's up with that?" Concern clouded Schuyler's hazel-green eyes. "You're not sleeping well, are you? I bet you miss Dale and the McGoos. It's a lot to deal with, and change can be hard. Want to do a sleepover this weekend?" She nudged Lucy with her shoulder. "It'll be fun!"

"Sure. My life is imploding again. Yeah, let's do a sleepover—that should fix it." Lucy offered a weak smile and prodded Paul under the table with her foot. He looked up from his book. "Want to join us at the Carriage House to study? We can order pizza and get those chocolate volcano brownies you like."

"Yeah, that'd be great." Paul grinned and bumped Mathias with an elbow. "Join us, dude. It will be fun."

"You've got to be kidding. Studying is fun? You're as crazy as she is," Mathias said, gesturing to Lucy with a raise of his chin. "But sure, why not? It will be a diversion from the macabre antiques and the equally weird people." Mathias leaned back in his chair, crossing his foot over his knee. He studied the girls with furrowed brows. Then he flinched suddenly, stuck a finger in his ear, and wiggled it.

"Great!" Paul wadded the paper remains of his lunch and stuffed them in the lunch bag. "Lucy opened my eyes to history last school year—now I enjoy it." He grinned at her. "When are we doing the group study thing?" He offered his last cookie to Lucy, but she declined.

"Dunno." Lucy hunched her shoulders with a glance at Schuyler.

"Friday! We can stay up late and sleep in on Saturday." Schuyler's head bobbed eagerly.

"Uh, okay, Friday it is." *Yay. Group study with Grumpy and a sleepover with Benedict Arnold*, Lucy thought. *It's a wonderful life.*

"Maybe you can give me a tour of the old house, Lucy," Paul said, munching on the cookie.

"You should see the chandelier in the foyer and the monstrous clock. I'm surprised it hasn't collapsed the floor into the basement." Mathias made a face. "Or the freaky lamp in my bedroom. It's like living in a nightmare. Bleh." He grabbed his throat and pretended to gag.

Thinking Mathias was trying to be funny, Paul laughed at his antics. "I can't wait to see the house. Can you imagine the stories it could tell? The hardships of the early settlers of the area, or Civil War soldiers returning home from battle—"

"No! No soldier stories, okay?" Lucy pinched her lips, running her thumb and index finger across them in a zipping motion. Schuyler looked aghast, waving her hands. Mathias gave them both a dubious stare.

Paul rose, grabbed his backpack, and toed Mathias's chair. "Come on, dude, or we'll be late for class."

Without saying a word, Mathias got up and followed Paul from the cafeteria. Lucy watched them leave and wondered about Mathias the Grump.

Lucy saw Schuyler hanging out with Madison two more times that day. It made her feel confused, discouraged, and distracted. She trudged up the turret staircase from the lower level after the last class of the day, her backpack bumping the steps where it dragged along beside her. Science lab had been a disaster with her thoughts so clearly scattered, which annoyed the teacher.

She wanted to see Mr. McGoo. He was usually in the utility room or the custodial staff lounge. He could always cheer her up, and she hadn't seen nearly enough of him since moving to the Carriage House. Hopefully, she would see more of the McGoos when the stable conversion was done.

Lucy bumped her way through the horde of students milling about, laughing, chatting, and scurrying to catch their rides. Schuyler wasn't waiting at the lockers like usual, which was odd. Lucy spun the dial on her lock, tugged it open, and dumped her textbooks to the bottom. A familiar giggle caught her attention. Schuyler walked with Madison down the corridor. She giggled again at something the other girl said to the group following them.

Lucy felt a pang of jealousy when Schuyler dropped an arm around the girl's shoulder and whispered in her ear. Madison stopped abruptly, causing the others to bump into her or swerve around. An odd expression flickered over her features, then the snarl was back in place as she spied Lucy watching. Grinning, Schuyler ducked into the girl's bathroom. Madison walked on and passed Lucy with barely a glance in her direction. Lucy felt bewildered and more than a little betrayed by Schuyler's actions—not unlike how General Washington must have felt when his general in charge of West Point committed treason and defected to the British during the American Revolutionary War. The general whose name became forever synonymous with treason and betrayal.

Benedict Arnold, she thought and slammed the locker door.

Life with Grumpy

"Hey, Lucy," Paul said, coming up behind her, his expression mimicking that of the bemused onlookers in the corridor. "Everything okay? How was science lab?" She grimaced, rolling her eyes. "Ouch. That bad, huh? It's not one of my favorite subjects either." He hefted his backpack to his shoulders, shrugging to get it settled and comfortable. His deep lake-blue eyes clouded with concern.

"Yeah, you could say that. The teacher kept calling on me to identify the specimen in the on-screen presentation, and I got every one of them wrong. The multicolored blobs all look the same to me. Science isn't my favorite. I usually do okay, just not today." She slung her backpack on a shoulder and trudged toward the exit. Paul fell in step with her.

"It will never be my favorite subject, but it's the one subject I am good at," Paul said, a small smile hovering on his face. He bumped his shoulder into hers. "Want me to tutor you?" He pushed the door open and waited for her to squeeze through.

"You might need to. Think you're up to it?" She gave him an amused smile, but it dropped from her face when Schuyler came running up.

"Hey! Wait, guys!"

Paul held the door for Schuyler, but several students burst through ahead of her. He grinned. "Hey, yourself. Where've you been?"

"I've been waiting by the lockers. I thought Lucy was late coming up from the science lab, then I saw you both heading for the buses." She frowned at Lucy. "Why didn't you wait? I always wait for you." She adjusted her quilted bag over her shoulder.

"She didn't wait because she's mad at you," Mathias said, joining them. He stuffed his hands in his pockets, as usual, and sauntered past them to the bus. Lucy curled her hands and hissed.

"Grr. He is so annoying!" she harrumphed as she followed him to the bus.

Paul hunched his shoulders, tilted his head toward his bus, waved, and walked on. Lucy rolled her eyes and climbed onto the bus. She walked to the back, slouched in a seat, and crossed her arms, sulking. Mathias had chosen a seat over the wheel well, and his outstretched legs prevented others from joining him there. He scowled at anyone who chanced to look in his direction. No one did. His grumpy demeanor fairly radiated from his every pore like toxic gas.

"Sheesh," Schuyler said, glancing from Lucy to Mathias. "What was in the water? Maybe it was something you ate for breakfast. Both of you have been grumpy." She held up a finger. "No, wait, my mom supplies the pastries, so I know it wasn't the food. So, what gives?" She dropped into the seat beside Lucy and turned toward her. "Spill it, girlfriend."

"Why are you suddenly hanging out with Madison?" Lucy said. "She's as mean and snarky to you as she is to me. Now you're best friends? I don't get it." She slouched farther into the seat.

"Are you daft? Madison? I haven't seen Madison all day, let alone hung out with her. You better get some glasses, girlfriend. You're not seeing straight. I don't know who you saw, but it wasn't me."

"I saw you! Like several times today."

The Ghost You Can't See

"I am not hanging out with Madison. I'm hurt that you think I would do that." Schuyler slumped into the seat and crossed her arms. "You're right though. She doesn't like me either. Why would you think I'm suddenly her friend? We've both tried to be nice to her, but it doesn't work."

"Whatever," Lucy said, trying not to sniffle. It hurt that her best friend would deny what she knew to be true. She had seen it for herself, hadn't she?

"See? Told you." Mathias smirked, a know-it-all look on his face.

"You stay out of this!" the girls said in unison.

Lucy held up a fist. Schuyler bumped into it with her own.

"You're both weird." Mathias said as he slumped into his seat. He ignored everyone and remained that way for the rest of the ride home.

After a quiet dinner, Lucy cleaned up the kitchen and placed the dirty dishes in the dishwasher. She overheard her mom and grandma talking in the breakfast room about the renovations to the stables. Her eyebrows shot upward when Grandma Elliot said, "That Mathias is such a delightful young man." Grandma detailed all the wonderful things about Mathias, saying that he was helpful, polite, and congenial. Lucy's jaw clenched, pinching her face into a grimace as she slowly shook her head. *Blah, blah, blah.* She trudged up the tiny back staircase to her room. *If they only knew,* she thought. When she got to her room, Lucy realized she'd left her back-pack in the library sitting room.

Her head drooped, and her arms hung at her sides. "The old house is fit for something. Exercise!" Grumbling to herself, she went down the back stairs.

The library was off the foyer. Built-in bookcases, painted a grayish green, lined the room, their crown moldings hugging the high ceiling. The butterscotch-colored wide plank floors and cozy love seat and chair set a warm and welcoming atmosphere to the room.

Mathias sat at the large table in the center of the room. He had his back to the archway and his homework spread out before him. A lock of unruly brown hair fell over his forehead as he chewed thoughtfully on his pencil. Lucy paused, unsure whether to dart in and grab her bag or leave and come back later after he had gone to his room. She decided on the latter, but Mathias whipped his head around and saw her standing in the hallway. His brown eyes held surprise at seeing her there.

"Hey, Lucy. Want to study together? It's kind of quiet in here by myself. I wouldn't mind the company." He pushed a chair out at the table with his foot. "Maybe you could help me with history. Paul says you're great at it."

"Uh, sure. I guess." She retrieved her backpack from the small chair in the corner where she had left it when she came home from school. Mathias cleared a spot on the table, dropping his extra books to the floor. Lucy leaned over her science book and tried to concentrate on the text. They worked in companionable silence for several minutes. She even answered some of the history questions he asked as they reviewed the current chapter.

Then Mathias laid his pencil down and slouched in the chair, his hands stuffed in his pockets. He stared at the floor without saying a word. Lucy surreptitiously watched him while continuing to tackle her homework.

"So, what kind of name is Hornberger? It makes me think *hamburger*, then I get hungry."

Lucy chortled. "Wrong burger. It's spelled *b-e-r-g* and, depending on who you ask, it either means 'horn blower' or 'horn-shaped hill.' Personally, I'm going with horn blower. I'm always spouting off about something. At least I can claim I come by it naturally."

"Huh. Fair enough." He twirled his pencil between his fingers, watching it flip. "What did you mean when you said your life was imploding again? What happened?"

His sudden interest and quiet demeanor took Lucy aback. *He remembers what I said at lunch?* This was unexpected. She'd been ready for a snarky, grumpy remark, but not this. "Well, Mom lost her job, then our house burned down, my cat died in the fire, then we had to live with the McGoos, and now we live here. So, yeah. Life imploded." Doodles filled the margins of the workbook. She concentrated on the squiggles; it was easier than admitting she liked this quiet version of the grumpy boy.

"Oh. I'm sorry. That's a lot to deal with. Why didn't you go live with your grandmother?"

"Grandma lives way up north, in Grand Traverse Bay. Mom didn't want to displace my brother, Dale, who was in his last year of high school, so the McGoos offered to let us live with them. It was kind of fun if I'm being honest. I love the McGoos—they're family now."

"Why are you living here? What's up with that?"

"Mom received an inheritance. She always loved the idea of a bed-and-breakfast, and now we live with strangers. Yay. No offense," she said, pushing her workbook aside and shrugging her shoulders. "So, how did you end up in Grand River Valley?"

Mathias didn't answer her question; he gazed at the floor instead. Intrigued, Lucy wanted to keep him talking. Maybe she could understand why his attitude was flip-flopping.

"I'm curious. What does the name Sasson mean?"

"Joy."

Her eyes flew open, and immediately, a dozen snarky comments popped into her brain. She clamped her jaw shut, dipped her head nearly into the workbook, and concentrated on the lesson instead.

After a few minutes, Mathias pushed back from the table and stood. "I'm gonna get something to drink. I'm kind of thirsty." He waggled his thumb toward the breakfast room. The small refrigerator contained a variety of drinks for their guests. "Want me to bring you anything?"

Confused, Lucy shook her head, her mind trying to comprehend his change in behavior. "Why are you being nice suddenly? You were obnoxious all day. I don't get it, and frankly, I'm confused with your Dr. Jekyll and Mr. Hyde routine." She closed her textbook and stood, facing him.

"Whaddya mean Jekyll and Hyde? You blew up when I asked if you wanted anything. I thought we were getting along fine. Now you're yelling at me. What's your problem?" His face was surly again. "I'm not a monster, you know."

"You! You're my problem, and now I am yelling. Ever since you came here, every day it's the same routine! You are nice one minute and grumpy the next. You act fine when we are here at the Carriage House, but as soon as we get to school or on the bus, you get grumpy, short-tempered, and obnoxious."

"Yeah, well, it's no picnic living with you either, Lucy the Magnificent."

"What? Lucy the Magnificent? What's that supposed to mean?" She threw up her hands. "Look—I get it, okay? You don't want to live here, and I don't want to live with strangers. Your life imploded just like mine did. So, let's just try to make the best of it, okay?"

"You're right—I don't want to be here!"

"Well, I don't want you here either!"

"Lucy Hornberger!" Mom bellowed from the doorway, anger and disbelief distorting her face. "You apologize to Mathias right this minute! He's our guest, and you know better than to treat him with such disrespect. What has gotten into you?" Shaking, Mom put her hands on her hips.

Mr. and Mrs. Sasson hurried from the parlor where they had been relaxing. Mrs. Sasson glanced dubiously from Jeannie to Lucy. Mr. Sasson gave his son a hard stare.

Feeling cornered and somewhat ashamed for her blowup, Lucy turned several shades of pink and quickly stuffed her books back into the backpack. Clutching it tightly, she swallowed, tilted her chin up, and looked Mathias in the eye.

"I'm sorry for my outburst. I probably shouldn't say such things, even if they're true." Lucy turned to his parents. "I apologize, Mr. and Mrs. Sasson. I was out of line. I hope you can forgive me." She eased by her mom, who was tight lipped and furious. "I'll just send myself to my room for the rest of the evening," she said, waggling a finger at the stairs. She took the steps two at a time, leaving everyone to stare after her.

She could hear her mother apologizing for her rude behavior, but the murmur of voices died away as she got to the top of the stairs. The private sitting room on the third floor felt like a welcome sanctuary. The tall floor lamp next to the couch cast a warm glow over the room, changing the light-blue bookcases to a blueish gray.

She hugged one of the decorative pillows and curled up in a corner of the couch, her emotions vacillating between sobbing into the pillow and beating the stuffing out of it. The pillow offered a safer alternative to vent her anger and discouragement. She knew if she threw something break-able, she would have to clean up the mess and face more of her mother's wrath. She buried her face into the soft fabric.

The couch sagged as someone settled into it. Then she felt an arm slip around her shoulders as someone pulled her close. She expected Grandma Elliot, but the fragrance of peppermint candies and spice wafted to her nose. Iam was sitting beside her. He wore his usual brown tweed suit, and his white shirt was open at the top. Lucy hiccuped, sniffled, and grabbed his lapel, hiding her face in his shoulder as he patted her arm. If she had a grandpa, he would be like Iam.

"Want to talk about it?" Iam said, leaning close. He gave her an encour-aging smile.

Eyes burning with tears, Lucy marveled that the High King of Ascalon would take time to comfort her. She didn't even know what to say, so she nodded instead. She brushed away the tears lingering on her lashes and hiccuped again.

"I don't think I even know where to begin."

"The beginning is a good place to start, don't you think?" His blue eyes twinkled, and his white mustache wiggled like a caterpillar.

"I don't know. It's just that—everything is changing again! I loved living with the McGoos after the fire, and now I miss seeing them every day." She tossed the pillow aside and paced back and forth in front of the windows, waving her arms in frustration, sadness changing to anger. "Now we're living in this huge, rambling old house with strangers! Mr. and Mrs. Sasson seem nice, but we don't really know anything about them. Dale is at college. I hardly ever get to talk to him. Schuyler is drifting away from me to become friends with the enemy. It feels like my life is imploding again. The old foyer clock has a portal. And, oh yeah, Mathias is driving me crazy!"

"Is there anything else, dear one?" Iam asked gently. He folded his hands in his lap and waited. His white hair was longer than usual and hung over his collar.

"Where have you been recently? I think you're drifting away from me too!" Lucy rounded on him with her hands on her hips, glaring. "I haven't heard from you in weeks!"

"I have been here. I will never forsake you, dear one." Iam patted the cushion. "Come, sit. The more you pace, the more frustrated you get, preventing your heart from hearing me." She opened her mouth to protest, but seeing his stern expression, she clamped it shut and sat next to him.

"Sorry."

"So, you say you haven't heard from me in weeks. I wonder, have you called out to me?" Iam's eyebrows floated benignly upward.

Lucy opened her mouth several times to respond, but each time, nothing came out. Her lips pinched together as she dropped her gaze and shook her head.

"You think that might be a problem?"

She briefly glanced at him, then dropped her gaze again. With her bottom lip poked out, she nodded. "Maybe."

"Uh-huh. I am always here, dear one. I'm always listening, even when you think I'm not. You can call to me whenever you need to talk. I may not answer as you want me to, but do not think that I don't care." He turned to face her. "Lucy, you must remember, orison is our way of communicating. Orison keeps your heart open and uncluttered when you tell me your deepest concerns. And I tell you mine."

"So, you will always answer if I call?"

"Yes, dear one. I will tell you things that you don't know." He smiled, a playful twinkle in his eyes. "And probably remind you of a few things too." He waggled his brows.

"Iam?" Lucy chuckled, thinking again that his brows were like furry caterpillars dancing on his forehead.

"Yes, dear?"

"Can you come talk to me now? I really need to talk."

Iam laughed and touched a finger to the tip of her nose. "You're irreverent, you silly girl. What would you like to chat about?" He reached into a pocket and pulled out a roll of peppermint candies. "Want one? These are quite wonderful. So minty."

Lucy shook her head. "No, thanks. I can't talk and chew at the same time. Besides, I need to talk." Agitated, she grabbed the pillow from the floor and paced the room. "I don't understand why Schuyler is suddenly friends with Madison and her groupies. Those girls are always spiteful to us. They say horrible things and lie to the teachers. I don't get it. Is Schuyler becoming one of them? She's drifting away from me, and I don't know why."

Lucy flung the pillow about furiously as she paced. Iam ducked the missile several times. He finally grabbed it from her and placed it back on the couch.

"Does this behavior seem characteristic of your dearest friend?"

"No—not really. That's why it's so confusing. One minute she's my sweet friend, then she's making mean, jeering faces at me from across the room or hanging out with the enemy. I don't know what to think." She dropped onto the couch and turned a hopeful gaze at him. "You're the King of Ascalon. Can't you tell me what I need to know?"

"I could; but what's the fun in that?" His eyes twinkled above a lop-sided smile. "Lucy, you know in your heart Schuyler is truly your friend, and she is also a child of mine. You've known each other since childhood. Do you think perhaps you are not seeing the entire picture?"

Lucy nodded. "Maybe," she said, slouching back into the comfortable couch, her arms crossed.

"You must remember, dear one, you are my Bachar—a chosen one, and a Sho-are—a Gatekeeper. Darnathian is our enemy, and he will use any means he can to defeat you, to destroy our relationship, and to cause as many problems in the kingdom as he can. One of his favorite ploys is HALT. It means hungry, angry, lonely, and tired." He slipped an arm around her again, and she rested her head on his shoulder. She felt the anger go out of her as she rested against him. He cupped her head with his hand.

"What does that mean?"

"Think about this: when you're hungry, you are weak. When you're angry, you make poor decisions. Loneliness makes you imagine things, and when you're tired, you are vulnerable. You can never forget that Darnathian is powerful and will not rest until he finishes what he has started. If he can cause you to HALT, your defeat is close at hand."

"Okay, I understand the anger, loneliness, and vulnerability parts. But food? What does food have to do with it?" A calmness permeated her spirit, and she relaxed further. Iam chuckled and patted her shoulder.

"Hunger isn't just about food. It is many things. It depletes your strength, making you weak, and it can make you long for something you once had. You are worried about Schuyler. You see your friendship slipping away. There is nothing more enduring or valuable than a friend. They lend us their strength, give us encouragement, and come alongside to help and restore and to guide. To be without a friend is to be truly hungry."

"You're right. It's just—I don't know. Did I offend Schuyler somehow, or are we just growing apart? Change is so hard."

"I think you may not be seeing things correctly. Perhaps you should wear your Spectacles."

"Schuyler said the same thing today!" Lucy got up and grabbed her backpack from the floor where she had tossed it, removing the case that protected the strange steampunk-like eyeglasses. Lifting them from the case, she turned to show Iam, but he was gone.

"Aw! I wish he wouldn't do that!"

Benedict Arnold's Blond Curls

On Wednesday morning, breakfast was a gloomy affair. Lucy sat quietly at the island counter, eating her oatmeal. Her phone beeped, and she checked the message and harrumphed. "Seriously?"

The message read, *Don't forget to put your dirty dishes in the dishwasher.* Lucy scrunched her nose and squinted at her mother, who was leaning against the counter on the far side of the island, ignoring her.

"A text? I'm sitting right here!" Her mom tapped furiously at the screen, and Lucy's phone beeped again.

I'm so mad that I can't trust myself to speak to you. I'm sure the Sassons must be equally mad at you because of your behavior! What a fine way to run a bed-and-breakfast!

Lucy snorted and laid the phone down. She glanced up as Mr. and Mrs. Sasson entered the kitchen. They both looked relaxed and rested.

"Good morning," Mrs. Sasson said, smiling at Jeannie. She patted Lucy's shoulder affectionately as she passed through into the breakfast room. Mr. Sasson followed his wife, a magazine tucked under his arm.

"Good morning, ladies!" Mr. Sasson greeted. "What a charming place. I love the relaxing and comforting atmosphere. I haven't slept so well in ages!" Jeannie smiled hesitantly, astonished by his remarks.

Mr. Sasson leaned toward Lucy conspiratorially and whispered, "Don't worry about what you said to Mathias. He's had a difficult time with the move, and he's been acting out his frustrations lately. It's not pleasant when you feel displaced." He patted her shoulder and smiled, reminding her of Iam. "I think you're good for him. Keep him on his toes, so to speak." He joined his wife in the breakfast room. The Sassons made their selections from Rebecca Williams's warm, jam-filled croissants and then took their coffee and croissants to one of the cheery dinette tables.

Lucy grinned, glanced over her shoulder to where Mr. and Mrs. Sasson sat quietly chatting and enjoying their pastries, and grabbed her phone. Her fingers flew over the screen's tiny keyboard, typing a message. It read, *I guess they're not mad after all! It's not my fault they have a surly son!*

"Lucy!" Mom bellowed, breaking her silence and causing everyone in hearing range to jump. Mr. Sasson spilled his coffee, and Mrs. Sasson tossed her fork in the air.

"Fine! I'm leaving!" She picked up her dishes and dropped them carelessly into the dishwasher. Grabbing her backpack, she stomped down the hallway to the foyer. As she passed the old clock, she heard a faint squeak. Her backpack fell to the floor, and she quickly opened the door and peered inside. Nothing was happening inside the clock.

"Lucy Hornberger! Get away from that clock!" her mom yelled from the kitchen.

"I thought I heard a mouse squeak. Fine by me if you want a mouse in the house!" She grabbed her bag and stormed out the door, the screen banging shut behind her. Mathias was sitting on the steps, waiting for the school bus, arms crossed again. At least they weren't stiff like a barrier.

"Oh, uh, hi." Lucy sat on the step next to him, clutching her backpack for comfort. "I'm sorry about last night." Mathias lifted a shoulder without saying a word. "You know my name means horn blower. Sometimes I can't help it. My brain sets my mouth in motion and then goes off and leaves it running." She dipped her head with a sideways glance and rested her chin on the backpack. "Forgive me?"

Mathias snorted but still avoided eye contact. He held up a fist. Lucy smiled and did an exploding fist bump with him. Mathias gave a weak smile, but it was a smile.

The school bus rumbled and creaked to a stop, and the driver opened the door. Schuyler waved from the back seat, and they climbed aboard. Lucy plopped into the seat next to Schuyler and scooted over so Mathias could sit with them, but he chose his usual seat over the wheel well. The surly expression was back. Lucy shook her head.

"Look what I did!" Schuyler waved a pink lock of hair at Lucy. The neon pink contrasted against her shoulder-length natural blond curls. It was the only straight lock of hair. Once, she'd used a curling wand to straighten her curly locks, and the length fell nearly to the middle of her back. But it had been time consuming, so now she never did more than one curl. It was unique, but that was Schuyler.

"Mom finally let me get it colored! She said I deserved a reward for making the debate team," she said, pulling the lock forward to admire the color.

Lucy laughed, glad they seemed to be back on friendly terms. "Congratulations! You've been hoping to make the team all summer. I was tiring of the prep work. Are we done now since you're on the team?"

"Nope. We'll have to work harder, do more research. You can help me write opposing arguments for each of our topics, and you can edit my speeches. You're good at that kind of stuff. I'll practice my speeches, and you can give me your opinion." Schuyler pushed a stack of papers into Lucy's hands. Lucy gaped at them. "Oh, don't worry. It's only the highlights."

"Oh, good—only the highlights." Lucy made a goofy face and shoved the papers in a pocket of her backpack. "I'll review them tonight." The bus bumped over some deep potholes in the road, nearly tossing the girls from their seats.

Schuyler leaned over the seat and nudged Mathias. "Good morning, Mathias! Are you trying out for any teams? I made the debate team! I'm so excited—I love to do research and writing and—"

"And talk, apparently. Do you ever stop talking?" he snarled. "Try practicing that."

Schuyler's jaw dropped, hurt glazing her eyes. Her cheeks flamed red, and she closed her mouth without a word and leaned back against the seat. Mathias's actions made Lucy so mad that she reached over the seat and snapped him in the back of the head.

"Ow! What did you do that for?" he demanded. A few snickers echoed through the bus, his cheeks flushing when he realized others were watching. He rubbed the sore spot on his head.

"Why do you think? You're doing it again! You're snarly and surly and bad tempered, and you need to apologize to Schuyler." Lucy's mouth compressed in a firm line. "You made her feel bad, and it was uncalled for. Apologize now!"

"I didn't ask her to bother me," he whispered with a hiss. "She got what she deserved. Maybe next time she will think twice about getting a stupid crush on me!" His brown eyes were dilated and angry. "Girls!" he spat. He turned around and slouched into the corner of the seat by the window. "What are you staring at?" he groused at another boy, who was smirking. The student whipped his head forward and ignored the angry teenager.

Lucy splayed both hands and mimed a grabbing motion behind Mathias's head. "Are you okay?" Lucy asked, noticing tears hovering on Schuyler's lashes. "I'm sorry I apologized to him this morning. He is such a crank." Taking a pastry snack from the backpack, she offered it to Schuyler, but the other girl shook her head. *No food? She is upset. Now I'm really mad,* she thought. Lucy handed Schuyler a tissue instead.

Schuyler sniffled, dabbing at her eyes. "Why did you need to apologize? What did you do now?"

Lucy rolled her lips. "I yelled at him last night for being cranky and bad tempered, and told him I didn't want him living with us. Mom and his parents heard all the yelling, and I got in trouble. Mom is furious with me. I may need to sleep at your house for a few days, or I might try vanquishing Mathias with the Spirit Sword." She snorted, took the Spectrescope from its pocket, and polished it on her shirt hem. "I wish we still lived with the McGoos. I didn't get in nearly as much trouble there. It helps to live with your guardian spirits." Lucy peered through the lens and searched the bus for anomalies. Everything appeared normal, no spirits or anomalies. There wasn't any purple spirit residue either.

Last, her search glanced over at Mathias. His ears were an odd color— not purple, exactly, but an odd dark red. As she watched, he rubbed his ear. The motion was oddly familiar, but she couldn't remember why. Outside of the lens, they appeared fine. Lucy checked the runes on the handle. They seemed warm but unchanging. She hid the scope when Mathias suddenly whipped his head around, expecting her to smack him again.

She waggled a finger at him. "You can turn back around and mind your own business, Dr. Jekyll. Until you apologize, you can sit by yourself at lunch. I doubt even Paul will put up with your attitude, and he's easygoing."

"Whatever," Mathias snapped, turning forward and slouching in his seat.

"What did you see?" Schuyler whispered. She reached for the bracelet on her wrist. "Please say you didn't see any spirit activity. You didn't, did you?"

"It's Mathias," Lucy said, pointing at his head. "His ears are a weird color, sort of dark purply red." Schuyler's eyes popped open, her eyebrows raised in query. Lucy shrugged. "Dunno. Frostbite maybe?"

"Did you see any spirits?"

"Nothing, nada, zilch. Only his weird ears showed up in the scope, but I don't know if what I'm seeing is spirit activity. I've seen nothing like it."

"Is it possible that it means something?" The bus halted at the curb in front of the school. Schuyler grabbed her bag and waited. The driver finally swung the door open, and the students disembarked.

"Well, one thing is for sure. We have work to do. I'll ask the Spectrescope when I get a moment alone."

"Okay, I'll catch up with you after my debate-team meeting after school. We can ride the last bus together."

"Perfect. I kind of messed up on my test yesterday, so I have some extra-credit work to do for science lab anyway." *And I have some sleuthing to do.*

Lucy was not looking forward to science lab with Mr. Hewitt. Based on the way his monotone voice usually droned, the teacher wasn't excited about the subject either. She wondered about his understanding of science. He once said rabbits laid eggs. She sighed and took her science books and lip gloss from her locker. Someone giggled. Peeking around the locker door, she saw Madison and her groupies coming down the hall, students stepping out of her way.

Schuyler was with Madison again. She grinned right at Lucy, waggled her fingers, and flipped her curly locks over her shoulder like Lucy had seen Madison do a thousand times before. Disappointment tumbled over Lucy like a wave at the beach and left her feeling unsteady. Lucy felt her cheeks flushing with humiliation. Apparently, her friend preferred someone else's friendship.

Schuyler seemed to be slipping further away, morphing into Benedict Arnold. This behavior was so alien to Schuyler Williams. It hurt to think their friendship may end. In her mind's eye, Lucy saw a gaping sinkhole opening at her feet without her best friend to anchor her.

Lucy sighed, shook her head, and turned away. She uncapped the lip gloss tube and swiped the moisture across her dry, chapped lips. A nervous habit, she constantly chewed her lips whenever a troublesome spirit problem arose—and nearly every spirit encounter was troublesome. Now Mathias might be affected somehow. She just didn't know. The locker door squeaked as she eased it shut, triggering a memory.

Lucy frowned. *Something about Schuyler was different. And what happened to Schuyler's dyed-pink hair?* She didn't remember seeing it. The lock clicked on the latch. She hurried through the crush of students, trying to get to class before the bell rang. In the next corridor, she caught sight of Madison and her groupies. Her friend wasn't with them.

Then she saw Schuyler chatting amicably with another girl as they entered a classroom, unaware that Madison or Lucy was nearby. Her bright neon-pink lock was prominent against her shoulder. Lucy was confused. *Schuyler has lots of people who love her and friends who enjoy being with her. Why does she need to be friends with someone who is so disagreeable? It makes little sense. We've been besties since grade school, and this is so out of character for her.*

The groupies circled Madison, who was bullying a younger girl with a beleaguered expression. Madison towered over the girl and squeezed her arm. The young girl flinched and tried to pull away, but Madison maintained her grip. Lucy scowled. Straightening her shoulders and settling the backpack firmly across her back, she plowed through the groupies, bumping them out of her way. Other students saw the commotion and gathered to watch.

The Ghost You Can't See

"Excuse me! We have an appointment in the principal's office." Lucy removed the bully's hand, flinging it back at her. "You should come too, Madison, since this will concern you." She wrapped a comforting arm around the young girl, then propelled her clear of the group before turning to face Madison.

"Oh, now you've done it, Hornberger," Madison snarled. "You better watch your back. I'll be coming for you when you least expect it." She leaned close and hissed, baring her teeth.

"Sheesh, eat a breath mint or something," Lucy said. "And thanks for the warning. When I least expect you, then I'll be looking for you." The observers snickered and whispered among themselves. A few even clapped.

"Huh?" Madison looked stupefied. "I don't have a clue what Paul sees in you. It's disgusting." She flipped her perfect hair, titling her chin.

"Whatever." Lucy snorted, put an arm around the young girl's shoulder, and walked her to the principal's office. The girl glanced hesitantly over her shoulder. Madison stood alone, her gaze ricocheting around the hall. Her groupies had left her.

Lucy was tired and discouraged as she leaned against the lockers, waiting for Schuyler at the end of the day. Science lab had been grueling. She had given the hall pass from the principal to Mr. Hewitt, but the teacher was still upset over the interruption. He gave her extra study work that left her more confused over the identification of those little blobs. *Paul's offer to tutor me in science lab might not be a bad idea*, she reasoned. *It would be weird to be tutored. But with Paul, it could be fun.* She gazed unheeding through the lens of the Spectrescope, searching the hallway for any anomalies.

Last school year, Lucy and Schuyler were chasing ghosts throughout the school. They'd fought and vanquished numerous ghosts in the gymnasium, the science lab, and even the girl's bathroom. The poor old building had taken quite a beating, but the High King's power had restored it before anyone was the wiser.

Still leaning against the lockers, she slid to the floor, stretched out her legs, rested her head against the metal, and closed her eyes. She was so tired. Her head started to droop. The Spectrescope lay in her lap. The backpack was next to her, so she leaned on it, propped her head in her hand, and waited. Soon, she was asleep.

Someone was giggling in a weird, manic kind of way, and the Spectrescope was vibrating. Lucy's eyes popped open. Schuyler stood over her, giggling uncontrollably, blond curls shaking from the motion. Lucy saw the runes on the Spectrescope changing, but they didn't settle into a message. She frowned, bewildered at what it meant.

"What's up with the giggles, girlfriend? Did you eat too much sugar today?" She got up and hefted the backpack to her shoulders. Schuyler kept giggling. It gave Lucy an uneasy feeling. "What happened to your hair? Your pink lock is gone. Come to think of it, your hair is shorter. What's up with that?"

Schuyler turned and ran down the corridor, waving a hand to urge Lucy to follow. The few students who lingered in the halls were oblivious to her as she hurtled by, hair streaming behind her.

"Where are we going?" Lucy rushed after her. Schuyler ran down the hallway into the next corridor, toward the natatorium. Lucy smelled the chlorine as Schuyler dashed through the doors to the girls' locker room. The locker room was empty.

"Schuyler?" Lucy yelled. "Where are you?" She heard giggling coming from the poolroom. A loud splash erupted and the giggling stopped. "Schuyler!"

The pool glistened under the lights, the chlorine stench filling her nostrils and burning her eyes. Something splashed in the water near the deep end. Avoiding the puddles along the edge, Lucy leaned over and searched the water. Schuyler floated near the bottom of the pool. Lucy tossed her backpack aside and prepared to leap.

Suddenly, she felt two hands hit her hard in the back, driving the breath from her lungs and pushing her into the pool. Sputtering and splashing, her head broke the surface, and she gulped for air. The room was completely empty. Treading water, she tried to see the bottom. The overhead lights glared off the water's surface, obscuring her vision. She dove under and swam the length of the pool. It was empty. Had she really seen her friend at the bottom of the pool?

"Lucy! What happened?" Schuyler rushed from the locker room to the edge of the pool and reached a hand toward her. "Are you all right? Why are you in the pool?"

With help, Lucy scrabbled from the water and sat on the pool's edge. "Someone pushed me! Was it you?" She stood and shook off some of the pool water. Schuyler leaned away, dodging water droplets.

"No! Are you daft? Why would you say such a thing? I would never do something so despicable. After debate practice, I went to the lockers and saw you charging down the hall. I followed and found you floundering in the pool."

"I followed you into the locker room, but the room was empty, and you were gone!" Lucy sloshed to the towel rack, grabbed a fresh towel, and blotted the water from her stinging eyes. "What's up with you, Schuyler? Aren't you my friend anymore?" Water dripped from her clothes, forming puddles around her feet as she dried her face and arms.

"What a thing to say!" Schuyler went to her. "Of course we're friends, and we always will be, but it hurts to have you think I would betray you. You're like my sister." Her lip quivered. Tears welled and threatened to spill from her eyes. She sniffled, her nose turning pink.

"Lucy! Schuyler! Oh, thank goodness you're both all right," Mr. Bill exclaimed. Coming from the utility room, he hurried around the pool. He was clearly flustered, his hair tousled. "I spotted the daemon earlier, then I saw Lucy run into the natatorium and knew he would be about somewhere. He is a nasty piece of work, that one. I had him, but he fought hard, and then he got away."

Schuyler turned away, sniffling and dabbing her eyes with a tissue. Bill raised an eyebrow. "Did you decide to take a swim with your clothes on, Lucy?" Bill handed her another towel from the rack.

"Someone pushed me into the pool! I didn't see who it was." She dried her hair, then wrapped her cold shoulders with the towel. "Wait—you were fighting with a daemon?" With dread, reality dawned on her, pushing the breath from her lungs for a second time in minutes. Suddenly, things made sense, and the suspicious, giggling Schuyler was at the center of it all. "What did this daemon look like? It didn't have blond hair, did it? Was it dressed like Schuyler?"

Schuyler whirled around and regarded them both.

"Merbas is a shape-shifter," Mr. Bill said, picking up Lucy's backpack and handing it to her. "He can take almost any animal form, but mimicking a human requires a powerful cloning elixir made from an item belonging to the human target. Only an herbologist could make such an elixir. Merbas was morphing when I caught up with him in the pool utility room. His actual form is an enormous cat with a lion's head and a humanlike face."

He rubbed his chin thoughtfully. "You know—there used to be an herbologist who worked with plants and herbs, concocting salves and medicines. He went bad and got banished from Ascalon. He became a follower of Darnathian." He peered at the ceiling, deep in thought. "What was his name, I wonder?" He tapped a finger against his chin. "Stolas! Strange little dude. He took an owl form, like a northern saw-whet owl, but he had the longest, scrawniest legs you ever hoped not to see."

The Ghost You Can't See

"Aw, those owls are so cute," Schuyler said, imagining the cute little owl with the big, startled expression.

"Nah, not this one. Stolas was quite the divo." Mr. Bill chuckled. "He wore a tiny little jeweled crown on his head. Dumbest thing I ever saw. I bet it was him who made the elixir for Merbas."

Mr. Bill's words were daggers to Lucy's conscience, pricking her heart. She took one look at Schuyler and knew she had deeply wounded her best friend. She felt so ashamed. Schuyler had a good heart, and she bore the Triune seal of the High King. *How did I not see this? All the signs were there. Haniel said evil is all around us. If I had trusted what I knew to be true, I wouldn't have hurt my best friend.*

"Aw—I am so daft! Schuyler, can you ever forgive me? I should have known you wouldn't act so out of character, choosing friends like Madison, a manipulative, self-absorbed fake and a bully. I am so sorry I hurt you." Tears welled in Lucy's eyes this time, spilling over and trickling down her cheeks. She set her backpack down and waited.

Schuyler nodded and sniffled, blinking rapidly, but kept her gaze averted.

"I guess even a Bachar is not immune to evil," Lucy said with a lopsided smile and a sniffle. "There is so much to learn about the spirit realm. I was confused and hurt when I thought our friendship was ending. It was like you turned into Benedict Arnold and Dr. Jekyll and Mr. Hyde, all rolled into one. I guess Darnathian got me to HALT after all."

"What?" Schuyler scrutinized Lucy with watery eyes rimmed with pink under pinched brows. Lucy explained the acronym.

"You were so upset with me. You kept asking about Madison. I didn't know what was going on. I should have known something was wrong. You're impulsive and incorrigible sometimes, but never like this. I guess the Dark Prince was working his HALT magic on me too. Are we okay now?"

"I am if you are," Lucy said, her heart lighter. Schuyler fist-bumped her hand, and she gave Lucy a hug.

"What are you saying, Lucy?" Mr. Bill asked. "Do you think Merbas was imitating Schuyler?" He dropped into a nearby chair, running fingers through his mussed hair. "Is that what's been happening between you two?"

"Mr. Bill, you're looking at a complete idiot. I know it was Merbas. Well, now I know it was Merbas. My best friend would never betray me. After all, she's a child of the High King."

"That she is, and she's a keeper!" Mr. Bill smiled, his head bobbing.

"I'm confused though. Why could I see the fake Schuyler, and no one else seemed to notice?"

"I'd say your eyes are beginning to see." Mr. Bill grinned.

"So, what are we going to do about the daemon?" Schuyler asked, her posture relaxing.

"We're going to have a pool party." Lucy bounced her eyebrows, a sly smile on her face.

Time for a Pool Party

"Merbas is downright nasty, Lucy, and dangerous," Mr. Bill whispered. Most of the staff had left for the day, but they were still discoverable by the dark forces. "You will need help to vanquish him, so you must include Paul. He needs to learn how to ghost hunt."

Lucy, Schuyler, and Vivian McGoo pulled their chairs closer to lean their elbows on the table in the staff lounge. An odor of stale burned coffee permeated the air in the lower level of the old school building.

"What?" Lucy bolted upright in her chair. Schuyler's eyebrows shot upward.

"Shh! We don't want to be overheard," Mr. Bill said. Vivian, who still wore her uniform from the cafeteria, put a comforting hand on Lucy's arm and nodded her agreement.

Lucy clamped her mouth shut, held up a finger, and retrieved the Spectrescope. "Spectrescope, please seal this room." The room took on a gauzy quality, the air muffled. Now, to the casual observer, the room would appear empty, and something would magically encourage them to move along.

"Paul is still new at this," Lucy said. "He was with us when we vanquished a couple of minor daemons, but he hasn't had to fight yet. I don't want to put him in danger."

"Mr. Bill is right, Lucy," Schuyler said. "We got dropped into the middle of an ongoing supernatural battle we didn't believe existed. Paul has the AnaPiel Rod, his armor, and weapons, the same as we do." They had found the AnaPiel Rod in the ashes after Lucy's house burned down. It survived the fire, though no one knew how it had gotten there.

"And he has the Triune seal," Vivian said. "He accepted the High King, and he has all the armor he needs. He'll be fine." She patted Lucy's arm. "Bill and I will be nearby protecting your backs and preventing any more daemons from showing up at the skirmish."

"Skirmish?" Mr. Bill said. "Aren't you being a little overconfident, Vivian? Merbas is cruel. Stolas, that old herbologist master, must have created a powerful cloaking tonic to hide him from us—even we didn't detect him hanging around the school and pretending to be Schuyler."

"Oh, posh!" Vivian said, waving a dismissive hand. "The Defenders have power given to them by the High King. If they get into trouble, the King will save them."

"I'm sorry—the who?" Lucy turned a puzzled face to Mrs. McGoo.

"The Defenders," Vivian said. "It's what I call you. After all, the circle is growing, and you need a proper name. We can't keep referring to you as the ghost hunters." She gave a sharp nod to emphasize her point.

"You're right, Viv. I guess I'm being a little overprotective, that's all." Bill shrugged.

"They should be fine if they remember not to vent their rage."

"What do you mean, Mrs. McGoo?" Schuyler asked. "Wouldn't we be a stronger, more fearsome adversary if we let our anger show?"

"Oh no, dearie. You must never vent your rage—only fools do that. You will lose control and your advantage if you do such a thing. It's wise to remain calm if you want to bring down an adversary. You must never openly rebuke Irredaemon or Ormarrs. Remember, your power comes from the High King; it is his right to judge the fallen, and it is he who enables his Defenders."

"Do you think Paul is ready for this?" Lucy asked. "Seeing his first daemon made him squeamish. And we haven't needed the AnaPiel Rod—yet."

Mr. Bill chortled. "I remember you being scared, too, Lucy. You and Schuyler screamed like little banshees when you saw that chandelier in your foyer, and it wasn't even a daemon!" He guffawed and slapped his knee. "It was hilarious."

"Hmm, excellent memory for someone as old as dirt." Lucy turned and smirked at him.

"Gee, thanks for the reminder, young one," Mr. Bill said. Vivian chuckled and cupped a hand to her cheek. Bill scowled at her. "You can stop laughing, Viv—you're as old as I am." She stopped laughing.

"Question—what does the AnaPiel Rod do?" Lucy waited for Mr. Bill or Vivian to answer. They both remained silent. "How do you not know? We have an artifact, and we don't know what it does?"

Mr. Bill hunched his shoulders nearly to his ears. "Well, no one rightly knows. The High King created the rod from the remains of the Tree of All Knowledge after its destruction. When Ealasaiden was first created, the rod guided the Oracles. Some say it performed incredible miracles, but over time, the rod became lost. No one has seen it in recent memory."

"Ealasaiden? I've never heard of it. Where is it?" Lucy looked from Mr. Bill to Vivian.

"Ealasaiden was the name of Earth at the beginning. But that was a long time ago." Vivian smiled sadly. Ealasaiden was a much lovelier name than Earth.

"You mentioned miracles, Mr. Bill. What kind of miracles did it perform?" Schuyler asked.

"Legend has it that the rod polluted and cleansed the waters of a great city, parted the water to create a dry road through the middle of a sea, and cracked open a rock in the desert, producing a fresh source of water."

"I'm sensing a water theme here," Lucy said, her lips pursed in a lop-sided pucker. "It will come in handy if we have to fill the swimming pool."

"Can you drown a daemon?" Schuyler asked, a simple look on her face.

Lucy, Mr. Bill, and Vivian regarded her suspiciously.

"Just wondering . . ."

Thursday morning, the Schuyler impersonator showed up several times, antagonizing Lucy whenever the real Schuyler wasn't around. Lucy could now easily recognize the disguise, distinguishing between her sweet friend and the entity. The subtle difference was in the eyes; they were cold, calculating, and uncaring. Lucy acted disheartened, her face downcast in the daemon's presence. Consequently, Merbas gleefully jeered, sneered, taunted, and mocked Lucy.

Lucy went to her locker and retrieved the books for her afternoon classes, then waited around the corner with the Spectrescope. The daemon sauntered down the corridor, heading for the lunchroom, unaware Lucy was spying on it. She nearly dropped the Spectrescope when she saw the specter in the lens. It was hideous. Mr. Bill wasn't being facetious when he said it was ugly.

Its body was that of a large, emaciated lion, gaunt and unkept, covered in russet fur with a great shaggy mane. It walked upright, swaggering like a cocky human. The revolting face was like a Picasso painting, distorted and exaggerated in strange configurations. Lucy was dizzy, her stomach queasy, from looking at it.

The daemon Schuyler entered the lunchroom, and as it had previously, went to Madison's table and sat with the girl who was lovely and poised on the outside but mean and conniving on the inside. Lucy followed at a distance, then slipped into the empty chair and joined her friends.

Schuyler was notably late, Paul was reading a graphic novel, and Mathias was ignoring Lucy, as usual. She opened the lunch she had made and nibbled at her sandwich, casting furtive glances at the daemon. The Schuyler clone casually whispered in Madison's ear, and the girl flinched. Lucy wondered what that was about. After a few minutes, the daemon left.

Schuyler dropped into the chair beside her, and Lucy nearly upended her soda.

"Sorry," she said, opening her lunch bag. "I got stopped by one of the debate-team members and lost track of the time. I'll have to snarf my lunch down." She took a bite from her sandwich and reached for a carrot. "Everything set for tonight?" she mumbled around the carrot stick.

"Uh-huh," Lucy said, chewing and glancing sideways at her friend. She swallowed, leaned next to Schuyler, and whispered, "Mr. Bill was right. Merbas is super hideous. I would have lost my lunch if I had already eaten."

"That bad?"

"Worse."

"Yikes. Glad I didn't see it."

"You probably will later." Lucy reached for her soda. Mathias was watching.

Lucy leaned against the lockers, waiting for Paul. She needed to know he was ready for this next-level confrontation. He had come a long way since his own hauntings and the episode in the science lab last year. She had texted him before school this morning, asking him to bring the AnaPiel Rod and his wristband. She'd also spent time in orison with Iam, and he had insisted Paul bring the artifact.

Schuyler was hiding in the girls' locker room. Mr. Bill and Vivian watched from the pool utility room, where Bill had encountered the daemon the day before. The remaining students had filed out moments ago, and the corridors were empty.

Paul plodded toward her. He was nervous. His lake-blue eyes had a startled expression. His backpack swayed on his shoulder. Though he was trying to appear nonchalant with one hand stuffed casually in his jeans pocket, the white knuckles on the hand gripping his bag strap belied that impression.

"Does this get any easier the more you—you know—do it?" he stuttered as he joined Lucy. She nodded and gave him a reassuring smile. It eased the tension slightly. They walked to the natatorium and stood in the antechamber.

The natatorium, which housed the pool, was added during the last renovation to the old school building, built in the late eighteen hundreds. The historical society was adamant that the structure should replicate the design of the original building. Looking at it from the curb, the building was identical. Inside, it housed the latest technology for the pool and its surrounding structures. Lucy preferred this pool over the public neighborhood pool.

Lucy peeked inside the girls' locker room. It was empty. Wherever Schuyler was hiding, Lucy doubted the daemon would detect her.

"I won't lie to you and say vanquishing gets easier; it doesn't. A spirit is still a living entity, and it's horrible having to vanquish it. But they became evil. They want to hurt and destroy us. We must remember we are not killing it, thank goodness—I don't want that responsibility. We are sending it back to Shinar."

"What is Shinar?" He let his backpack slip to the tile and rolled his shoulders, easing the tension knots in his muscles. "Do you know where it is?"

"It's like a prison, a place the High King sends the fallen angels. There, they are separated forever from the High King. I imagine it's hidden somewhere in the universe. Someday, Darnathian will cross a line, and he will go there too." She grabbed his hand and squeezed it. "Thanks for coming. I know it sort of takes a leap of faith at first, believing in the supernatural. There's a lot to take in." She took a deep, cleansing breath. "Wait—where's Mathias?"

"I saw him get on the bus. He should be home by now."

"Good. Got your armor?"

He held up his arm, showing the leather wristband he wore. It was magical, like hers and Schuyler's bracelets, and contained his shield and sword.

Lucy tapped a finger on the leather wristband. "Always wear your armor," she said, peering up at him. He was several inches taller. Her face flushed as she realized how silly she sounded.

"I'm sorry, Paul," she said. "You know this already. I get anxious when we're ghost hunting." She gave him a lopsided smile.

"It's okay, Lucy. I don't mind. I've been hesitant to take it off, anyway," he said, with a faltering smile of his own. "I'm kind of nervous, too, in case you didn't notice."

"Did you bring the AnaPiel Rod?" Paul nodded, took it from his backpack, and handed it to her. Beautifully detailed carvings of almonds and flowering branches filled most of the rod's length. On top was the head and face of a deeply wrinkled old man with long wavy hair and a beard. His eyes were closed.

The rod was currently no larger than a rolling pin. Iam had shown her how to reduce its size so it was easier to hide. Gripping a series of almonds along the staff, it burst to full size. With its length at nearly five and a half feet, it was round, stout, and quite a handful. The wood grains gleamed in the light.

"Oh, cool!" Paul exclaimed. "It's kind of like a lightsaber!" He gladly reached for it. Lucy shook her head and grinned. Paul was the most unlikely ghost hunter yet. This would be his first time using the AnaPiel Rod.

"Paul, your artifact has great power and knowledge. From now on, keep it with you, like I always carry the Spectrescope." Lucy took her vest and floppy brimmed hat from the backpack and put them on.

"Knowledge?" Paul said, laughing. He scrutinized the carvings, which were easier to see now, especially those of the old man. "What's it gonna do? Talk to me?" he asked, grinning.

"Yes, I talk to you, silly boy," AnaPiel said, opening his eyes and blinking. "How else would I convey knowledge to you?"

"Whoa!" Paul screamed, throwing the rod. It remained upright and floated above the floor. It drifted back and hovered in front of him. Paul leaned away from it.

"Wonderful," AnaPiel said, curling his lip. "They bequeathed me to a vacuous boy."

Paul's eyes were about to jettison from their sockets. Lucy snickered, thinking if he leaned any farther backward, he would topple over. It reminded her of her own reaction upon discovering the magic in the Spectrescope.

"This is what we do, Paul," Lucy said with a laugh. "We have special tools, and we hunt ghosts and spirits and daemons and creatures and—"

"Okay—I get the idea," Paul said, eyeing the staff. He shook his head and blinked several times. The old man still glared at him.

AnaPiel levitated between the teenagers, glancing between them as if he were assessing them both. "I am AnaPiel, the Keeper of Knowledge." His eyes were intelligent, and his hair rippled like ocean waves. "What do you wish to know?"

"I'm—I'm not sure," Paul stuttered.

The Ghost You Can't See

"How surprising," AnaPiel said. "When you figure it out, wake me. I'm going back to sleep." He closed his eyes briefly, then opened them again. "I am your responsibility. Do not lose me or mistreat me." He floated around and frowned at Lucy. "And news flash: I don't enjoy lying about on the cold ground or being kept stuffed in a trunk," he groused, "or a backpack." With a tilt of his nose, he went back to sleep, still floating in the air.

Lucy harrumphed. "Charming fellow, isn't he?"

She poked the sleeping AnaPiel Rod. It drifted toward Paul. He watched it for a moment, then grabbed it.

"Paul, I know this ghost hunting business is still new to you, but please be brave. This may be horrendously scary to you, but we need to get rid of this daemon. His name is Merbas. You have the Triune seal and protection from the High King. It's the daemons who need to fear you."

"I think I can be brave," he said, his voice an octave higher than usual. He cleared his throat, swallowed, and lowered his voice. "I trust you, Lucy. If you think I can do this, then I can."

"I'm not sure what AnaPiel will do for you, but keep him ready." She pointed at the wristband. He nodded and tapped the nameplate.

A large silver kite shield, emblazoned with a white fox holding a purple flag baring a golden cross, erupted from the wristband. Paul jumped, awkwardly holding his piece of armor. It startled him each time. His broadsword was sheathed in the back.

"It's cool," he squeaked. Lucy knew exactly how he felt.

"Do you have a plan?" Paul asked, holding the AnaPiel Rod in one hand and the shield in the other. Both shook.

"This is where I say, 'Yes! I'm making it up as I go,'" she said, thrusting a fist in the air. He didn't laugh. She shrugged a shoulder and flashed him a goofy grin. Paul was so tensed up he was breaking out in a cold sweat. *Okay, pleasant talk*, Lucy thought.

"Spectrescope, I need the Belt of Truth. Paul has a shield and weapons, but he still needs more armor. Will you equip him, please?" The Spectrescope vibrated, the symbols glowing. She watched as a golden breastplate appeared on Paul's chest and a helmet materialized on his head.

A snort escaped her lips. The memory of Paul's startled expression would keep her laughing for days once this was over. *At least he didn't faint*, she thought. The ring settled on her finger.

"Spectrescope, I forgot the new shoes for each of us. Would you bring them, please?" No sooner had she asked than the sandals appeared, comfortably snug on her feet, like any common, everyday sandals. The dryad had said they would provide a firm footing. "Thank you, Spectrescope. We need all the help we can get." Paul was wearing them too.

"Paul, you go to the boys' locker room, but wait until you hear me shout—then coming running. Keep your shield up and your sword in front of you. Schuyler will enter from the girls' side. Mr. Bill and Vivian are protecting us. If any other daemons show up, they will handle them. Our job is to vanquish Merbas."

Paul took a deep breath and squared his shoulders. "Ready."

"Oh, one more thing. Don't freak out, but the daemon is a shapeshifter impersonating Schuyler. Be sure you don't vanquish the wrong girl. Schuyler will be the one wearing armor." She dashed from the antechamber and into the girls' locker room.

"Schuyler, are you in here?" Lucy yelled. She and Schuyler had discussed the prearranged dialogue last night as they made plans to vanquish the daemon. They chose the pool since the chlorine would help mask the stench until they could cleanse the air. A vanquishing was always stinky. Mr. Bill and Vivian had thought the plan was a good one. But even the best plan could go horribly wrong.

The Ghost You Can't See

The glare from the overhead lights bounced off the surface of the water. It was eerily quiet, the air stagnant with apprehension. Nothing moved, not even the pennants that hung over each end of the pool.

The Olympic-sized pool had a motorized movable wall, dividing it into swimming lanes for competitive swim meets. Bright-orange safety cones blocked each end of the motorized platform. Puddles lay along the edge from swim practice earlier in the day. Tonight, the room was empty—no swim practice on Thursday or Friday evenings.

Lucy advanced into the natatorium and sniffled. The chlorine was strong; it made her eyes burn. The Spectrescope was in the waistband of her jeans, hidden under the vest. She pushed the hat back on her head so she could see past the floppy brim. There was no sign of the daemon Schuyler, so she walked around the pool and sat in the side chair permanently bolted in place. Her backpack dropped to the floor.

Movement caught her eye on the other side of the pool. The fake Schuyler had appeared and stood on the platform of the motorized wall near the shallow end, giggling. *Seriously?* Lucy thought. *Do daemons think we're just silly little girls? He will be surprised.*

"Spectrescope," she whispered, her hand on the artifact, "seal this area." Immediately, the atmosphere changed. The Shimmer Shield was in place. Merbas didn't notice the change in the room; he was watching Lucy.

"Schuyler!" Lucy said cheerfully. She stood and waved at the daemon. "I thought you had forgotten about our swim party. Are you ready to have fun?" The daemon giggled louder. "Righto, here we go," Lucy said softly, still smiling at the entity. She whipped out the Spectrescope.

"*Armor!*" Instantly, her armor appeared, including the Belt of Truth. She raised her shield. Her spare sword, Ratha-nael, was in its sheath if she needed it. The lens disappeared from the Spectrescope, and the Spirit sword flowed from the handle. The metal gleamed under the bright lights.

Schuyler charged from the girls' locker room, holding the Zazriel sword and her shield high. Her armor gleamed, the light bouncing off her helmet and breastplate.

Paul entered from the boys' side, wearing armor and clearly uncomfortable. He ran forward, placing the daemon between them in the center.

Merbas was surrounded.

Schuyler's Ultimate Dunking

Merbas growled, low and ominous. He crouched and crawled across the top of the barrier and stood on top of the motorized wall in the middle of the pool, his hands gripping the rails. Lucy shuddered. While she knew it was the daemon, it was disconcerting and utterly creepy to see a replica of her best friend act in such a manner. The hairs on her arms stood up.

Lucy paced slowly toward the barrier and the daemon, her shield and sword ready. The real Schuyler, clad in full armor, advanced slowly to the end of the pool. She gave her doppelgänger standing in the middle of the pool the stink eye. The only difference between the two was that she was wearing her magical armor and had one pink lock. The imitation Schuyler was a slightly younger version, like when they'd fought the ghost of Darwin Stewart in the humongous castle dining room.

Lucy grimaced. Paul stood frozen, his shield and the AnaPiel Rod drifting slowly toward the floor as he gaped at the two nearly identical girls. He glanced at Lucy, and she indicated the rod with a dip of her head. He nodded and rolled his head, stretching his neck before squaring his shoulders and raising his weapons.

Paul whispered to the artifact, and AnaPiel's eyes popped opened, his expression intense, not missing any details as he floated next to the teenager. AnaPiel nodded at the shield, and Paul unsheathed a sword with a muted rasp of metal against leather.

Now that Paul was focused, Lucy watched the daemon glance maliciously at each teenager. She could almost see what Merbas was thinking, and she wondered what the daemon would do next. With the current positioning of the Defenders, they trapped Merbas in the middle, creating a standoff.

Merbas stood and swayed back and forth, fists clenched. He'd clearly underestimated his opponents.

Lucy mounted the motorized wall and tilted her head toward the opposite end. Schuyler nodded and climbed up on the platform. The daemon had nowhere to escape except into the water. Schuyler tossed the safety cone. It bounced off the clone's back and fell into the pool.

"Stupid humans!" the spirit hissed, his head swiveling to glare at each girl. His feet morphed to lion paws, the claws gripping the rails. He had to get to firm ground. He turned and charged at Schuyler. Suddenly, the facsimile lost cohesion and segmented into unnatural configurations, one eye above a bent nose, the other above an ear.

Schuyler braced her feet for impact, and a moment later, her imitator scudded into her. The daemon grabbed the shield and howled as it burned his flesh. He pushed the girl backward.

Lucy charged after the daemon, her sword raised. Merbas somersaulted over Schuyler, grabbed her arm, and tossed her to the platform. Her helmet banged against the rail, making a sound like a ringing bell.

Merbas landed on his feet and darted away.

"Are you all right?" Lucy extended a hand, pulled Schuyler to her feet, and guided her poolside.

"I'm okay, just dazed a bit." Schuyler shook her head to clear the brain fog. A form flashed past them as Paul chased after the fleeing daemon.

"Go with him! I'll take the other side!" Lucy dashed across the motorized platform and kicked the orange safety cone aside as the daemon slid to a stop in front of her. Schuyler and Paul closed from behind.

Merbas ripped the poolside chair from its bolts and tossed it at the two closing Defenders. They dodged the chair. Lucy lunged with the Spirit Sword. The daemon swayed sideways, narrowly avoiding the deadly weapon. He streaked to the towel rack, picked it up, and tossed it at her.

Next, Merbas tore the pool ladder from its mounting and hurtled it at the Defenders. Paul's sword knocked it away with a loud clang. Schuyler dove to the floor and landed on her shield arm, letting out a yelp of pain. The entity grabbed Paul's shield, scorching his hands again. Paul shifted his weight and thrust his sword forward. The entity sidestepped the sword, seized Paul, lifted him, and threw him into the pool. Paul spluttered and coughed as he climbed out of the water.

The spirit grabbed Schuyler and laughed as the girl kicked and squirmed while he dragged her to the opposite side of the pool. The Shimmer Shield left him no other place to go. She beat at him with her shield, but this time, he didn't react to the burning pain.

Merbas took a vial from his pocket, yanked out strands of Schuyler's hair, and then tossed her aside. She landed in a heap against the wall. He dropped the strands into the vial, swirled the contents, and drank it before smashing the empty container to the floor. Roiling clouds of purple-tinged smoke obscured the daemon and his hostage. When the smoke cleared, two identical Schuylers with armor and swords faced off across the room. Lucy looked at Paul, gobsmacked.

The Schuylers lunged at each other, their swords clanging together, rasping and screeching. They copied each other's moves. It was like watching a dangerous but well-choreographed dance.

"How are we gonna tell them apart?" Paul exclaimed, shutting his gaping jaw with a pop.

One of the Schuylers waggled her shield. "Lucy, I'm here!" she shouted. "It's me!"

"No! Lucy, I'm here!" the other Schuyler yelled. "I'm the real me!"

"Oh, you've got to be kidding!" Lucy shouted, racing across the platform again. "Spectrescope! Please, show me the real Schuyler." The Spirit Sword retreated into the handle, and the big lens reappeared. Lucy waited, but nothing appeared in the glass except swirls of blurry images.

"Lucy, can't you tell who the daemon is?" one of the Schuylers yelled.

"Seriously?" the second said. "Even the Spectrescope doesn't know?" The twin girls scrutinized each other.

"The cloaking elixir Stolas used must be extremely powerful if the Spectrescope can't penetrate it. Belt of Truth, please help us!" Lucy waited, but the stones didn't react. She wiggled the belt, but no stones fell out.

Paul charged one girl, his sword raised menacingly. The Schuyler in front of him squealed and darted aside, using the sword to block.

"Don't!" the girl said. "Paul, it's me."

Lucy advanced on the second armor-clad girl and lunged. The girl squealed, her sword clashing into Lucy's, blocking the strike.

"Lucy! It's me," she screamed. The swords screeched and clanged, metal against metal.

Her opponent was strong, but Lucy still couldn't tell if she was the real Schuyler. The girl moved so quickly, reacting to each thrust with a counter cut. The moves were defensive, so it could be the real Schuyler, but she wasn't sure.

"Tell me this—where did we first meet Malpar?" Lucy stepped back and balanced on her rear foot, her body angled and her sword arm pointed straight at the girl. It was a weak stance, and one she hoped showed a desire to talk.

The Ghost You Can't See

"In my bedroom!" the girl said, imitating Lucy's stance.

"He was in the closet with two doors," the other Schuyler yelled as she deflected Paul's thrust.

"This is ridiculous," Lucy huffed, still pointing the sword.

"Lucy, what're we going to do?" Paul asked. "I don't want to hurt our Schuyler."

Nearby, AnaPiel hovered over the pool, then dropped with a splash into the water. He remained submerged momentarily before surfacing and floating out of range of the skirmish.

"Oh, that was quite refreshing. I really must get out more." He hovered over the end of the pool, observing the fight.

"Paul!" AnaPiel shouted. "They must both go into the water!"

"No!" the Schuylers yelled in unison. They each scrutinized their opponent, desperation etching their features. Schuyler Williams could barely tread water, and daemons didn't swim at all.

"Now!" Lucy yelled, charging the unsuspecting facsimile. She grabbed its arm and dove into the pool. Paul did the same with the second girl, and they all splashed into the water and disappeared below the surface. The pool water spouted and bubbled before it settled to a frothy simmer. Moments later, three heads in helmets broke the surface, their owners spluttering and treading water, blinking water from their eyes.

Merbas popped up, screaming in agony, and scrambled to the edge. His nails clawed the cement wall for purchase. The water had neutralized the concoction, revealing his true form.

The soaked and matted russet fur emphasized the hideous face on the bulbous head. The daemon's skin bubbled and churned, like marbles rolling about under a wet fur blanket. He howled as the boils erupted, tearing the skin, the poison leaching into the pool water and turning it a vile yellow.

Paul grimaced and swam for the edge, an arm wrapped around Schuyler. He steadied her while she got out of the pool, then he hauled himself onto the ledge. Lucy swam to them. They grabbed her outstretched arms and yanked her from the water.

AnaPiel floated to Paul and nodded. "Well done, boy. Now take the Briathos sword and finish your work. I am here if you need me."

Paul stood and picked up his sword; he had dropped it with the shield when he dove in the pool. He gulped, cleared his throat, and strode to the pool's edge where the daemon struggled in the water.

"You are worthless, vile pieces of human muck, and I curse you!" Merbas swiped a ragged claw at the boy. "The wretched High King you serve denied our master his rightful—"

"Enough of this," Paul said, jabbing the daemon in the chest with the Briathos sword. The daemon exploded into black and russet grains, imploded to a pinpoint, and disappeared with a pop. The air stank of sulfur.

Lucy walked up to Paul and nudged him in the shoulder.

"Hey. Are you okay?" Lucy asked, gazing up at him. He seemed different somehow, more mature. *I guess it's what happens when you live in two realities*, she thought. "I'm so glad you're here. It's a lot to take in, but you did good."

She stretched out her arm. The shield and the Ratha-nael sword transmuted back into the bracelet. The Spectrescope returned, and she tucked the artifact in the waistband of her jeans. The muffled quality from the Shimmer Shield abated, and the sound returned to normal. Schuyler joined them, wearing her magical clothes.

Lucy watched as Paul studied his sword. Leaves and vines etched the broadsword along the entire length of the metal on both sides, the edges razor sharp. It was both magnificent and terrifying. Written in script under the hilt was the name Briathos. "Wow," Paul whispered.

"I wonder what Briathos means," Lucy said. A tiny flame appeared and licked the metal, etching words into the surface. *It means "punisher of daemons."*

Paul grinned. It seemed he was getting used to the many supernatural surprises. "Uh, thanks. I'm glad you're on our side." *You're welcome*, the flame wrote and flickered out. The words disappeared.

Paul sheathed the Briathos sword and tapped the shield. It changed to the leather wristband. His magical clothing was back too; he wore a baseball cap and a hoodie. He pulled the cap off and stuffed it in a pocket.

The AnaPiel Rod floated to Paul, hovered, and studied the boy's face. "I am waiting," he said.

Paul glanced at Lucy and raised his eyebrows, clearly perplexed at what he was supposed to do next. "Um. Waiting for what?" he said.

AnaPiel rolled his eyes and huffed. "My job is complete. Press the almonds and shrink me. I'm tired, and I want to go back to sleep."

"Well, before you take your nappy," Lucy said, staring at the AnaPiel Rod, "I have a few questions. Why did the water affect the daemon? It's only chlorinated water."

"No, it's not," he said, gloating. "I turned it into holy water. Evil entities cannot abide holiness or goodness. It is as vile to them as evil is to me." AnaPiel floated to Paul. "Now?"

"Wait," Lucy raised a finger. "Schuyler and I were the only people in her room when Malpar showed up. How did the daemon know the details of the closet with two doors?"

"Everything that makes you who you are is in your DNA. Even your memories are encoded." AnaPiel said. "Stolas, the potion master, needed something from his human target to generate the cloned image. Do you know what he might have used?"

Lucy thought for a moment while AnaPiel waited impatiently, his eyes slowly rolling about in his head. "Schuyler's hair! When we fought the daemon in the huge dining room of Darnathian's castle."

"Oh my goodness!" Schuyler exclaimed, her eyes widening. "I'd forgotten—when your sword sliced through the ropes tying me to the chair, I lost a lock of hair. The ghost of Darwin Stewart snatched it up. I don't know what happened to it afterward."

"The Dark Prince would have kept it for such a use as this," AnaPiel said. He raised a dubious eyebrow at Lucy.

"Okay, last question. What are you going to do about the water?" Lucy asked, pointing at the pool. "We can't leave it all nasty and neon yellow. Aren't you going to clean it like you cleaned the waters of the great city in the Oracles' time? Mr. McGoo told us all about the miracles you performed."

"McGoo talks too much. Besides, I was a younger branch back then. You clean it. I'm going back to sleep." AnaPiel closed his eyes and slept.

"He's so likable, isn't he?" Lucy grinned and poked Paul in the arm. "I'm glad I don't have to live with him. He's your responsibility now." The Belt of Truth vibrated around her waist. A white stone wiggled and popped into her hand.

The words inscribed inside the stone glowed brightly. Lucy squealed and showed the stone to Paul so he could read the message.

"It's incredible," he gasped. Schuyler peeked at the inscription and nodded at him with a grin.

"Okay, watch this." She held up the stone and read the inscription aloud. *"He will sanctify and clean it and wash the water with his word."* She tossed the stone into the polluted water. Steam rose from the pool like a cool mist in the morning, the water bubbling and frothing. The gurgling noise filled the room, and the pennants danced on their strings. The gurgling stopped, and the water settled down. It was clean, and a vibrant shade of Caribbean blue.

Lucy fisted her hands. Paul and Schuyler bumped their fists into hers and each did an exploding fist bump. "Boom!" Lucy said.

Mathias boarded the school bus and waited until Paul disappeared back into the building. He got off, pushed through the throng, and followed Paul at a distance. He kept to the shadows behind the big columns in the main hallway. He saw the boy join Lucy, and they went to the natatorium. The inner hallways had changed to power-saving mode, every other light fixture darkened. The remaining lights would dim after midnight. The witching hours. Mathias scoffed at the idea, not knowing why he knew that or why he should care.

He stayed in the shadows as the two friends entered the antechamber, the doors swinging closed behind them. His ears itched, so he stuffed his hands in his pockets. Anything to keep from itching. He should probably see a doctor, but it was one of the last things he wanted to do in this stupid town.

They had itched for weeks now, ever since his dad took the promotion and moved the family several hundred miles away from home. Why couldn't things stay the way they were? Why was everything constantly changing?

It annoyed him. No, he was angry. He thought Lucy was his friend, but she accused him of being Dr. Jekyll and Mr. Hyde, like he was some kind of monster. It pricked his conscience when she called him those names.

Because some days, he didn't even recognize himself in the mirror. Maybe he was a monster.

More often, Mathias did things he didn't want to do, like now, betraying his friends, traipsing after them like a lying spy, or having strange thoughts that popped in his head. He felt weak and ashamed.

And it scared him. Maybe he was losing his mind. Maybe he was losing his soul, whatever that might be. He didn't want to lose his mind or his soul. He could hide for a while, sitting in the dark auditorium before class, but too many times he felt like he was being pulled from his body, then suddenly, he would snap back in. He felt like he had lost something each time that happened.

The only time he felt normal was in his room at the Carriage House. It felt like coming home—welcoming, peaceful, and comforting. It soothed him to be there—he didn't know why. It was a bed-and-breakfast establishment, a mom-and-pop hotel, but with the best breakfast pastries he had ever eaten. He wished he could stay in his room and never come out.

Edging closer to the doors, he heard muffled voices but couldn't make out what they were saying. After a moment, the voices stopped. He eased the door open and stuck his head in. The antechamber was empty. Lucy and Paul must have gone through one of the locker rooms to the natatorium. The boys' locker room was empty, so he tried the door to the pool-room. It was unlocked, but it would not open. They were up to something, but what?

The door had a narrow window of clear safety glass for viewing the natatorium, but he couldn't see beyond the glass; everything was blurry. Something strange was happening, he was sure of it. He waited and watched. The locker room was eerily quiet, the silence hinting at danger. Or maybe he was just feeling frightened and alone.

Mathias rubbed his sleeve against the glass to scrub off the film obscuring the window. Suddenly, it cleared. He peered through the glass. His eyes were playing tricks on him.

Lucy, Paul, and Schuyler stood together near the shallow end of the pool. Something long and brown floated in the air, but the three friends didn't seem to notice. The object was too far away for Mathias to see what it was; it was probably a balloon of some sort. Lucy was wearing a glittering belt he didn't remember seeing earlier.

He watched as she tossed a large rock into the yellow pool water. Why was it yellow? The water bubbled and roiled, and a mist rose from the surface. Mathias took a step back. He rubbed his eyes and looked again. The pool water was now a sparkling blue, and the belt Lucy had been wearing was gone.

"I am going crazy." He turned and fled.

A Dissonant Chord

"*Mom!*" Lucy shouted as she ran through the hallway to the kitchen. "Pizza is here! Can I borrow some money? I left my babysitting money in my room." Her stocking feet slid to a stop at the island counter. The kitchen, breakfast room, and sunroom were all empty. "Mom!"

"I'm in the office, for goodness' sake," Jeannie said, tapping away on the calculator, her budget book laying open in front of her. While most people used an app or a program to keep track of finances, she preferred the bookkeeping method. It kept her mind sharp.

Lucy entered and leaned over the stylish wood desk in the center of the room and rapped her knuckles on the top. Days after Lucy's outburst at Mathias, her mom was still ignoring her. "May I please borrow twenty bucks? We're all pitching in for pizza, and I left my money in my room."

"I guess you will just have to run upstairs and get it. If you start now, you should be back before the pizza gets cold." She gave Lucy a hard inspection over her reading glasses and laid the pencil into the journal's open spine.

Lucy pursed her lips and returned the stare. She had apologized numerous times for her behavior, but Mom wouldn't let it go. "Fine. I'll just take the elevator, shall I?" She spun on her heel and crossed the hall.

Mom grumbled to herself as she went back to her budget book. "Wait," she called after Lucy, "take what?"

Lucy threw open the cupboard doors and climbed into the dumb-waiter. Numbered buttons on the side of the cabinet matched the floor stops. She slapped number three, folded her legs in, and hoped the little elevator didn't drop her into the basement.

The motor whirred to life, and the dumbwaiter rose slowly at first. Just as the lift disappeared into the recesses of the old house, her mother appeared in the office doorway, her face contorting as she yelled, "Lucy Hornberger!"

The lift shook its way to the top floor and stopped with a bump. Lucy's stomach lurched into her throat. It was pitch dark inside the dumbwaiter. Inanimate objects didn't need lights to quell their fears. Thoughtless teenagers, however, did. She placed two quivering hands on the flat vertical surface in front of her and hoped it was the cabinet on the third floor. She gave a firm push. The doors swung open, and light spilled into the small space. Relief flooded through her as she tumbled from the lift and gulped air.

"I don't think I will do that again." Quaking, she stumbled to her room, opened her desk drawer, and paused. Sounds murmured through the wall vent near the floor next to the desk. Someone was talking. She knelt and leaned close to listen, the angst with her mother forgotten. Mathias was in suite four, located under her room. No wonder she could hear him.

Mathias was talking to himself.

Lucy frowned; she couldn't make out the words, but the tone was hard to miss. He sounded angry and sad, and he argued with himself. Empathy pricked her heart. She retrieved the twenty dollars and took the front staircase down to the second-floor guest level. She knocked on his door, then took a step back.

"Who is it?" he answered.

"It's Lucy."

Lucy heard him fumbling with the lock before he opened the door. *He keeps his door locked. What's up with that?* she thought. *His parents are the only guests in the house. Who is he keeping out—me?* She pasted on a smile when the door creaked open. Mathias stood in the doorway. His tousled hair and wrinkled shirt and jeans made his face seem haggard and drawn.

"Did you want something?" he asked, stuffing both hands in his jeans pockets. He leaned against the doorframe and waited, avoiding eye contact.

"Did you forget the study group?" Lucy placed her hand on the newel knob of the railing that circled the loft, the solidness somehow comforting. "Paul and Schuyler are here. We ordered pizza, and we're about to eat. Don't you want to join us? It will be more fun than being alone. I promise."

"Well, maybe for a little while." He ran his hand over his hair. "Uh, thanks. I'll be down in a minute."

"Great." She smiled, then clomped down the stairs to the foyer. Schuyler and Paul were already munching pizza in the main dining room. "Who paid my share for the pizza?" Lucy held up the money.

"Paul did. You owe him twenty bucks," Schuyler said, chewing a slice of pepperoni pizza. She snatched the bill and gave it to Paul. Lucy rolled her eyes. Schuyler squinted at her. "What? Do I have sauce on my nose?" She shoved the pizza boxes across the table and handed a paper plate and napkin to a grinning Lucy.

"I've got to ask. What did you do now?" Schuyler said, wiping sauce from her nose. "Your mom was yelling and grumbling again."

"I used the dumbwaiter." Lucy sat and inspected each of the three pizzas, trying to decide what to eat.

"Okay. Why would using the dumbwaiter upset her?" Schuyler took a sip of soda and reached for another slice of pizza.

"I was in it."

Schuyler choked and coughed. "You did what?" she said, wiping the spittle from her face. "Why would you do that?"

"Cool!" Paul said, grinning. "Was it fun? I've always wondered if it was possible to fit a person in one of those."

"Eh." Lucy shrugged. "More like scary and dark."

"I'd worry it would drop me into the basement and splatter my remains across the cement floor!" Schuyler said.

"Well, yeah, there was that," Lucy admitted, hunching her shoulders to her ears with a goofy grin. She plopped a slice of Hawaiian pizza on her plate and reached for the last soda. "It was fine until it started moving. Then I wondered what the weight limit was." Paul laughed; in fact, he couldn't stop laughing. Lucy eyed him dubiously and changed the subject.

"Mathias had holed up in his room. I asked him to join us. He should be down in a minute." She popped the can open and took a swig while watching Schuyler's smile expand. "I'll go get more drinks from the kitchen."

Lucy filled a tray with cold soda and carried it back to the dining room. Mathias came down the stairs just then. He had combed his hair and tucked his shirt into his jeans. Water droplets dampened his shirt collar. She tipped her head toward the dining room and he followed her to the table.

The tastefully decorated dining room between the parlor and the breakfast room was spacious. Archways connected it to both rooms, creating an open feeling without changing its Victorian flare. Its white beadboard, trim, and crown molding offset the wide band of red patterned wallpaper on the top third of the wall. The mismatched antiques and warm honey-colored pine plank flooring were unassuming and homey.

Mathias slid into a chair across from Schuyler and nodded his thanks when she handed him a plate and pushed the tray of soda toward him. He ate his pizza while the others chatted about the debate team.

Mathias's parents were relaxing in the parlor; his mom read a book while his dad, deep in thought, studied something on his laptop. His mom glanced up, waved, then went back to reading. They both appeared well rested and content. The atmosphere of the old house seemed to agree with them too.

"We're gonna study in the library room. It's quiet in there with fewer distractions. Coming?" Lucy said, picking up her used plate and napkin. She thumbed toward the library across the foyer. Paul and Schuyler had already cleared their places and waited in the library room.

"Fewer distractions?" Mathias said. "What's that mean?"

"It's the only room in the house where I can't get an internet connection, so I can't surf the net while I'm studying. Therefore, fewer distractions." She shrugged, walked to the kitchen, and dumped the trash in the bin. Mathias followed and sat at the island counter. Lucy rummaged in a cupboard until she found a tin of Mrs. McGoo's bar cookies. She waggled it in front of him.

"Wait till you taste these. They make doing homework worth the effort. It's like a flavor explosion in your mouth—chocolate, butterscotch, and pecans—so yummy." She grabbed some napkins from the basket on the counter. "C'mon. Schuyler and Paul are waiting. If we don't get these to Schuyler, she'll faint from hunger."

"She just ate pizza." Mathias shoved his hands in his jeans pockets and loped down the hallway behind Lucy.

"For Schuyler, that's like hours ago." Lucy entered the library, but Mathias didn't follow. He paused, then started up the stairs instead. "Aren't you coming?" Lucy said, disappointed by his change in plan. "I thought we were all going to study together."

"Uh, sorry. I'm not feeling good. I'll just go to my room and read a bit before bed. I'll catch up with you tomorrow. Um, thanks for the pizza." He trudged up the stairs and passed the small sitting room. Lucy watched as he rounded the balcony, his hand on the railing, then heard his door click shut. She frowned and joined the others in the library.

"Where's Mathias?" Schuyler said. "I thought he was joining us tonight for study time and a movie afterward."

"He decided he wasn't feeling good," Lucy said. "I hope that's all it is."

Schuyler's disappointment was palpable. She opened her workbook and leaned over it, her face downcast. Paul, on the other hand, was already absorbed in his study and didn't seem to notice. Lucy slipped into a chair at the table, selected a dessert bar, and passed the tin to Schuyler.

"Here, you should have some chocolate," Lucy said, waggling her brows.

"Yes! Mrs. McGoo's Chocolate Revel Bars. Chocolate makes everything better." Her face broke into a smile as she bit into the crunchy bar with rich chocolate and butterscotch flavors. Mrs. McGoo's bars were a taste experience unlike any other.

"If chocolate makes everything better, maybe we should slather some on Mathias."

"He was pretty quiet today, especially at lunch," Schuyler said. "He's usually snarling at all of us, but today he was different. He pressed his hands to his ears, so I asked if he had a headache. He walked away and acted like I had the plague. Did something happen at school, I wonder?"

"Dunno. He was his usual grumpy self this morning. You're sleeping over. Maybe we can figure it out this weekend."

"Maybe. What do you think, Paul? You have classes with Mathias." Schuyler finished her dessert and selected another. "Have you noticed anything different about him?"

"Yeah, but I really hope it isn't true." Paul hesitated. He tapped a finger to his lips, tipped his chair back on two legs, and glanced across the foyer. Lucy and Schuyler turned, following his gaze. Mr. Sasson was asleep on the couch in the parlor, his stocking feet propped up on the armrest. Mrs. Sasson was entertained with a novel. "You know," he whispered, "he reminds me of how I was last year."

Lucy and Schuyler considered his words. Paul beckoned them to lean in closer.

"What do you mean?" Schuyler whispered. Her eyes went huge. "Oh—"

"No. You're not saying . . ." Lucy said, leaning forward, elbows on the table, close to bumping heads with Paul and Schuyler.

"Yeah, I am. I think Mathias is being haunted."

"What are you seeing that makes you think that?" Lucy was getting cold chills. It frightened her to think another friend was being touched by evil.

"His behavior changes by the moment. He's skittish, and he's always tired. He has dark circles under his eyes—he's sleep deprived, just like I was."

"Okay, he might have trouble sleeping. He is living in a strange house in a new town. It can't be easy for him to adjust."

"Nothing can haunt him in the house," Schuyler said, "right?" She looked at Lucy as she pushed her cookie bar away, having seemingly lost her appetite. Never a good sign.

"No, nothing can haunt us here in the house. The dryad Haniel knew that too. You know, the house has a blessing forever from the High King. But evil leaves an imprint. It could explain Mathias's bizarre Dr. Jekyll and Mr. Hyde behavior."

"You saw something the other day when you scoped the bus." Schuyler looked at Lucy, her face anxious.

"You scoped the bus?" Paul said. "I know you don't get along with Madison, but really?"

"Well, yeah. You can't be too sure." She wrinkled her nose at him. "I saw something strange, but I didn't think much about it. His ears were a deep purple, with a red tinge, like they might have frostbite damage. It could happen. My ears got frostbit once; now they hurt like crazy whenever it's freezing outside."

"Do you truly think he's haunted?" Schuyler twirled a lock of hair. "If he is, at least he's safe in the house."

Lucy waggled her head. "Think about it. Haniel said evil is everywhere. Mathias would be an easy target. I doubt he believes in the supernatural, much less knows about the High King, not like we do." Lucy took a bite of the cookie bar, licking the chocolate from her fingers. "I think it's time I find out what the Spectacles do. Maybe they can help me see things I'm missing."

Lucy sighed. They needed to find out what was happening with Mathias. Fast.

Saturday-morning breakfast consisted of a delicious, jam-filled pastry, so light it nearly melted on the tongue. Lucy and Schuyler were in food heaven. The Sassons sat at a table in the breakfast room beneath the stylized sign that read Lunch Served Today, enjoying their juice and pastry. They waved to Lucy and Schuyler, beckoning them to join their table, which the girls did. The sun shone through the window into the cheery room. Mathias sulked in an overstuffed chair in the corner.

"Good morning, girls." Mrs. Sasson patted Lucy's hand. "Your dear mother graciously offered to take us house hunting today. Doesn't that sound like fun? We love the Carriage House, and it pains me to think we will need to leave one day. The house is so beautiful, and we feel right at home here. I hope we can make our new home so welcoming. Promise to come to visit us when we're settled?"

"I will, and if you need any antiques for your new house, trust me, Mrs. Sasson—we have antiques. We have them in storage while those gargantuan stables out back are under construction. Mom is opening an antique store soon. She loves antiques and inherited a bunch from her auntie, who was a collector too."

"Oh, please don't tell my wife that, Lucy." Mr. Sasson laughed. "She will buy stuff before we get a house to put it all in!" He finished his pastry and glanced at his empty plate.

He was so relaxed these days, and Lucy was glad. She thought of the day when his eyebrows surged together. The house, or perhaps its blessing, influenced people. Well, maybe not her mom. But her mom was working hard to make the B and B a success.

Lucy went to the sideboard and poured fresh coffee for the Sassons, then placed the brimming cups in front of them. "You know, Mr. and Mrs. McGoo will need to sell their house soon and move to the Carriage House. The stable lofts are being renovated into apartments for Grandma Elliot and Bill and Vivian. Grandma is selling her house in Grand Traverse Bay, and the McGoos are downsizing."

"Oh, Lucy! That's a great thought. You should mention it to your mom and Mrs. McGoo." Schuyler buttered her scone. "I think you would love the McGoos' house, Mrs. Sasson." She took a bite and chewed.

Lucy passed the plate of pastries around the table, selected a scone for herself, and placed it back on the sideboard.

"Their house is beautiful," she said. "We lived with them for several months after the fire destroyed our home. Mrs. McGoo has a wonderful flair for decorating. She had quite an influence in this house."

"Then I must chat with her. It would be such a blessing to get the house issue settled soon. Is their home close by?" Mrs. Sasson licked the crumbs from her lips, then patted them dry with the napkin. She wore her hair tucked into a French twist in the back, elegant but simple.

"Yes, they live only a couple of blocks over," Jeannie said, entering the breakfast room. "I didn't mean to eavesdrop, but Lucy's right—it's a lovely home and the right size for your family. I don't know why I didn't think of it before. I can call the McGoos right now if you're interested. I'm sure they wouldn't mind if we stopped by to see it. I've been checking the listings. There are several others I can show you too."

Mr. and Mrs. Sasson both nodded vigorously and grinned at Lucy. Jeannie stepped into the kitchen to call Vivian.

Lucy glanced at Mathias. He had slouched further into the chair, his arms crossed over his chest. She took the case with the Spectacles from her pocket and laid it on the table. "If you like antiques, Mrs. Sasson, look at these. Aren't these the coolest eyeglasses you've ever seen?" She slid the case to Mrs. Sasson, who studied them intently.

"My goodness, these are unique. I've never seen anything like them." She pointed to the minute details of the vines and leaves. "The workmanship is beautiful. Wherever did you find them? Among your aunt's antiques?" She handed them to Mr. Sasson. He scrutinized them too. Then he gave them back to Lucy with a grin and picked up his coffee, nodding his thanks.

"We've kept some of the antiques, but these were in an old trunk I bought at the flea market." Lucy slipped them on and glanced around the room. She placed a hand on her cheek, tilted her chin, and feigned a superior attitude. "Darling, don't you agree these are ever so sophisticated? I must have more of these spectacles." Everyone laughed at her antics, except Mathias. Continuing the charade, Lucy let her gaze drift over the teenager. The Spectacles illuminated the bruised flesh around his ears.

"Oh, do tell, dear Mathias, whatever do you think of my special eyeglasses?" She studied him, manipulating the articulating arms to drop a small lens in front of her eye. His ears were darker than they'd been earlier in the week, when she first spotted the ailment. He glanced at her but said nothing. She folded the glasses back into the case.

"We should leave in a few minutes. The McGoos are expecting us," Mom said, clicking off her cell phone. She poured a cup of coffee from the sideboard and joined the group at the table. "Lucy, I need you to dust and polish the clock while we're gone. The dust is getting heavier. I haven't had time to do it. The polish and cleaning rags are in the cabinet at the registration desk."

"Do we have a ladder?" Lucy asked. "I'll never reach the top of that monstrosity without one." She smiled benignly. Schuyler rolled her eyes and concentrated on the juice in her glass.

Mr. and Mrs. Sasson busied themselves with their plates or adding cream and sugar to their coffees. Mathias sauntered to the parlor. He sat in a chair in the turret sitting area and started typing away on his phone.

Jeannie's lips were in a state of agitation; pursed, puckered, and pinched. She was probably still simmering over the dumbwaiter incident. "The carpenters will have a ladder stashed somewhere in the stables. I'm sure they won't mind if you borrow it. Just be sure you put it back where you found it when you're done." She sipped her coffee.

"Wonderful." Lucy smiled weakly and drank her juice.

"And make sure you're careful using the ladder around my clock." She rose and patted Lucy's shoulder. "There's my good girl," she said with a smirk and picked up her cell.

Lucy squinted at her mom's retreating form.

"Come on, Lucy. We can check the progress on the stables," Schuyler said. "I'll help you carry the ladder."

"You're not helping here," Lucy groused. Schuyler grinned at her. "Fine. Let's go find a ladder." She gathered her dishes and placed them in the dishwasher. Schuyler brought the used dishes from the breakfast room. Lucy put those in, too, and set it to run.

Mr. Sasson leaned toward his wife and whispered. Mrs. Sasson giggled and tried to hide a smile.

Jeannie grabbed her keys and chatted to Mr. and Mrs. Sasson as they beckoned the surly Mathias to join them. The family left with Jeannie. Lucy heard the car doors slam shut and the SUV leave the garage. The house was quiet except for the hum of the dishwasher. Schuyler pushed ahead of Lucy and scurried down the hall to the library.

"Okay, they're gone," Schuyler said, watching as the group drove down the road and receded from view. She dropped the curtain, curled up on the library loveseat, and waited. "Spill it, girlfriend. What did you see in the Spectacles?"

"Don't you want to visit the stables?"

"It can wait. What did you see in the Spectacles?" She pointed at the bulge in Lucy's shirt pocket.

"His ears have damage, I'm certain of it. The color is getting darker. I just don't know how they got damaged—by frostbite or the supernatural." Lucy removed the decorative pillow and sat in the overstuffed chair with her legs tucked beneath her. She played with the button on the pillow.

"I'm worried, Lucy." Schuyler removed the throw blanket from the back of the loveseat and snuggled into it with a shudder. "Paul thinks Mathias is being haunted. I'm afraid he might be right."

"Well, he's safe for the moment. There are no spirits or ghosts in the Carriage House, and I didn't see any spirits on the bus the other day. If he's in the house, he's protected. But outside? Not so much. It must happen to him at school."

"Oh, great. What is it about that old building?" Schuyler curled her hands into the yarn and hugged it tighter. "So, another school haunting?"

Lucy shrugged. "Maybe. It could happen anywhere, but only one way to find out. I'll have to use the Spectacles on him again." Her face pulled into a grimace. She heaved a sigh. "C'mon. Let's go find that ladder."

"How's that look?" Lucy stood on top of the ladder, holding a polishing rag and a tub of wax. Her fingers felt greasy, and her arms ached from rubbing the wood. The instructions said to swipe on a thin layer of wax, let it dry, then buff for a high sheen. She was tired and sweaty from the exertion. It was almost lunchtime, and her stomach was growling.

"The top half looks fine from here." Schuyler held two thumbs up with a grin. She supervised the work from her perch on the stairs, a nail file in one hand. She swirled a finger at the clock. "You need more wax on the door. It is a little dull."

"Fine, but just for that, I get two of Mrs. McGoo's Chocolate Revel Bars. I've earned a treat after this." She tugged the ladder away from the clock. Schuyler held one side as Lucy folded it, and they carried back to the stables.

Lucy yawned and swiped her damp handkerchief over her face as they entered the kitchen. She opened the fridge and sighed. The refreshing, cool air rushed at her with a strawberry scent from the bowl on the shelf. She grabbed two waters and handed one to Schuyler.

"Okay, let's go finish the clock, then we can grab dessert," she said, taking a swig before setting the water bottle on the check-in desk counter. She buffed the door and rubbed the waxy rag over the old wood on the inside. The interior smelled old and musty. She set the can down and slathered the interior walls with wax, hoping it would mask the odor. The brass works hung heavy and silent.

"Hand me a dry rag, please?" Lucy dropped the soggy rag and took the dry cloth from Schuyler. "Thanks. Wowza, I'm stiff." She stretched, flexed her wrists, and swung her arms about, the cloth waving like a pennant, then her hand slammed into something solid.

The giant brass pendulum.

It clanged into the weights, the noise thunderous and dissonant, a portend of disaster. Lucy skittered away from the cacophony to stare in disbelief. Schuyler held her breath.

The two weights swung precariously on their chains in constant motion, banging and clanging. The pendulum quaked, swaying back and forth. It fell from its mounting hook, flipped through the opening, and hit the floor. It broke apart, the pieces sliding across the floor. Lucy gaped in horror.

She had broken the monastery clock.

A Curse with a Devious Plot

Lucy was gobsmacked, her face frozen in disbelief. Her knees buckled, and she dropped to the floor beside the bob of the pendulum. The huge bob was as round and shiny as a giant's food platter. Schuyler stared, wide-eyed and open-mouthed, at the brass pieces gleaming in the sunlight.

"This is it! She's gonna disown me this time!" Lucy hadn't blinked in moments, and her eyes were drying out. Trembling, she picked up one end of the hefty pendulum rod and gulped. She didn't see any way they could fix it on their own. She blinked as tears suddenly filled her eyes. "Iam! Help!" she yelled. "I broke Mom's clock!"

"Lucy! Look!" Schuyler slid to the floor next to her and pointed at a slip of paper peeking from the inside of the rod. She tugged on it. The thick scroll, which appeared to be more than a single page, wouldn't budge.

"What is that?" Lucy laid the rod in her lap and stuck her fingers in the tube. The paper's texture was strange, thick, and a little slippery. As she gently tugged the paper, it moved, and together, they eased the roll from its sheath, where it had possibly spent centuries undetected.

The paper was heavy. Gently laying it on the floor, Lucy slowly unrolled the sheets, smoothing them with her hand. They were supple. The sheets

The Ghost You Can't See

were large, nearly two feet by three feet. Script filled the pages with an unknown language. The ink was so vibrant and rich, someone could have written only it yesterday.

Lucy shuddered. There was something eerie about the manuscript. The red ink reminded her of blood.

"I wonder what it says," Schuyler whispered, leaning in to study the characters. Drawings of vines and leaves shaped like snakes' heads surrounded the script. She leaned away and rubbed the goose pimples on her arms. "I don't think I like this," she said.

"Neither do I. Wait right here, and keep an eye on them." Lucy hurried to the desk for the Spectrescope. The backpack was in a cabinet. The glasses were in their case on the shelf with the bag. She grabbed them too.

The Spectrescope hovered over the manuscript as both girls, their heads together, viewed the pages in the lens. The telltale purple residue of spirit activity was all over the pages, even after centuries secreted away inside the pendulum rod. Lucy splayed her fingers and eyed them with apprehension. Her hands were clean, but it felt wrong to handle something touched by evil.

"I don't know what to do with these," Lucy whispered. The clanging pendulum and weights had startled her and zapped her strength. Her heartbeat was almost back to normal. Thankfully, the room was quiet now.

"Put the Spectacles on." Schuyler took them from the case and handed them to her. "Maybe they will help you read the script."

"Do you really think I should? Maybe we shouldn't read it." A chill gripped her. "Someone hid these for a reason. I don't know . . ." Lucy stared at the pages on the floor. Schuyler nodded encouragingly, so she put the Spectacles on.

And gasped.

Lucy's hands were shaking. The hoods of the Spectacles blocked her peripheral vision, the magnified the script nearly filling her view completely.

The red script leaped off the page and hung like small holograms before her eyes. She gulped and grabbed Schuyler's hand.

"You can read it?" Schuyler said, squeezing Lucy's hand in both her own. Lucy gave a brief nod. "Wait. You should seal the room, or the entire house, in case someone comes back. We don't want anyone to find out."

Lucy nodded and picked up the artifact. "Spectrescope, please seal this house." Her voice was weak and squeaky, like a cartoon mouse. The atmosphere changed, reassuring the girls of the protection inside the bubble.

The words wavered in front of Lucy's eyes, making her lightheaded. She wasn't sure whether it was the Spectacles or the evil in the manuscript, but it was disconcerting.

"Go ahead, read it. I think we need to know what it says."

Lucy took a deep breath and slowly released it. "Here goes," she said, clearing her throat of bile. She swallowed and began to read the script titled "*Darnathian's Lament.*"

"*I was the symbol of perfection. I was in Ealasaiden, in the very meadow of the High King, on the day he created me. My attire was the purest of linens, my sandals the softest leather, and my breastplate was solid gold adorned with every precious jewel: carnelian and chrysolite, emerald and topaz, lapis lazuli and turquoise, and the purest beryl, like the foundation stone of the city of Ascalon.*

"*I was his anointed one, the High King's guardian. I walked with the High King on the beautiful mount of Ascalon, along the path paved with the fiery red jewels of ruby, garnet, and prismatine. I was blameless in everything I did until the High King accused me of wrongdoing and expelled me in disgrace from his presence and from the city of Ascalon.*

"*For his treachery to me, the anointed one, I will destroy his kingdom and take the throne from the High King. I will be Highest.*

"*I will ascend back to the heavenly kingdom and walk its streets as before.*

"*I will raise my throne above the High King's.*

"I will sit among the stars and rule the universe and everything in it.

"I will be revered and adored.

"I will be KING!

"What I have said, I will do!

"I was and always will be full of wisdom and knowledge and beauty.

"I will recruit my Murmidones, my creatures, spirits, and ghosts, to achieve my goal. I will instruct them in the art of whisperings and influences to lead the people in self-destruction and thus destroy the kingdom of the High King from within his own creation. I will use self-deception, confusion, jealousy, anger, self-love . . ."

"I can't read any more of this." Lucy's skin crawled with goose bumps. She took the glasses off, letting them fall to her lap as she rubbed her eyes. She was cold. So cold. Beside her, Schuyler was rocking back and forth, her arms wrapped tightly around her body. The parchment curled back into its original form and lay like a tube on the floor. "It goes on. Darnathian plans to destroy everything: the kingdom, the city of Ascalon, and—he plans to kill Iam!"

"What? Lucy, what are we going to do? We need to warn Iam and Ishi!"

"There are details about how the King will die. Darnathian will kill him on the altar of the sanctuary. We must destroy this thing. It's evil and hideous." Lucy tucked the glasses in her pocket, got to her feet, and pulled Schuyler up with her. "Stand back. The Spectrescope will get rid of it." She pointed the artifact at the scroll. "Spectrescope, in the name of the High King, destroy this evil!"

The symbols on the ring began glowing and spinning, and the big lens illuminated. The runes spun faster and faster until they were a blur of golden light. The handle vibrated in her hand. The lens grew so bright they had to shield their eyes. Suddenly, a laser-focused energy beam blasted from the lens, narrowed to a pinpoint, and seared the pages with fire.

The parchment caught fire with a whoosh. The script burst into flames. The words became hideous forms and leaped from the pages, screeching and writhing as the scroll unfurled. Flames reached for the ceiling. The intensity and searing heat scared the girls, forcing them to step away. The fire cast a peach-tinted hue, flickering wildly across the foyer's white walls.

The scrolls flamed and sputtered, then flared up again, the enchanted parchment refusing to be destroyed. The screeching increased, and a sulfurous stench filled the room.

And then it was over. The words turned to vapor and dissipated. The cursed parchment, reduced to a pile of ashes, lay smoldering on the floor. Lucy and Schuyler gaped at it, their faces pink and warm from the heat. Then, out of nowhere, a puff of air lifted the ashes, swirling them around until they completely disappeared. The Spectrescope returned to normal. Shaking from what had just happened, Lucy and Schuyler sat in silence on the steps.

After a few minutes, Lucy picked up the big pendulum bob and gawked at it. Someone had detailed it with intricate scrolls winding around the circle. It was beautiful, and it was a problem. Schuyler picked up the rod, surprised at the weight as she balanced it in her hands.

"No wonder this thing caused such a clamor," Schuyler said. "If you dropped it on your foot, it would break all the bones. Wowza."

"I've got to fix it. Hold the rod steady, and I'll try to put this thing back on. Maybe no one will notice." Lucy tried several times, pushing the brass platter-sized bob against the end. "It's no good. It won't go back on. It will probably have to be welded."

"Do you think the Spectrescope could fix it?"

"I can't expect to use its power to fix my mess. There's nothing else for it. I'll have to tell Mom how it got broke and hope she doesn't exile me to Siberia."

"Might I make a suggestion?" a familiar voice said. Their heads whipped in his direction.

"Iam!" the girls called in unison. They dropped the broken pieces with a thud and a clang and rushed to greet him. He sat on the staircase steps, his elbows resting on his knees and hands clasped. He was smiling and wearing the familiar brown tweed suit and the open-collar white shirt. He would always be a grandpa to Lucy, even if he was the High King. Schuyler reached him first and dove in for a hug. Lucy waited her turn, then hugged him tightly, joining them on the steps. He smelled of his beloved peppermint candies.

"Oh, Iam! We are so glad to see you," Schuyler said. "You won't believe it. A daemon cloned me!" She fidgeted, her hands worrying the hem of her shirt. "Lucy thought I had betrayed our friendship." Iam clasped Schuyler's hand and gave it a jiggle. She smiled back peacefully.

"And we found a manuscript of sorts," Lucy said. "I think Darnathian wrote it. You need to know about—"

"I know, dear Lucy. I was here, listening while you read it."

"You were?" Lucy was confused.

"You called me, remember?" Iam chuckled.

"Oh yeah. Then you heard?" Lucy said. He nodded. "Darnathian is plotting to kill you and destroy the kingdom. He wants your throne and to be King in your place."

"I've known this for some time. It's one reason I banished him from Ascalon. He is dangerous and violent. It is why he sent a daemon armed with a tonic from Stolas to imitate Schuyler. He tried to weaken you, destroy your friendship, and hurt me."

"Schuyler would never act like that. I should have known something was wrong," Lucy said ruefully. "Why does he want to destroy you? He knows how good and loving you are. Why would he think you would betray him?"

"His pride led to deceit and then to violence. His wisdom became corrupt. I had to send him away in disgrace for his evil. Now he seeks my life and my throne, but he will never have it. He knows he has already lost, but he doesn't want to admit it, and so he keeps on."

"I'm so sorry, Iam. I'm glad the Spectrescope could destroy those pages so you didn't have to see them. They were awful." He patted her hand, smiling ruefully.

"You must train your eyes to discern the truth, child." He sighed, leaned forward, and folded his hands, elbows on his knees. "Darnathian thinks he can pull the wool over your eyes and mine. Nothing that cherub does is unknown to me. But good news: my messengers are everywhere. They monitor him and report to me." He gave them a conspiratorial wink and a nod.

"Isn't there something we can do to stop him?" Schuyler said. Her worried hazel-green eyes fixed on him. "We want to help. Someone else knew, too, and they must have been worried, or they wouldn't have hidden those pages in the clock."

"You must listen carefully." He pulled them in for a huddle, and the three of them put their heads together. "I am about to tell you something Darnathian does not know, though he thinks he knows everything," he whispered, glancing around the empty foyer. Then he tapped a finger to his nose. "His power is limited."

"It is?" Lucy said. "But he still plans to overthrow your kingdom and destroy everyone who loves you." She grabbed his hand. "He must know his power is limited—he's searching for the ancient magic. Mr. Bill and Vivian said he is searching for a cipher to unlock the runes and learn the magic's secret. We can't let him win!"

"And he won't. The best way to defend the kingdom and wrestle against the dark powers and spiritual forces is to always wear your armor," he said, gently patting her hand. "It prepares you to defend yourselves and the kingdom. Whatever happens then, you must use orison to make your requests known. Help will always come to those who ask."

"But shouldn't we take the battle to Darnathian?" Schuyler asked, scooting closer to him. "I've heard the best defense is a great offense. He might not suspect we would come after him."

"You must not challenge Darnathian or rebuke him. When the time is right, I will handle him. For now, fight to defend yourselves and others. Resist him in *my* name. One day, there will be a battle, but first you must prepare. You still have much to learn."

"I guess," Lucy said.

"Lucy," he drawled, raising a brow. It looked like a question mark.

"I'm sorry," she said, raising her hands. "You're right. I have a lot to learn. Keeping my mouth shut is probably the first lesson." She smiled grimly, and Iam nodded.

"Lucy, Schuyler—I know you both are worried about Mathias. You need to vanquish his immediate need, then you must tell him about me. The promise will help him understand, and it is already helping him." A smile tugged at the corners of his mouth, his head tilted and brows raised to emphasize his point.

"Okay," Lucy said slowly. A frown creased her forehead at what he had said. "How can someone understand if they don't know about you?" Lucy tilted her head to look at him suspiciously. "Wait. There is a secret hidden in the promise mark, isn't there?"

"You are very perceptive. I haven't explained that yet, have I?" Lucy shook her head. Iam paused and pursed his lips. "The promise mark contains an inherent code. Some might call it your conscience or your heart. The code allows you to know good and evil, right and wrong. I encrypted the code within your DNA, and it gives light to the mind for understanding."

"Holy cow—that's brilliant," Lucy said, her mouth falling open. "I have never thought about how I knew those things. So, people should already know that what I'm saying about you is true. They just don't realize it. But they still need to choose to accept you, don't they?"

"Exactly."

"And that weakens Darnathian's power, doesn't it?" Schuyler asked, leaning into his shoulder.

"You are correct, sweet girl," Iam said, planting a kiss on top of her head. "When a person perceives the significance of what is true, their heart will want to know more. When they accept the Truth, then Dove can begin her work. It is she who places the Triune seal on your heart, and she helps you gain knowledge, understanding, and good judgment. These are the qualities of what we call *wisdom*."

"Who is Dove?" Lucy asked. "Will we meet her too?"

"Dove is my kinswoman. She works silently, mostly. She teaches and instructs. You must understand, Dove is an extremely powerful spirit, and she must be to accomplish her tasks. And, speaking of tasks, I believe you have one to accomplish yourselves."

"Yeah, that clock won't fix itself. Mom will be beyond furious, closer to a nuclear meltdown, and it isn't gonna be pretty." Lucy said that last part through gritted teeth.

"I think he means Mathias," Schuyler said, giving her an impish grin. Iam dipped his head, pressing his lips together as if holding back a laugh.

Cheerful voices chattered outside, accompanied by slamming car doors. Lucy tensed, her head jerked up, and her eyes widened. Schuyler ran to the window. Lucy's mom and the Sasson family were mounting the steps to the porch.

"Oh, Lucy, they're back. How will we ever explain the broken clock?"

"What broken clock?" Lucy said with a wide grin.

The brass pendulum and bob had reunited and hung solidly from the hook.

Another Brew, Another Tonic

"Grehssil! Get in here," Darnathian bellowed, rubbing the back of his neck and pacing the floor. A vein pulsed in his neck. The fireplace crackled and groaned, reflecting the Master's mood. The door creaked open. Long, bony fingers appeared on its edge, followed by a gaunt, rawboned face.

"Yes, Master? What does my Master need?" Grehssil remained hidden behind the door. A sheen of sweat beaded on his forehead. The master's foul moods never boded well for Grehssil. The room's temperature had risen since the last time he was here.

"Come in here, and close the door!" Darnathian stopped pacing, his feet planted wide and his nostrils flaring.

The creature squirmed around the door and closed it. His eyes widened at seeing the scorch marks on the door. Darnathian had tried to blast him many times, but Grehssil was always quicker. He scurried further into the room, twisting his hands in front of him, and stood before the Dark Prince.

"Who did we send to infect the boy?"

"Berbatos, my Master. You needed the boy to be greatly influenced," Grehssil said, his voice wavering.

"I don't recall choosing him."

"Oh no, Master. Grehssil selected him, he did," the creature said. He made odd noises in his throat, his lips moving as he searched for the right answer. A wrong answer would cause another unpleasant correction.

"Why choose him?" He ran a hand through his hair.

"Master needed a powerful daemon, and Berbatos is a master of secret counsels. He is. He knows a person's thoughts, and he can change those thoughts as he pleases. He can."

"Hmm, yes. Berbatos should have completed the task by now. We can't let the boy get too chummy with that Hornberger girl and her friends or they will infect him with their High King nonsense instead. He is in the perfect position to search for the key. I need him to find that artifact."

His lips flattened as he turned his head with a twist, cracking his neck. The habit was irritating. It was one of many that annoyed him. He had been cracking his neck since the High King took his magnificent wings.

"Get Stolas to create another tincture." He crossed his arms, his eyes glinting like hard flints. "The venom must be potent and irremediable. Then give it to the daemon. Be sure Berbatos understands that failure is not an option."

"Yes, Master. Grehssil will see to it. He will." Backtracking, the creature bobbed up and down in an obsequious manner. "Master can count on Grehssil." His hand fumbled for the doorknob.

"Now, you ingratiate dolt!" Darnathian launched an energy ball at the servant. Grehssil dashed around the door and shut it before the missile exploded. The door vibrated against his bony fingers.

"I enjoy scaring him," Darnathian murmured, a wide smile splitting his face.

Grehssil gulped and tugged at his ragged collar, chafing his skin. He trudged down the long stone servant's corridor, the floor rough and uneven, to the recesses below that castle. The door to the potion master's laboratory was closed, but the vapors permeated the passage, noxious and unpleasant. The herbologist was inside, twittering to himself. Grehssil could not make out the words. He knocked on the door.

"Who—who is it?" Stolas shouted. "What do you want?"

"Who do you think it is, you old bird? It's me. Now open this door. The Dark Prince needs an elixir." Grehssil heard sounds of scraping and scrambling behind the laboratory door. Stolas opened it and stepped out; his little jeweled crown perched at an awkward angle. He pulled the door shut behind him.

"What is it now?" the owl said. His big, black pupils had shrunk to mere pinpoints in the bright, golden irises. It was like staring into giant sunflowers.

Grehssil squinted at him, leaned forward, and sniffed his breath. "Are you imbibing your own tonics? You are crossed-eyed, you dumb bird." He smiled at what the Dark Prince was likely to do to the potion master when he found out.

"What? No, of course not. Who—who would blame me if I did? I must test them somehow. No one will try any of my tonics."

"Because most of your tonics grow extra limbs!" Grehssil declared. "Look what you did to Cerberus—the poor dog has three heads. I almost lost an arm trying to feed him."

"Get—get on—with it." Stolas burped, blinked, and wobbled on his scrawny legs. "What does the Master want now?"

"The Dark Prince needs a potent venom, he does. One that is incurable. Berbatos must not fail at his task. No, no. His venom must penetrate and poison the boy's mind against the wretched High King."

"Oh, goody!" Stolas twittered and hiccuped, unsteady on his toes. "I know just the tonic to use against weak minds. All humans have—have weak minds. The fools are fun to poison. Master will be so pleased with me; he may even drink a toast in my honor!" The owl squeaked, clapping happily, and taking a deep breath. Grehssil rolled his eyes and shook his head, muttering.

"Scoff if you must. You will see." Stolas twittered and scurried about the corridor. "The tonic is difficult to mix, but I'll have it ready within the hour. Berbatos must apply it slowly so the victim's spirit gradually becomes hard and darkens until it can no longer discern the difference between our lies and the King's truth. It's a wonderful thing to watch." Stolas slapped Grehssil on the shoulder and disappeared back into his laboratory, slamming the door.

Grehssil huffed and shuffled back along the hallway.

The Clock with a Secret in Its Walls

Lucy and Schuyler sat on the stairs, smiling like two Cheshire cats and not saying a word while the animated group entered through the front door.

Judging by the enormous smiles, Lucy guessed the house-hunting excursion was a success. Her mom crossed the foyer, followed by the Sasson family, who chattered excitedly, except Mathias. He passed the girls without a word or a glance and went up to his room. Lucy and Schuyler exchanged an uneasy look before turning to watch him traipse upstairs.

"Miriam," Mom said, addressing Mrs. Sasson. "I must show you the Scandinavian grandmother clock we have in storage." She passed by the monastery clock and retrieved a binder from the check-in desk cabinet. "It would be lovely in the living room."

"I hope it isn't as large as this one," Mrs. Sasson said, admiring the workmanship of the old clock. She ran a hand over its sleek surface, intrigued by the blue blotches.

"Goodness, no. I'm not even sure what to call this one, it's so huge," Mom said.

"You could call it the great-great-great-grandfather clock," Lucy quipped.

Mom jovially waved a dismissive hand at her and flipped through the pages. "Lucy and Schuyler did a thorough job of photographing and cataloging the antiques and knickknacks. It was tedious, and I hadn't a clue how to organize it all." Mrs. Sasson winked when Lucy grinned and patted herself on the shoulder.

"Wait—the living room?" Lucy said, sitting up. "Does that mean you found a house, Mrs. Sasson?"

"Your suggestion, Lucy, was perfect. We just love the McGoos' home. The house is as lovely as could be, and we came to a mutual agreement with Bill and Vivian. So, we're buying their house! Isn't it exciting?" She gleefully waved her hands.

"Mrs. Sasson, how wonderful!" Lucy hurried to hug her. "I'm so glad for all of you."

"Wowza. That's great!" Schuyler added. "When do you move in? Can we help decorate?" Her enthusiasm for decorating had only gotten worse after seeing the country-chic designs used for the Carriage House.

"We will need to remain here for several more weeks. I hope we're not overstaying our welcome," Mrs. Sasson said with a grin.

"Oh goodness, you and Mr. Sasson are welcome to stay as long as you need. I admit, it's been weird living with other people in our space, but I'm glad you came," Lucy said, smiling at the wife and husband. "This bed-and-breakfast thing isn't as bad as I thought." Mrs. Sasson laughed and joined Jeannie at the desk to search the catalog.

"And Mathias, maybe not so much?" Mr. Sasson whispered with a wink. He glanced at his wife. She was deep in conversation with Jeannie.

"Eh," Lucy said, hunching a shoulder and smirking. "He's okay. We're friends, and we're getting used to each other."

"I know it's been difficult," he said, sighing. "I have seen some disturbing changes in him recently. Outwardly, he's relaxed here at the Carriage

House, but he withdraws in public and keeps to himself a lot. He's probably the same way at school. Am I right?"

"Yeah, sort of. Paul is his friend too. Mathias joins us for lunch, but he doesn't say much." *Unless he's being surly, snarky, and mean to me*, Lucy thought.

"He always sits alone on the bus," Schuyler interjected. "We have invited him to sit with us, but he never does."

"I'm glad you try to include him. I think he may be lonely. The move upset him deeply, leaving his friends, his school, and everything familiar. He's like a turtle—any attempt to draw him out of his shell causes him to retreat further."

"Yeah, we've noticed," Lucy said. "Don't worry, Mr. Sasson. We'll keep an eye on him."

Mathias leaned on the balcony railing, listening to his father discuss his attitude problems with Lucy and Schuyler. His emotions vacillated between anger, betrayal, and hopelessness. He wanted to speak up, but something prevented him from reaching out.

Discouragement washed over him, leaving him cold and alone. The voices in his head were silent when he was inside the Carriage House. If only his parents knew.

Maybe the voices were right.

Lucy rolled over, checked the time, and sighed. She was still awake after two o'clock in the morning. The conversation with Mr. Sasson had nudged her spirit, reminding her of the conversation she'd had earlier with Iam. Mathias and his family had the promise but not the seal. And what was up with his attitude? Was it loneliness, as Mr. Sasson suspected? Or was it something else? It scared her to think of the *something* else. It was more than just the move; she was sure of it. But what could she do?

"Schuyler," Lucy whispered. "Schuyler? Are you awake?"

"I am now," she grumbled. "Did something happen?" Schuyler sat up, yawned, and stretched, scratching her head and flipping her wavy blond locks around. "Why are we whispering? Nobody can hear us."

"I don't know. It's what you're supposed to do in the dark." She heard a snort. "Whatever."

"So, what's up, girlfriend?"

"I'm hungry."

"Seriously? You woke me up to tell me that?"

"Well, yeah. A glass of milk and Mrs. McGoo's Chocolate Revel Bars are calling my name." Lucy strapped her sandals on and tucked the Spectrescope into the pocket of her pajamas under her robe.

"Hmm—that's odd. I hear them calling me too." Schuyler snickered, slipped into her sneakers, and followed Lucy down the back staircase to the kitchen. She grabbed napkins for their snack and sat at the island counter.

Lucy got the dessert and milk. Moments later, they were licking gooey chocolate from their fingers, enjoying the delicious cookie bars Mrs. McGoo had sent home with her mom.

"So, what's keeping you awake, girlfriend?" Schuyler said between bites. Her feet hung loosely over the rungs of the chair.

"I've been thinking about what Iam said earlier. Mathias has the promise but not the seal. I would love to tell him about Iam, but Mathias is so surly all the time. It's like he has a split personality, or maybe he just enjoys being disagreeable. Did you know he called *me* disagreeable?"

"No! He called *you* disagreeable?" Schuyler feigned a shocked expression with a hand to her cheek. Lucy pinched her face and squinted at her, and Schuyler giggled in response.

Lucy waved two fingers back and forth, showing she would be watching.

The Ghost You Can't See

"Anyway, I mean, remember how gobsmacked we were at the beginning? We had no clue about spirit beings." Lucy sipped her milk. "I can't exactly say, 'Hey, Mathias, there's another realm filled with ghosts and spirits—'"

"And giants," Schuyler said. "Don't forget the Grigori."

"Exactly. Who would believe it?"

"Wait." Schuyler held up a finger, listening. "Did you hear anything just now?" It was impossible there were any spirits in the hallway and foyer. The blessed house was entity free of them, after all.

"What did you hear?" Lucy set her milk on the counter and immediately reached for the Spectrescope. Ever since the Grigori had stalked her last year, she kept the artifact on hand.

"I swear I heard something in one of the other rooms. Uh, the hair on my arms is standing up. Ooh, that feels so creepy."

The sunroom was clear of spirit activity, as was the breakfast room. Lucy walked through the dining room to the parlor, Schuyler following close behind. The Spectrescope wasn't revealing any activity. The ambient light from the streetlamps filtered through the front door sidelights, casting shadows of varying depths around the room. The foyer was clear too.

The monastery clock loomed over them in the shadows. Lucy opened the door. It creaked ominously.

"Spectrescope, a little light, please." The brass pendulum and weights were missing, but the scope was clear of any purple residue. Lucy glanced anxiously at Schuyler. "Okay, that isn't good."

The beam of light illuminated the carvings inside the clock. Lucy gulped. The woman's sad face was downturned. When Lucy had seen the effigy before, the woman's eyes were closed, not gazing at the stone floor as they were now.

"Aw, she seems so sad," Schuyler said. "I wonder why someone would carve such a sad face. Looking at her, even I feel sad."

Lucy moved the beam along each of the carvings. The light revealed the edge of an open door between the columns with the man and woman effigies. Schuyler grabbed Lucy's sleeve and stared.

"Oh, wow," Lucy said and reached for the door.

"Wait! Do you think it's safe to open it?"

Lucy swallowed hard. "There's only one way to find out," she said and pushed it. The door swung open, revealing a polished stone balcony and a staircase.

"Shall we?" Lucy asked, and without waiting for an answer, she stepped into the clock.

Painful Discoveries

Lucy and Schuyler stood on a landing at the top of a staircase inside a tower. The smooth, carved stone steps were wide, with a wrought iron railing and balustrades. Reminiscent of a grand old European castle, its sweeping design was simple, yet elegant. It spiraled down into the shadows. Behind the girls was the portal through the clock. Lucy could see the foyer.

"Lucy, we should go back. We don't have our armor," Schuyler whispered, her voice barely more than a mouse squeak. "I feel so exposed without it."

"If we go back now, the portal may close. The Spectrescope can get it for us." Lucy glanced at the scope. It was quiet. "Spectrescope, can you get our armor, please?" The lens clouded with swirling mist, like the Augur Sphere when it activated. Faint golden letters appeared in the glass.

He knows the way that you take. Then the message faded away, and the lens went dark.

"Spectrescope?" Lucy jiggled the artifact but got no response. The lens remained dark, and the runes were dull.

"What do you think that means?"

"I . . . don't know. I don't understand why the Spectrescope won't answer," Lucy said, tapping the scope. "Come back, Spectrescope, please. We need our armor." Still, no answer appeared. "Spirit Sword, come forth." Again, there was no answer. Lucy's knees trembled. She was unsure and scared.

"I don't like this, Lucy. We can still go back."

Lucy nodded, her heart beating hard in her chest. Next to her, Schuyler's eyes were enormous orbs in her pale face, and her hair was a wild mess.

"Maybe this was a bad idea after all." They hurried across the platform toward the portal. "I am sorry—I thought it would connect to the other portals and gatekeepers. Or at least, I hoped it would."

Suddenly, the door slammed shut, and the portal disappeared.

Schuyler flinched and opened her mouth to scream, but Lucy clamped a hand over her face, preventing her from uttering a sound. Schuyler grabbed Lucy and clung to her, shaking, then shoved Lucy away and glared at her.

"Why do you always rush into things!" Schuyler hissed, flinging her hands about. "This is all your fault! You had to know this would happen. The first night the clock arrived, Grehssil entered the portal." Schuyler's face reddened. "Of course it would connect to something evil." Her body tensed. "How will we get it back?"

"What do you mean it's my fault?" Lucy said, her whisper harsh. "You're in this ghost hunting thing, too, you know! Why don't you figure it out for a change? If you're so smart, you get us out."

"Maybe I will figure a way out. I am in it because of you. Do you know what your problem is? You make snap judgments and don't consider the fallout. How could you think I was that fake Schuyler, that I was someone who could betray our friendship? Did you even once consider me—the person you know me to be? No!" She stomped around, flinging her arms. "Why am I even talking to you? You're never going to change." She kicked the wall, then leaned against it, her arms crossed. The sleeves and legs of her flannel pajamas quaked.

"Look—I'm sorry, all right?" Lucy threw her hands up, palms out. "I should have known it wasn't true, should've known you wouldn't hang out with bullies. You're such a know-it-all. Maybe you thought you could teach me a lesson, but it didn't work, did it?" Her thoughts were all scrambled, and betrayal gripped her again, flooding her cheeks with heat. "I was so confused and hurt and—wait." She paused, her heart pounding. Something was wrong. "Why are we fighting? We settled this. We've forgiven each other. Why are we dredging up all the hurt feelings?"

"Oh, you're right." Schuyler wrapped her arms around her body. "I don't want to fight with you! You're like my sister from another mother, remember?" Schuyler laughed nervously; an impish grin mixed with remorse trembling her cheeks.

"I don't want to fight either," Lucy said, folding Schuyler in a quick hug. "This place is affecting our thoughts and emotions. We need help to find a way out." She grabbed Schuyler's hand. "We need to call Iam. I only hope he can hear us from wherever we are. Orison?"

"Orison." Schuyler gripped Lucy's hand tighter.

"Iam, can you hear us? Please, we need your help. I made a mistake, and I am so sorry."

"Iam, you will help us, won't you?" Schuyler asked. "We're alone, and we don't have our armor. Please, come help us!"

Iam's voice, the timbre soft and comforting, whispered in their ears. "I know the way that you take. You have called, and I will answer. You began this journey in haste; now you must follow through to the end. There is much for you to learn. I have given my spirits charge over you to keep you safe in the way. Wait, I say, on my spirit."

"Follow through?" Lucy asked, waiting expectantly. Iam had shared the same message as the Spectrescope. "What does that mean?"

"Follow through," Iam whispered again.

Schuyler ran her hands over the wall where the portal had disappeared. There would be no following through it; the wall was solid stone. She leaned over the railing and grimaced as she looked down. "Any thoughts, girlfriend?"

Lucy gripped the railing, peering into the shadows below. "I am so sorry, Schuyler. I didn't mean to get us trapped wherever this is."

"Yeah, I know. Hey, at least we're together," she said, a lopsided grin bunching her cheek.

"For which I am truly grateful. I can't imagine doing this ghost hunting thing without you. Forgive me?"

"Well, yeah." She lightly punched Lucy in the shoulder. "I've told you before, girlfriend, you need me. And right now, we need each other. Don't lose me, okay?"

Lucy flattened her lips, nodded, and walked to the steps. The height was dizzying. She was getting nauseous, and it was a long trek down to the bottom. "Iam said to wait on his spirit, so we know help is coming. The question is, do we go, or do we stay here and wait?"

"Iam said there was a lot to learn. So, I guess we follow the staircase and see where it goes." Schuyler lifted a shoulder. "After you, Grand Poobah," she said, sweeping a hand toward the staircase, then followed Lucy down the steps.

"Stay close," Lucy whispered.

Their rubber soles gripped the stone. Brandishing the Spectrescope like a baseball bat gave Lucy a modicum of comfort. She kept her back against the wall and led the way down the steps. Torches burned in iron sconces, leaving oily soot on the walls. The orange glow mingled with the candlelight from the immense wrought iron candelabra that hung from the recessed ceiling, dripping wax.

The staircase ended, and a tunnel began. A variety of rough-cut stone formed the sidewalls. The chinking had oozed and lay frozen like silver neoprene worms crawling over the walls. The rounded arch ceiling, chiseled from white stone, reflected the flickering light and illuminated the passage.

The passage ended with an elegant door. Its refinement was stark against the tunnel's rough construction. Lucy grimaced at the ugliest door knocker she had ever seen, alarms going off in her head. Schuyler shuddered at the sight.

It was a bronze cast of a man's face, wrinkled in pain with the eyes pinched tight. The nose was chipped and blackened. Positioned over the man's forehead, which formed the striker plate, was a large iron knob on the end of the striker arm. He had a permanent indentation on his forehead.

"Ouch. Who thinks of these things, anyway?" Lucy said, disturbed by the imagery. Goose bumps formed on her arms.

"Oh, that would be the Dark Prince. He has no end of ideas for causing pain." The bronze man opened his eyes and studied the two intruders. "What is your business here?" His eyes raked over the Spectrescope in Lucy's hand, and a hard gleam filled his eyes. "You are a Bachar! You have no business here. Go away."

Lucy glanced sideways at Schuyler, deciding against revealing too much to the talking door knocker. She straightened her shoulders and tilted her chin.

"We have orders to follow through," she said, reaching for the doorknob. She turned the knob. Locked.

"Whose orders?"

"The King's."

"The King's orders," the face spat. "If you have orders to follow through, then you must use the striker."

"Why do I need the striker? You know we need to follow through. Now open the door." She twisted the knob again. The robe's belt tightened around her waist. Schuyler clutched the tail like a lifeline.

"Use the striker!" he commanded.

"Why?" Lucy asked, jiggling the knob.

"Pain opens the door," the face snarled at her. "The Dark Prince has cursed it, and it will not open unless you use the striker to cause me pain."

"That's horrible!" Schuyler said. "It's such a wicked thing to do. There must be another way." She gripped Lucy's belt a little tighter.

"The Dark Prince *is* wicked," the face replied. "By deceit, he causes confusion. A little bending of the truth leads astray. He uses jealousy to effect loneliness, and with pain comes disillusionment. These are his tools." He gave a hard laugh. "Use the striker if you will pass."

Lucy sighed. "I am sorry to do this to you," she said. She dropped the striker. It smacked the bronze face, and the face howled. The lock clicked, and she opened the door. The howling stopped. The face was silent and still as they stepped through into another corridor.

The door locked behind them.

"I'm sensing a theme here," Lucy said, jiggling the knob. Schuyler was still clutching Lucy's belt. It was about to fall off. Lucy retied the belt in a tight knot around her waist, then anchored the other end around Schuyler's wrist, binding them together.

"Thanks." Schuyler gave the belt a tug. A weak smile flashed across her anxious face.

"No problem. I don't want to lose you, you know." Lucy scrunched her nose, then glanced around as lights flickered on. "Oh my." This hall differed from the rough-cut stone corridor they had just left.

The elegant hallway boasted high ceilings, polished marble floors, and mahogany paneling. Along one side, illustrated tapestries of inhuman creatures being hunted by daemons and snarling dogs adorned the recessed wall, and electric sconces paced the length of the walkway.

A series of floor-to-ceiling french doors were open to the stone balcony that ran the length of the corridor. The view of the mountains from the balconies was amazing. Green, rolling hills under blue skies stretched as far as they could see.

Schuyler tugged on the belt. "Lucy, I think I know where we are," she whispered. "We're in Darnathian's lair. It must be a castle of sorts. Those windows are familiar. Remember?"

Lucy nodded, pointing to the door at the end of the corridor. She put a finger to her lips and slowly approached it. The door stood ajar, light spilling from the opening. She peeked inside. It was unoccupied.

And it was Darnathian's office.

Lucy tugged Schuyler inside and eased the door shut. The immensity of the library, the opulent furnishings, and the frescoed ceiling were astonishing. Lucy felt small in comparison, and Schuyler looked stupefied. Wandering farther into the room, they tried to take it all in.

The room filled Lucy with dread as it brought back painful memories. It was here she had fought with Darnathian over the Spectrescope. Her mind's eye replayed the struggle between Malpar and the Dark Prince. That day, she thought Malpar had died. He had, but he now lived with the High King in Ascalon, serving and loving his King. His physical death brought her a way of escape. Malpar was alive, restored, and redeemed at home with his family. The thought brought a momentary smile to Lucy's lips, then her eyes rolled.

"Schuyler, how dumb can I be? The Spectrescope knew this place. And the Spectrescope mustn't risk falling into Darnathian's hands. The power transferred—I don't know where, but it's not with me. At least, without its power, he's less likely to take it."

Schuyler's shoulder bumped into her. "Well, we're together, and Iam knows where we are. He said help was coming too. Now, we trust and follow through."

"You're pretty smart, you know that, right?"

"Yeah, just making sure you do," Schuyler said, smiling smugly.

Darnathian's rune-carved wood desk sat in the center of the room, the french doors open behind it. Opposite the desk, the enormous fireplace belched heat into the room, its cursed logs burning perpetually. The mantel and fireplace surrounding it had carved effigies, the animals, tree spirits, and creatures so realistic, they nearly leaped into the room. It was unnerving.

Floor-to-ceiling bookshelves, overflowing with tomes, manuscripts, and books, lined the walls. A balcony circled the upper half of the room. A wrought iron spiral staircase wound its way to the upper level, where a large rune table sat in the middle of the space.

The room was altogether beautiful, gruesome, and evil. Red was everywhere, adding to the uncertainty. The color saturated the chairs, the curtains, and the plush area carpet underfoot. Schuyler's face radiated like a sunburn with the garish color. Lucy worried her skin would stain.

A large, gilded cage hung suspended under the balcony in the opposite corner in full view of the desk. The cage was empty except for a roundish brown blob in the middle of its floor.

"Oh. My. Goodness. I would love to have my very own library. Just think of all the knowledge in these pages." Schuyler gawked at all the volumes and books peeking from the overburdened shelves. The amount was staggering. Her eyebrows furrowed as she squinted, released, and shot up her forehead in surprise as she read some of the names. "There are a lot of creepy titles here."

"There are thousands of books and manuscripts." Amazed, Lucy wondered what it all meant. The sheer vastness of the room, and the information it contained, was overwhelming. It raised another, more immediate concern. "Why does Darnathian need all of this? I doubt he reads for fun. He is trying to increase his knowledge, but what is he looking for, I wonder?"

"He's searching for clues," the brown blob said, sitting up and stretching. "He needs the fruit from the Life Tree and the ancient magic to defeat the High King."

Lucy yelped, and Schuyler squealed, her eyes wide. She tugged Lucy's belt and bolted for the door, dragging Lucy with her.

"Wait—don't go! Please, keep me company for a little while," he pleaded. "I can't hurt you. I am a mere shadow of a man in a gilded cage." The earnest longing made Lucy pause, her hand on the doorknob, the shock and the heat of the room forming a bead of sweat on her lip. The owner of the voice rose. Lucy realized the man was a monk and wondered how he'd come to be trapped in a cage.

About middle aged, he was pale and wore a hooded cloak with a rope tied around his waist for a belt. His shaven head was bare except for a ring of hair cut in a tonsure. The sleeves of the cloak slid from his arms as he gripped the bars. Lucy gasped; the man was translucent. The bars were visible through his hands.

"You're a spirit—in a cage. How does that happen?" Lucy asked, getting her voice back. She edged closer and regarded the robed figure; Schuyler straggled behind on her tether. "Why don't you leave, float away, or go into the light?"

"It is a cursed cage. I cannot leave."

"Of course, it is," Lucy said with a sigh. "Darnathian's handiwork, I suspect." He nodded.

"What happened? How did you end up here?" Schuyler said, folding her arms in a protective huddle.

"I died centuries ago." Sadness tinged his voice. "I traded my eternal soul for a pittance, a few extra years of life," he said with disgust, his head bowed. "A single moment, a wrong choice, and remorse. Though I regretted my actions, I didn't repent. I knew I would do it again. Now I am trapped here for eternity. It is a familiar but painful story."

"Who are you?" Lucy said. The entity looked harmless enough, but they were in Darnathian's office in a castle populated by daemons, spirits, and entities. "I'm Lucy, by the way."

"I am Herman the Recluse," the spirit said with a bow.

The Man in the Gilded Cage

"And you, Lucy, are the Bachar, the chosen one of Issachar and an avenger who carries out the High King's anger on wrongdoers. The friend with you must be Schuyler. The King chose her too."

"How do you know that?" Lucy's breath hitched, and she clutched her throat. Uneasy, she glanced around. There were two possible exits: one door and the open windows. She heard Schuyler shuffling from foot to foot, ready to bolt.

"I have learned much over the centuries," Herman said. "I listen, pretending I am asleep. When Darnathian isn't raging or belittling me, the Dark Prince reads to me from the scripts. He drills me with questions about the text, then gauges the writing's importance from my answers. I've become very good at deception."

His head bobbed slowly, and he considered the two humans before him. "Darnathian is in turmoil over you. It makes me glad." His steady eye contact seemed to say, "*Thank you.*" He dipped his head and let a smile crease his face. "The High King is still on his throne."

"I don't understand. How do you know about us? And about the High King?" Holding the Spectrescope with two shaky hands, Lucy eased forward to a nearby bench, sat, and considered the spirit. Schuyler sank down beside her.

"The Ormarrs and the Irredaemon have known about the power of the Spectrescope for centuries. It is the tool Darnathian has searched for most diligently." He pointed at the artifact clutched in her hand. "However, his focus has recently centered on something else, a key of some sort. I know nothing about a key. The scripts never mentioned a key."

"Scripts?" Lucy asked.

"I am a monk—or was when I was alive. It was my holy calling to preserve ancient writings by transcribing the precious text to new parchment to maintain an accurate recording of the Chronicles." He grinned. "I loved it. To me, it wasn't working. My knowledge of the High King greatly increased."

His smile suddenly fell, replaced by sadness. "But in the end, I chose to believe a lie and turned away. Pride wouldn't let me admit I was wrong." He hunched his shoulders. "So, here I am. A doomed soul in a cursed cage of my own making." He slid to the floor of the cage and sat, regarding them. "Enough about me. How did you come to be here?"

"We came through a portal inside an enormous clock," Lucy said.

"It's the biggest clock anyone has ever seen," Schuyler added. "It's one of a kind, for sure. Lucy's mom calls it the monastery clock."

"What? Is this true? You must tell me, girl—is it about ten feet tall and big enough for a person to stand in? Does its middle section have blue blotches on it? Like blueberry stains?" Herman leaned closer, a sparkle in his eyes. He looked anxiously from one girl to the other.

Lucy blanched. "How could you know that?" A queasy feeling roiled in her stomach.

"Because I hid something evil inside of it. The evil cursed the clock and twisted it inside out. Its mechanisms never worked again."

"We found the pages of a manuscript inside the pendulum when I accidentally broke it," Lucy said. "There were horrible things written against the High King. Is that what you hid?"

"Dear girl!" Herman tensed and pressed his fists to his temples. "I stole 'Darnathian's Lament' and hoped the pages would remain hidden for eternity! I tried to destroy them, but Darnathian's spell protected the pages. So, I hid them inside the clock." He raised his hands, despair contorting his face. "Oh, what have I done? What have I done?" Herman fell to the floor, covered his face, curled into a fetal position, and sobbed.

"Herman! It's all right. I destroyed the pages." Lucy stood and reached a hand toward the cage but drew it back, wary of the curse. The monk sniffled, wiped his eyes, and sat up.

"You . . . you destroyed the pages?" His eyes were wide and skeptical. "But how? He cursed them! Darnathian's spells are impossible to break." A tremulous smile tugged his mouth. "Indeed, you must be a powerful Bachar. How I wish I had been as bold as you." He clasped his hands.

"No, I am not powerful or bold, but I have special tools. They get their power from the High King. We told the High King too. It seems he was already aware of the manuscript."

"Amazing! Thank you, Lucy. You have made this poor soul glad." Herman's smile turned to bewilderment, and he crawled closer and peered at her through the cage bars. "Did you say a portal was how you came here?"

"Yeah, we couldn't go back because the portal inside the clock suddenly closed. We're trapped here until help comes."

"I wonder. Were the carvings still on the inside? They were the most magnificent carvings Brother Thaddeus ever did. A monk's life is simple, you know. We have only the barest necessities so worldly things do not distract us. The carvings brightened a bland existence. Thaddeus put so much imagination in them."

"Yes, we saw them. They only appear when the portal opens. What else do you know about the clock?"

"Thaddeus was a tinker and craftsman," Herman said, his eyes brightening at the memory. "He loved working with metal but especially wood, seeing the images in the grains. 'They wanted to come out,' he would say. The furniture in the scriptorium and the abbey were all his handiwork, but he was particularly fond of that clock." He chuckled and held up a hand as he ruminated through a memory.

"Thad read about a similar clock in the scripts. They were originally water devices. They were called horologes back then and could tell the time and the seasons. Thaddeus was clever. He used metal to accomplish the same. He made the mechanicals and cobbled the cabinet together from discarded pieces and even carved the effigies for it too. Those wonderful tones echoed through the abbey and the hallways. It stood in the main hall near the scriptorium. Oh, how I would love to see it again and hear those rich notes."

"What is a scriptorium?" Schuyler said. Her leg bounced uncontrollably, shaking the bench.

"Why, it's a library, dear girl," he said, smiling and sweeping his hand toward the books in the room. "The scriptorium is where we did our transcribing. We kept the ancient writings there, along with the new translations and parchments. It was a beautiful room, long and narrow, with arched windows. It even had frescoes on the ceiling. Thad's writing tables lined the center of the room, and when we weren't writing, we relaxed in the comfy chairs and benches Thaddeus made." His smile faded quickly. "Thaddeus was a good brother to me. It was so long ago, it's probably all gone now."

"I'm sorry. You really miss it, don't you?" Lucy said, noticing the melancholy furrowing his face. He slowly nodded, then he got a hard glint in his eyes.

The Ghost You Can't See

"The Dark Prince has his Codex because of me," he spat. "Evil thing that it is." He gave a disgusted snort, and ugliness twisted his mouth. "Darnathian waltzed into the scriptorium one evening, demanding we scribe for him. We refused, of course, so he cast a spell on me and my brothers, forcing us to write the heinous book—in his handwriting, no less." His head waggled; his anger spent. "I was the transgressor! I had already traded my soul. But my dear brothers!" Shimmering tears trickled down his translucent cheeks. His hands tugged at his cloak.

"The ink kept flowing, and the quills never stopped that night. I can still hear the whimpers, the quills scratching at the parchment. The repulsive words punctured our minds, and we could not fight it. He forced us to write until our bodies weakened, the bloodred ink staining our fingers. The book's atrocities cancel out all the good we did." He closed his eyes and pinched the bridge of his nose. His shoulders slumped in defeat.

"What is in this Codex?" Lucy said. She was curious, but as a ghost hunter, she had learned to be wary. Herman seemed genuine, but he was a trapped spirit. "Why was it so important to Darnathian?"

"It is a record of Darnathian's knowledge. It contains lists of beneficial and poisonous plants and herbs, remedies for illnesses, spells and incantations, and even a copy of the Chronicles of Ascalon. He filled it with monstrous drawings on every page." Herman snorted again.

"You must remember—Darnathian is a created being," he said. "The benevolent King gave him knowledge, understanding, and great responsibility. But Darnathian became obsessed with himself. He believed he was the most important being in the universe. Eventually, he caused a war in Ascalon with his derisive attitude. The King had no choice but to throw them all out to restore harmony." A doleful expression shrouded his eyes as he gazed at Lucy.

"Now, Darnathian and his followers want nothing more than to seek, kill, and destroy. Not just the kingdom—but all of creation. He would exterminate all the stars and planets, the creatures, spirits, and beings—everything that has life. He despises anyone who follows the King." He leaned closer and earnestly searched her face. "Did you read the pages, Lucy? Do you know the horrible thing he has planned?"

"Yes, and I am sorry I did. It was like reading a mad-man's ranting decree. It was awful, and now those words are stuck in my head. When the pages got destroyed, images of screaming daemons appeared in the flames before it all disintegrated."

"Dear girl, I hope it did not infect your mind, or yours, either, Schuyler. Do not focus on Darnathian or his nefarious plans. If you want to cleanse your mind, focus on the love of the King. If I had allowed the truth of the scripts to penetrate my hard heart, I would not be here, punished for eternity. The scripts reminded me of my bentness and my need to ask for the King's forgiveness. It was easier to believe a lie, that it didn't matter, than to repent. I regret rejecting the true King. Now I am separated from him forever."

"Is there no hope for you, Herman?" Schuyler asked.

"No, dear girl. The King will forgive anything except the rejection of his son, the true King. But remember, where there is life, there is also hope."

"Where is the Codex?" Lucy plastered on a benign smile. She was curious to see if the book really existed. "Could we see it?"

His demeanor changed, and he eyed her suspiciously. "Why do you want to see it?" Herman said gruffly. "It is evil; evil made it, and evil sustains it!" he spat. "The Codex caused terrible harm to my brothers. Everything Darnathian does is evil. He lied, I believed, and I am lost!"

He heaved a sigh, his gaze searching from one girl to the other. "Have you ever wondered why there is turmoil? So much darkness in the world? It is because he influences people to do wrong. A random wrong thought or a desire may seem harmless, but it will always lead astray. Even now, the book is calling to you, isn't it? You are curious. His words cannot harm a Bachar or one who has the Triune seal, but they can influence you. You must not listen. And don't forget his lament."

"Is it true, Lucy? Is it calling to you?" Schuyler shifted on the bench seat. "You destroyed the pages; you know it exists." She darted an uneasy glance around the library. They'd been in the castle too long. "We should go. I know I don't want to see it. I don't think we should."

"Yes. It is here," Herman said darkly. "Darnathian consults the book often. I hear him laugh every time he sees his noxious self-portrait. It presents him as a creature with a forked tongue, claws, and wearing an ermine diaper. He wants humans to think of him as this ridiculous thing so they are less likely to believe he exists. It's all part of his cunning." He frowned and held up a finger, listening.

Satisfied, he gazed earnestly at Lucy. Then he resignedly pointed to the spiral stairs in the corner.

"Go, if you must," he said sadly. "It is upstairs on the rune table. You may see it, but do not touch it." He grasped the bars and pushed his face close. "But remember this—your failure will serve the Dark Prince. Exercise caution, Bachar." He crawled back to the center of the cage floor and sat cross-legged. He closed his eyes, head and shoulders slumping forward, and chanted quietly.

Lucy considered him for a moment, then stood. She climbed the spiral stairs and followed the walkway to a sizable loft area. It was lit by electric candelabrums on bronze poles shaped like human arms wrapped with snakes, the hands holding the bulbs. They stood at intervals along the balcony railing, circuiting the room.

Thousands of books and manuscripts, written in various languages, stuffed the polished mahogany shelves. Lucy did not recognize most of them.

"Herman," Lucy called, leaning over the railing. "Are the books cursed too?"

"Oh no," he replied. "They're just old books Darnathian has collected over the centuries. He steals them, mostly from churches and monasteries. The only danger is the layers of dust on them. You may touch them if you like."

"What about the Chronicles of Ascalon? The book you mentioned is here. You're sure it's okay to touch it?"

"Oh, definitely. Be sure to take it with you when you leave. Darnathian stole it from the High King's library. So, it really belongs to the High King. Perhaps you should read it—it will help you prepare for what is coming."

"Uh, okay. Thanks, Herman." Lucy reached for the book. It was a thick volume with gold lettering, otherwise simple and unadorned. She flipped through the pages, scanning the phonetically written text. The stories piqued her interest, but she was getting tired, and it had been late when they came through the clock portal. She yawned and placed it back on the shelf.

The room's atmosphere changed slowly, the air getting heavy and sweet. She hadn't noticed the scent before. It wasn't unpleasant, but it made her nauseous. It tickled her nose, and she waved a hand before her face to dispel the too-sweet odor. She'd expected Darnathian's office would smell more eau de burned ash.

Schuyler wandered along the balcony, her hand trailing along the rows of books. A recessed display shelf in the wall held a vase of dead black flowers, and another contained a bench with pillows.

Lucy stepped to the rune table that stood prominently in the center of the loft. The Codex lay open on the table; the pages glistening in the light. The writing was the same as the destroyed pages, the ink vivid. Schuyler came and stood next to her, staring with fascination at the humongous book. Voices whispered, hushed and incoherent. They came from the book.

Lucy's hand gripped the Spectrescope, and she gazed through its lens. It was only a large magnifying glass and no longer a powerful artifact. Her eyes were heavy, and she yawned.

Beside her, Schuyler's eyes became glassy, her head tilted sideways. The murmuring voices were speaking to her too, calling her, urging her closer.

Illustrated vines filled the margins around the twin columns of text. Each vine ended with an oddly shaped leaf. A sketch of a trumpet-shaped horn with the vine-and-leaf motif adorned the heading of a column. As she watched, the images lifted and floated off the parchment, holograms hanging in the air. One vine became a snake, but it purred like a kitten. *How fascinating*, she thought. *It doesn't seem evil at all.* More vines morphed into snakes, lifting from the parchment, murmuring and moaning.

The holograms circled and coiled around one another in a choreographed dance. It was fascinating and lovely in a strange way. It was hard to look away.

Lucy's thoughts were in a jumble. An overwhelming urge to run seized her, but she felt rooted to the spot. Her hand reached for the book. She wanted to touch it, to feel its texture beneath her fingers, but something held her back. The book contained a vast amount of invaluable knowledge. It was right in front of her, calling to her. *Knowledge is good, isn't it?* Lucy wasn't sure. A stupor settled over her, erasing her thoughts and the concerns she knew she should have, but didn't. She simply couldn't remember them.

"You shall not touch it!" the High King's voice boomed in her ear, startling her awake. She squeezed her eyes shut and blinked to clear her vision. Her hand still hovered over the page, and she jerked it back, her face flushing with heat at what she had nearly done. Next to her, Schuyler's face registered shock for her actions too.

The dancing snakes had disappeared. The whispers were silent.

"What happened? Schuyler said, stumbling away from the table and shaking. "I heard Iam's voice! It was like I was sleepwalking. I saw myself reaching for the pages and tried to resist, but I felt so tired."

A sudden clamor from below made them rush to the railing. Herman banged the rungs of his cage.

"Bachar! The Master is coming. You must run!" Herman yelled.

A Trick, A Trap

"Run? Where?" Lucy said, rushing down the steps. The door they had entered earlier was across the big room. Schuyler, still tied to Lucy with the robe's belt, scurried to keep up.

Lucy reached for the doorknob and paused. She held a hand up, then tapped a finger to her lips. Two voices, one deep and the other mousey and obsequious, conversed on the other side of the door.

"Lucy!" Herman whispered, frantically waving a translucent arm through the bars, urging them to him. "Quickly! Upstairs behind the fireplace is a false wall. Press the center panel and wait for the click. There is a hidden passage that leads to another door, and it should lead you back to the portal. Hurry!"

"Thank you, Herman! I wish we could—"

"There is nothing you can do." He smiled tremulously and waved. "Goodbye, Bachar. Be happy knowing you brought me joy for a little while. Now go!" he said, urgently pointing at the stairs. He smiled at Schuyler, too, and waggled his hand. Schuyler smiled sadly and dipped her head.

"Goodbye, Herman." Lucy turned, grabbed Schuyler's arm, and propelled her toward the stairs. As she passed the fireplace, she saw that hanging on the wall next to it was a Crystalline mirror, exactly like the one in her trunk at home. "Herman, could we?" she asked, reaching for the mirror.

"No! There is no time. Quickly, you must go through the passage!"

"Are you certain it will take us to the portal?"

"I can't say for sure, never having seen it, but I hear Grehssil babbling to himself sometimes. Yes, I think it will work. Now go!"

Lucy followed Schuyler up the stairs to the wall behind the fireplace. Across the room, the door opened. Lucy and Schuyler pressed themselves into the shadowy corner and huddled against the panel, not daring to breathe. Darnathian strode to his desk, followed closely by Grehssil, who bobbed up and down like a pigeon, chanting, "Yes, Master."

If Darnathian looked up, he would see them. Any movement would catch his attention. He swung the desk chair around and sat in it, focusing on the servant.

"Yes, Master, Grehssil is sorry, Master. Grehssil should have told you sooner about Stolas and his potions." The cowed servant, head bowed, was sweating profusely, a glossy sheen covering his balding head. He stood in front of the desk, wringing his hands.

"You idiot. If Berbatos fails at his assignment, it will be entirely your fault!" Darnathian bounced a shimmering energy ball in his hand. "I should blast you to smithereens for your incompetence, you fool." He continued to rant at the servant, belittling the daemon's actions and threatening his destruction.

While Darnathian's focus was on the servant, Lucy reached behind Schuyler, who hugged the wall, and pressed the center panel. It didn't move. Alarm coursed through her, and her heart banged furiously in her chest. If this didn't work, it would trap them in Darnathian's office. They would surely be discovered. She pressed the panel again, harder this time, and heard a soft click.

Schuyler felt the panel give way and eased slowly through the opening into the dark passage.

Lucy inched her way to the opening, and then it happened. Her foot stepped on a weak spot. The floor creaked. Panic seized her, freezing her in place. Darnathian's head popped up, his eyes narrowing. He stopped talking and listened. Grehssil continued to apologize.

"Hush, you fool!" Darnathian barked.

Herman's cage creaked. "Fa la fa la fa la la la la!" Herman sang loudly and disturbingly off key.

"What the blazes are you doing?" Darnathian barked, his head rubbernecking toward the spirit. He stood abruptly, and the desk chair careened through the open french doors and out onto the balcony. "Stop that infernal noise!"

"Just felt like singing, sir!" Herman said. "I had a refreshing nap today, and these old bones feel like new!" He raised his arms over his head and waggled his hands. "Fa la fa la fa la la la la!"

"You don't have any bones, you idiot!" the Master yelled. "You're a spirit!" Darnathian stomped toward the cage. "Now, stop that this instant!"

Lucy suppressed a giggle, praising the old spirit for the diversion. She slipped through the entry into the passage. As she eased the panel shut, she spied the book. The Chronicles of Ascalon sat on a shelf near the door. Below, Darnathian's and Grehssil's attention was still on the caged singer.

Lucy hastily snatched the book and knocked a neighboring tome from the shelf. Her free hand caught it before it hit the floor. She froze, stiff as a statue. If Darnathian or Grehssil returned to the desk, she would be in plain view. Fear gripped her muscles, tingles spreading through her arms and back, locked in an awkward position and holding two heavy books.

Herman bellowed at the top of his lungs and marched around the coop, stomping his feet, swinging his arms, and making a ruckus. Darnathian pitched the energy ball at Herman. The missile hit the cage and dissipated.

Absorbed by the curse, it had no effect on the cage or its occupant. The gilded coop merely swayed on its mounting. Herman grinned and wiggled his fingers at the Master.

When Darnathian threw a second missile, Lucy dove through the entry and Schuyler quickly closed the panel with a muted click.

"What were you thinking?" Schuyler hissed. "You scared me half to death!" She reached out in the shadows and gripped Lucy's arm.

"Herman told me to take the Chronicles of Ascalon with us," she said, holding the volume. "Darnathian stole it from the King's library. I'm just taking what isn't his."

Schuyler blew out a breath. "So, what do we do now? I can't see anything in this passage; it's like pitch. I can barely see you." Schuyler fumbled for the wall, feeling her way along. Suddenly, torches flared to life, illuminating a rough stone passage. She flinched and shielded her eyes.

Lucy blinked against the harsh light, then heard someone yawn. She whirled about. No one was there. But now she noticed something else.

The door panel had a carving of a woman. And she was waking from sleep.

The face yawned again. She had long hair, parted in the center, and her carved braids lay beside her face. Surrounding the head was a series of rune symbols forming a square. The rest of the door was unadorned.

"Who goes there? Who woke me up?" she asked. Her eyes fluttered open, and her gaze settled on Lucy. Then they flew wide, round with shock. She opened her mouth, forming an exaggerated oval and prepared to scream. Lucy stuffed the heavy book into the woman's mouth, muffling the scream. The shocked look changed to anger as she flailed her head about, trying to dispel the tome.

"Time to go!" Lucy said. They ran through the shadowy passageway, torches flaring as they approached. A deep thud echoed from the darkness behind them, followed by the woman's scream.

"Master! Intruders in the castle!" her voice yelled. It repeated the phrase two more times. Lucy glanced back and saw the door crash open, spilling light from the balcony. Angry voices reverberated off the stone. The two Defenders ran faster, torches flaming after them. Rushing footsteps thundered through the passage.

They were descending further into the depths under the castle. The air was thick and stale. Dusty cobwebs hung suspended from the ceiling, the gooey strands snagging in their hair. The flickering light from the torches added to the malevolent atmosphere. The hunters knew exactly where they were. All they had to do was follow the sputtering torches.

The tunnel curved and cut off at a wooden door with another bronze face and striker.

"Oh, you've got to be kidding! You again?" Lucy said, reaching for the striker. The man's face awoke and glared at them.

"What do you mean, 'You again?' I've never seen you before!" the face snarled. "What do you want?"

"Whatever. We need to pass, and yeah, I know. Pain opens the door." She lifted the striker.

"Yes, it does," the face said, sniggering, an evil smile creasing his features.

Lucy frowned at him as the striker dropped with a thud. Excruciating pain seared her forehead. Schuyler screamed, grasping her head.

The lock clicked. Lucy groped for the knob, pulled Schuyler through the opening, and slammed the door. They were in another darkened hallway. The lock snicked behind them.

More torches sprang to life. They were in an identical passage. The light pierced their eyes with pain. Ignoring the pain, they clenched the belt that tied them together and stumbled along the passage. Lucy gripped the Spectrescope, the book tucked under her arm, and followed the descending tunnel.

This time, a series of doors appeared along the shadowy corridor, each one different and carved with effigies of ominous and frightening creatures. She paused and stared, unsure what to do. One door had a handle and no lock.

"This is so bad," Lucy said, rubbing her throbbing temples. "What is the right way to go?" Tears blurred her vision.

"I thought Herman said the tunnel would end with a door to take us to the clock portal," Schuyler said, panting, her breath hitching in her throat. "Lucy, how are we going to choose?" She rubbed her forehead with the heel of her hand.

Before Lucy could answer, she heard the face howl on the other side of the door. Whatever was hunting them didn't have to experience the pain as they did. The lock clicked, and the knob turned. Something was about to come through. Lucy stuffed the Spectrescope through a belt loop to keep from dropping it and clutched the book.

She ran for the closest door, opened it, and hurried inside with Schuyler right behind her. The passageway door crashed open, smacking the striker against the face again. The bronze face yelled expletives as something bounded down the passage.

Before they could completely shut the door, an enormous paw with lethal talons forced its way through the opening and raked the air. Lucy and Schuyler fought to close the jiggling door. The creature shoved it open enough to reach its arm into the opening. Their shoes gripped the rugged stone as they pushed and shoved. They pinned the beast's paw against the jamb. The creature screamed, the paw flailed, and then the beast jerked it out. They slammed the door and pressed against it, panting. The creature

growled and scratched vehemently on the other side. The sounds were terrifying in the dark.

A torch suddenly sputtered, spit, and flared a feeble, flickering light
over the stone. The door had to be centuries old, the wood dry and cracked.
It thudded in the frame as the creature lunged against it.

"I'm not sure we can hold this," Lucy said, sweating with the exertion.
"Now would be a good time for that help to show up." The door threatened
to shatter with each thrust from the beast. The book slipped from her arm,
fell to the floor, and flipped open. A line of text caught her eye. *My help
comes from the High King.*

"I've got splinters in my hands," Schuyler whimpered and turned her
back to the door, her feet braced on the stone. Bloody handprints smeared
the old wood. "Lucy, look!"

Standing in the corner near the door was a large timber. Glancing
around, Lucy noticed iron brackets protruding from the stone on either
side of the door. She grinned.

"Help me get this into place?" Still pressed to the door, she reached
for the timber, nudging the heavy beam toward her. It slid partway, then
tumbled onto her shoulder. She lifted the end of the beam and set it in the
nearest bracket. Schuyler lifted the other and slid it into place. The door
was secure. Breathing heavily, they leaned against each other and surveyed
their surroundings. They were in a large room.

"Where do you think we are?" Schuyler asked, stepping to the center of
the big room, the movement causing more torches to flare throughout the
chamber. "Each of the tunnels descended. I guess we're in the lowest part
of the castle. Maybe in the dungeons?" She grimaced.

Lucy studied the chamber. The arched ceiling was imposing, as if the
stone would press down on her, judging her. A door was centered in each
of the four walls, one of which they had just come through. Rows of pews

sat in galleries opposite each other to view the raised platform in the middle of the room.

A large ornate desk and a gold chair sat on the platform. Two more chairs were situated directly in front, facing the platform.

"It might be the dungeon level, but I'm not sure what they use this for," Lucy said, pointing at the raised platform. The detailed woodwork had a polished finish. It was incongruous with the rough-cut stone construction of the room. "It kind of reminds me of a playhouse or a courtroom. Whatever it is, it gives me the chills." The two viewing chairs were old and worn, the arms scratched and gouged. "We need to get out of here."

"I'm afraid that won't be possible. You are staying with me, as my guests." Darnathian laughed, but there was no humor in it, only venom. "How sweet of you to walk so boldly into my domain!"

Lucy whirled around. Her breath hitched, and her eyes widened. The Dark Prince stood in the aisle between the galleries, his feet set wide and arms folded over his chest. His eyes were glowing like hot coals. Next to him was a hideous creature with a lion's body. The human face snarled, its eyes hard and flinty, and a scorpion tail hovered over the creature's back, threatening and deadly. The Master casually caressed the creature's mane, running his fingers through the fur. The Spectrescope seemed to raise in front of her of its own accord, and Lucy's hands gripped it tightly.

"I see you found my courtroom," Darnathian said. "This is where we hold proceedings to decide the fate of wayward daemons but especially adversaries like yourselves. It's close to the correction chambers. Would you like to see one?" he said coyly.

Lucy tried to swallow, but her throat had gone dry. The Dark Prince was tall and lithe, with dark hair and perfect teeth. He wore an expensive light-colored suit and exquisitely detailed crocodile-patterned leather loafers. She had forgotten he was extremely handsome, but she would never forget his wickedness. She straightened her shoulders, lifted her chin, and returned his stare.

"My, but aren't you the brave one? I admire your courage though."

"Schuyler," Lucy whispered, scarcely moving her lips. "Check the door behind us. If it's open, run for it. I'll try to distract him." The pain was receding, making it easier to focus. She widened her stance, feinting with the Spectrescope. It was powerless, but Darnathian didn't need to know. He would find out soon enough.

"Uh-huh. You need me, girlfriend. We fight together." Schuyler stood beside Lucy and tugged on the belt. "Together, girlfriend."

Lucy sighed. Her nod was nearly imperceptible but grateful.

Behind them the door squeaked open, and two brilliant, white-winged entities flew past them. The entities stood between them and the Dark Prince. Their bright appearance made the torches seem mere candles in comparison. They folded their arms, wings extended, and watched Darnathian and the creature. Lucy and Schuyler huddled anxiously behind the guardians and waited.

Darnathian growled, and his fists clenched. The creature raised the hackles along its back, its body arched like a cat.

"What are you doing here, guardians?" Darnathian said angrily. "Aren't you afraid I will have you plucked like chickens and served for dinner? My pet carries quite a sting. It will paralyze you and pluck you before you know it."

"Still playing with the manticores, I see," one guardian said. "Are you not afraid they will turn on you and poke you instead?" The guardian smiled easily as the Dark Prince bared his teeth.

The door squeaked again, and Ishi emerged. He strode into the chamber, placed a comforting arm around each of the girls' shoulders, and dipped his head between them. Like his father, his attire never changed. His khaki pants, sandals, and baggy cardigan were comfortable and casual.

His comely appearance with a prominent nose, high cheekbones, and easy mannerisms belied that he was the son of the High King and a powerful entity. Relief washed over Lucy at his presence. Schuyler seemed giddy as she watched him, her eyes alight.

"Defenders," Ishi said. "I have opened a door. Go through it and follow on. Resist the evil that awaits you. Trust your armor and fight like warriors. Your High King has not given you a spirit of timidity but of power tempered by love and discipline." Beneath thick brows, his serious brown eyes looked evenly at Lucy and Schuyler, instilling a calm reserve in them. His winsome smile inside a wealth of rich brown beard was reassuring. "Remember, knock, and it will open for you."

"But, sir, we don't have our armor," Lucy whispered, casting a wary eye on Darnathian and his manticore.

"Are you sure about that?" Ishi smiled mischievously and tapped a finger on top of her helmet. He straightened with a chuckle.

Lucy gasped, her hand touching the smooth metal helmet. The breastplate, belt, and her bracelet were in place, and sandal straps wrapped securely around her calves. Schuyler was grinning, wearing her armor, too, though she was spinning her bracelet, a sure sign of anxiety. "Thank you!"

"Remember, you do not fight against flesh and blood. You fight against spiritual forces and the dark powers. Do not be afraid, Sho-are." He winked at her. The motion was so like the High King, Lucy grinned, and she realized she loved Ishi as much as she loved the High King.

"Shouldn't we stay here and help you and the guardians?" Schuyler asked, tucking a stray curl under the helmet. Ishi patted her shoulder but shook his head.

"I think we can handle a wayward angel who has lost his wings," Ishi whispered, a smile tugging at his mouth.

"I'm sorry you had to come rescue us. It was all my fault," Lucy said. Tears filled her eyes again.

"No need to worry." His hand offered the book she had dropped. "You may keep this. It is mine to give." Lucy sheepishly took it from him. He tipped his head toward the door and strode forward to join the guardians.

"C'mon," Lucy said, tugging the belt that still tied her to Schuyler. "I just want to get out of here." She tapped the bracelet, and as the shield emerged, the Ratha-nael sword appeared, too, sheathed on her belt.

As Ishi and the guardians confronted Darnathian and his pet, the girls slipped through the door and found themselves in another stone corridor. The battered wood door closed behind them, and the lock clicked.

The passage was lit by a series of torches and stretched away to the left and to the right. It was populated by several doors. Which way would take them back to the clock portal? The silence in the tunnel was eerie.

"How do we decide?" Schuyler said, her eyes wide in her anxious face. Her head rubbernecking, she glanced down the tunnel in each direction. "We're really deep under the castle."

"Darnathian said the correction chambers were nearby," Lucy said. "I'd like to avoid those if we can. Is there any sign the tunnel is leading upward?" The Spectrescope vibrated in her hand.

"Ishi must have restored the power! Thank you, Ishi!" The runes on the ring under the lens were glowing and transforming. The characters settled into different forms—a gargoyle and an owl with skinny legs. Lucy showed the scope to Schuyler, who grimaced.

"What are those?" Lucy said, staring at the rune symbols. "Spectrescope, is something coming at us? Which way should we go?" A message appeared in the lens. *Evil approaches on all sides. Stand your ground.* "Ew, okay. Thanks. I'm glad you are back though." *Me too. Don't lose me, okay?* A smile flashed briefly across her face. Nudging Schuyler with her elbow, she lifted the Spectrescope. The lens receded, and the Spirit Sword appeared with its ethereal blue light.

"Why are we raising our swords?" Schuyler whispered, lifting her sword, the hairs on her arms standing up. Zazriel glittered menacingly in the flickering torchlight. "What did the Spectrescope say?"

"Stand your ground." A door squeaked opened, and Lucy nodded down the corridor where two creatures matching the runes stepped out.

"Wowza!" Schuyler said, her eyes widening in disbelief. She clapped a hand over her mouth at the sight of the two hilariously preposterous creatures. Lucy would have laughed except for the fact they were being hunted like rats trapped under Darnathian's castle.

One creature was a miniature Grigori gargoyle with a squat body and bulging eyes and arm muscles. He was wearing a leather caplet, brown tunic, and knee-high leather boots and carrying a short, knobby club. Next to him walked a small owl with a tiny crown, huge yellow eyes, and impossibly long, skinny legs who was chattering away and hiccuping between sentences.

The owl glanced up, saw the armored girls, and screeched.

"Ow! What you dun do that for?" the small gargoyle groused, flinching violently and swatting the owl. He rubbed his ear and drew back when he saw the Defenders standing in the middle of the passage with their raised weapons. Then he said, "Stand back, Stolas. They're just puny humans. Ronwe got this." The creature seemed to be referring to himself. "You go fix up that potion. You got to put me back to right size." The creature gave the two girls the stink eye, his mouth twisting with annoyance. He smacked the club against his hand and crouched.

"Be careful, Ronwe," Stolas said, his startled yellow eyes darting like pinballs in his pinched face as he stared at them. "Those are the King's Defenders. I overheard the Irredaemon say they are formidable opponents." He squawked, scampering erratically back and forth behind the small Grigori. His crown slipped sideways. He shoved it back on top of his head. "Oh, dear!"

Ronwe growled and stalked toward the girls. He twirled the club in his hand, one hand cupped and ready to grab them.

Lucy stood sideways, shield forward, her sword pointed at the Grigori. Schuyler mirrored her stance.

Ronwe swung the cudgel at Lucy's shield. She swerved, and the club skidded harmlessly off the shield, but the action unbalanced the gargoyle.

Ronwe stumbled, the force of his thrust propelling him forward. Schuyler swooped in and struck the creature, her sword slicing through the gauntlet protecting his forearm. The creature howled with anger. Lucy flicked her wrist, circling her sword, and brought it crashing down on the knotty club, severing it in half. He threw the remains aside.

The creature roared, his gauntlet hanging from his arm. He bared his teeth and pulled twin daggers from his belt as Stolas twittered, "Oh, dear!" The daemon owl turned, clutched his crown, and skittered away. A moment later, the door slammed, and the lock snicked.

Lucy and Schuyler stood side by side, shields and swords raised. The creature lunged, stabbing the short knives at one girl, then the other. Swords clashed with the daggers, the metal screeching and clanging. The miniature Grigori was fast. The blades darted quickly in and out, only to be dashed away by their swords. The skirmish went on for several minutes. Each time, it was a draw.

"Enough of this," Lucy said. "Watch my back," she told Schuyler. "Down, shield!" The shield retreated to the bracelet. The Ratha-nael sword appeared in her hand. She stepped toward the creature with the two deadly swords.

His bulging eyes squinted, and he backed slowly down the corridor, drawing her further away from her friend. His hands were fast and as knotty as the club had been. The swords screeched, the metal sparking against the knives. Again, Lucy twisted her wrist with little effort, and the sword slipped under a dagger, which she flicked from his hand. It clattered along the floor, out of the creature's reach. He pitched the other dagger back and forth in his hands, crouched, and growled menacingly.

Lucy feinted with the Spirit Sword, aiming at his head. The creature turned quickly, throwing an arm up to block with the knife. As he swerved, Lucy thrust the Ratha-nael sword under the creature's outstretched arm. His bulging eyes nearly popped from his head as he imploded to a pinpoint and disappeared with a pop.

"Schuyler, did you see where the daemon owl went?" Lucy sheathed the spare sword, and the Spectrescope returned when the Spirit Sword retreated.

"Yeah, for a raptor species, he wasn't very brave. He scurried to a room and slammed the door. I don't think he will be a problem." Schuyler, her shield and weapon ready, reconnoitered further into the passage. "Which way should we go? I don't have a clue where this leads. It isn't familiar. I don't think it is the same passage we came through earlier."

"Spectrescope, can you help us?" The lens rippled for a moment like water, then words appeared in the lens. *Let the wise and discerning listen and get guidance. Run away from evil.* Lucy rolled her eyes. "Seriously? Now you're giving me riddles?"

"Another riddle?" Schuyler frowned, worry in her eyes. "What did it say?"

"Basically, it said, 'Listen and learn and run from evil.'" Lucy's jaw dropped, and she tapped a finger to her lips. Schuyler listened intently too. Footsteps and grunting echoed faintly along the corridor behind them. "We run this way!" Lucy said and darted in the opposite direction.

Torches flared up as they sprinted along the passage that seemed to run on indefinitely. Footsteps and grunting followed behind them, but the creatures weren't visible yet.

The Ghost You Can't See

The tunnel ended abruptly with another door and door knocker. Lucy clenched her jaw as Schuyler huffed next to her. Her hands searched the wood for a clue to open the door. The only hardware was the black iron hinges and a pewter door knocker. It had no latch or doorknob. Etched on the striker of the knocker was a message: *Knock, and I shall open it for you.*

"This is what Ishi meant," Lucy said. "He said to go through the door he had opened."

"I don't think Darnathian would be so accommodating." Schuyler nervously pointed at the knocker. "Hurry. It sounds like whatever is following us is getting closer."

Lucy dropped the striker with a loud clang. The rhythmic shuffle of the footsteps changed to boots pounding along the ground toward them. A series of clicks resounded in the confined space that echoed off the stone. The knocker disappeared, and the door opened, revealing the first passage. They ran until they came to the spiral staircase and charged up the steps. At the top was the clock cabinet and the foyer beyond. They scrambled through, and the door slowly closed behind them and disappeared.

Bunkum and Balderdash

"Lucy," Iam said, his voice whispering in her ear. "Wake up, dear one. We need to talk. Be sure Schuyler comes with you. I'll be waiting in the viewing room."

"Aw! We just got to sleep," Lucy whined, pulling the covers over her head and burrowing further into the sheets. "It's only five in the morning, and it's still dark outside."

"Now!" The sternness in Iam's voice made Lucy spring from her pillow in a tangle of blankets.

"I'm—I'm sorry. We're coming, Iam," Lucy said, pushing back the covers. Across the room, Schuyler yelped and flung the blankets off. There was a muffled grunt as she bumped her head on the slanted ceiling. "You got the same message, huh?" Lucy slid her feet into her slippers and reached for the robe on the floor.

"Yeah, and I think we're about to be sent to detention, don't you?" Schuyler had forgotten to bring a robe, so she pulled on an oversize fleece shirt to cover her pajamas.

The Ghost You Can't See

"That's putting it mildly. If anyone gets detention, it should be me. I'm the one who jumped through the clock. I am sorry, Schuyler. It put us both in danger."

"You didn't go alone if you remember, girlfriend," Schuyler said, stuffing her hands into the pockets as she followed Lucy. They padded quietly down the stairs to the viewing room.

A soft glow issued from the sitting room. Iam stood in front of the stained glass window, his arms folded and an uneasy expression on his face. His blue eyes usually twinkled mischievously, but they were clouded with worry. Lucy had never seen him that way.

Suddenly, guilt washed over her at the realization that her rash actions caused his furrowed brow and the concern etched in the lines of his face. She had placed herself and Schuyler in extreme danger, along with the Spectrescope and its secrets. It was the most foolish thing she could have done. Ishi even had to come rescue them.

Iam was clearly upset with her. Instead of rushing to greet him, she closed the door softly, sat demurely on the bench next to Schuyler, and chewed her lip.

"Good morning?" Lucy asked hopefully, with a tremulous smile.

"Do you still not understand?" Iam said, his gaze piercing. "How long before you believe? You went through the portal without your armor. Without it, you are vulnerable!" He slammed his hand into his palm, startling them. He paced the room. "You have been told three times, yet you don't believe."

The stained glass window behind him was active, its colors glowing. The dryad and faun were watching closely. Haniel's hair shimmered around her anxious face, her hands folded together in front of her emerald dress. Pheman held the flute, a frown puckering his forehead as he nervously wandered at the edge of the meadow.

"But I—" Lucy began to protest, but Iam held up a hand.

"Bunkum! Whatever excuse you are about to make, it's bunkum."

"Yes, sir," Lucy whispered and rolled her lips. Tears welled in her eyes. It grieved her that Iam was so upset with her. She would do anything for him.

"Lucy and Schuyler, you must always be on your guard. Darnathian wants to lure your conscience to sleep and desensitize you. The helmet protects your mind. The breastplate protects your heart—" He threw up his arms at their blank faces, then ran an impatient hand down his face.

"Okay, let's try this," Iam said. "Mrs. McGoo's chocolate chip cookies—they go into your mouth, you chew, you swallow, and then they go into your stomach. Right? They don't affect your thinking, do they?" he said, tapping his temple with a finger.

"Well, yeah, they kind of do," Schuyler said. "When I eat one cookie, I'm thinking about eating another." He pursed his lips and pierced her with a stern look. She dropped her gaze, dipping her head, and flinched when Lucy jabbed her with an elbow. Schuyler mouthed, "Sorry."

Iam stopped pacing, took a deep breath, and leaned against the wall, considering. "Darnathian whispers half-truths and deceptive thoughts to bend your thinking—a redirection, if you will. Unconsciously, you know something is missing, so you add your own interpretation to fill in the gaps. Then, instead of truth, you have a lie." Iam squatted, still leaning against the wall. "Don't you understand? What you let into your mind can change your thinking. It's like nourishment for those little gray cells. Therefore, your helmet is critical to guard your mind. The breastplate is another layer of protection for your heart."

"So, if Darnathian uses half-truths," Lucy said, "how do we know what is wholly true?"

"Remember the code? You must test what's given as truth against what you know is truth. The more truth you apply to your heart, the more the code expands. Dove will help you too. Darnathian is your enemy, and his half-truths will confuse you. What is good and right will no longer make any sense to you."

"Lucy," Haniel said, stepping closer to the window, "the battleground is the mind. It is why your magical armor is both physical and spiritual. If Darnathian can alter the way you think, he can change your heart. He wants you to doubt and disbelieve. The absence of dirt makes a hole. Your life without truth makes a lie. To love the King means knowing truth."

"Trapped as we were in the castle," Lucy said, wringing her hands, "I was so scared! Schuyler is right. I rush into things without thinking. I don't mean to cause a problem, but that's usually the result." Her cheek tickled, and the hand she swept across it came away damp. "And not using my armor was the dumbest thing ever. I am so sorry, Iam."

"Darnathian teaches his daemons and ghosts to whisper," Haniel said. "Whispers affect the hearing. Once the ear can't hear the truth, the mind won't recognize the seriousness of bentness. Eventually an inflexible attitude develops—"

"And they deny the High King," Schuyler said softly, her eyes moist. She wrapped her arms around herself in a huddle, nearly disappearing in the oversize fleece shirt.

"Lucy, Schuyler," Iam said, "the Triune seal gives you protection, but you can lose your effectiveness for the kingdom. Darnathian will be happy to see you defeated. When you feel you are being influenced, whisper my name, and focus on me. You will find peace. Darnathian and his Irredaemon never sleep."

"I don't know what else to say except—can you forgive me?" Lucy stood hesitantly, waiting. Iam stood and opened his arms, and she ran into them. He kissed the top of her head as he rocked her back and forth.

Schuyler watched them, her eyes filled with hopefulness. Iam motioned and pulled her in for a group hug, and she wrapped an arm around each of them. Haniel laughed lightly and clapped. Pheman took a deep breath and played a melodious tune, his fingers flying over the flute as he danced around the Life Tree.

"Lucy," Iam said, "remember the book that Ishi gave you? The one from Darnathian's office?" She nodded, looking up at him. "Good girl. I want you to read it. It will help you understand our history and what you and the Defenders are up against. Look in your trunk later. Each of the Defenders needs a copy." He gave them each a squeeze and released them.

"Now that *that* discussion is over." Iam grinned at them. "Why don't we meet in the kitchen for a glass of milk and Mrs. McGoo's chocolate chip cookies? I'm hungry too," he said, cupping his hand to Schuyler's cheek and smiling. "I'll be right along. I need to speak with Haniel."

"Awesome! You read my mind!" Schuyler said.

"Food, it—"

"Don't start, girlfriend!"

Mathias stood outside the viewing room, eavesdropping on the conversation, and wondered if he was still sane or if he had finally lost his mind.

He had been lying awake when he heard Lucy and Schuyler come down the stairs and tiptoe past his door, whispering. He'd watched them go into the viewing room and had heard several voices inside. A man's deep voice sounded upset. The woman's voice was pleasant and musical as she spoke. He didn't recognize either. And someone was playing a flute.

Though he didn't catch every word, it was enough to make him question his sanity. They spoke of spirits, battlefields, magical armor, kingdoms, and cookies. He must be hallucinating. His lack of sleep might be to blame, but what about the voices inside his head? The only time he didn't hear them was inside the B and B.

The man mentioned getting milk and cookies. Mathias hurried back to his room and hid on the steps to the third floor, listening. He peeked over

The Ghost You Can't See

the railing. Lucy and Schuyler went down to the kitchen. He waited several moments, but no one else left the room. He slowly approached the open door and looked in. The room was empty.

And yet, it wasn't.

He entered the room and closed the door. The room was peaceful, like something wonderful yet intangible had just been there. The peace lingered.

Where were the man and the woman? They hadn't left the room. If they had, he would have seen them. Dryads and fauns watched lifelessly from the window. It had to be backlit. The window was glowing softly, giving light to the room. *What was going on in here?* he thought.

His head dipped, and his fingers gripped handfuls of hair, tugging the roots as if he could pull the strange feelings and thoughts from his chest and his mind.

How much longer must I wrestle with my thoughts? Day after day, I have this gloominess. I don't know what to do. I wish I could stay in this room forever. These voices have me so confused.

He sat on the bench and stared forlornly at the beautiful window.

For a Sunday afternoon in late September, the weather was comfortably warm and sunny. Lucy had convinced Mathias to join them, and the group trudged across the yard to the old stables. She wanted to find the infamous teacup cat figurine. She had found it once in a box of Great-Aunt Isabel's antiques. After the fire and their subsequent stay with the McGoos, the little porcelain cat had been forgotten and lost among all the tchotchkes.

The long, two-story building was slightly larger than the house. It didn't have any turrets, but it had two octagonal-shaped cupolas on the roof. A newly constructed vestibule was a welcome addition over the main entry and shaped like a tiny house. Sidelights and a half-circle window above the antique door spilled light into the small room. Lucy pushed open the unlocked door.

Inside, the vestibule was charming with natural wood trims and a brown octagon brick floor. Two barn doors with black iron handles, each with a half-round window, glided on rails and opened into the foyer with a small hallway and an elevator. A staircase led to the second floor. The stair railing laid in segments against a wall, waiting to be installed.

The storage area on the right held remnants of lumber, planking, wiring, and aluminum ducting strewn about the space. Sawdust covered everything. Most of the stalls were intact; a large open area, now filled with boxes and broken equipment, had once housed the horses and carriages from the stagecoach route.

The other side of the foyer held an equally large space for the store. Lucy thumbed toward it and picked her way into the room, avoiding the debris scattered on the floor.

This side of the stable was taking shape. Lucy could envision the antique furniture and tchotchkes artfully arranged and attracting a buyer's attention.

Along one side of the room, individual stalls remained with their wrought iron dividers and more of the octagon brick flooring. The polished wood and the new custom shelving and cabinets in each stall gleamed, and pairs of semicircle windows let in the natural light. The exposed beams and rafters in the high ceiling were rustic and natural. Wrought iron chandeliers hung evenly spaced throughout the room. Stacked cartons of tchotchkes stood like soldiers in formation, ready to be unpacked and placed on the display shelves.

"Oh my goodness!" Schuyler said. "This is going to be awesome." She wandered through the units, admiring the new cabinetry and peeking into drawers and cabinet doors.

Lucy scanned the cartons. This was more difficult than she'd expected. It would be nearly impossible to find the box she was looking for until the renovation was complete. By then, the antiques would be sorted and displayed in the gift shop. She toed a stack of boxes, moving them around and checking the labels. Pursing her lips, she huffed and flung her hands up in defeat.

"Where are the guys?" Lucy asked, realizing Paul and Mathias had disappeared.

"They are over there." Schuyler pointed across the foyer. Long rows of stalls still waited to be renovated. The string of work lights suspended from the ceiling was lit. Swathed in cobwebs, it enhanced the mystery.

As they continued searching through boxes, they watched Paul investigate an empty horse stall. Mathias grabbed a dilapidated padded leather horse collar from the wall and dropped it over Paul's head. "Neigh!"

"Hey! Gross, dude," Paul said, flinging the collar off with a laugh. "It's covered with cobwebs and eons of grime." He shimmied like a dog and brushed the cobwebs from his hair. "Bleh."

"But it looked good on you," Mathias joked, a smile tugging at the corners of his mouth. He glanced over at Schuyler. A smirk dimpled his cheek.

"There's a lot of stuff here." Paul pointed to a line of dusty collars hanging on the wall. There were harnesses and yokes, a crusty old dresser or two, wooden barrels with iron bands, galvanized buckets, and feed bags and several huge carriage wheels leaning against the walls. Dust motes floated in the air. Years of undisturbed grime layered everything. "This was a busy stopover. I don't think a normal barn would have this much stuff."

"Hey, Lucy! What's the story with this junk?" Mathias yelled, waving an arm. She and Schuyler crossed the foyer and joined them, Lucy holding the porcelain cat figurine she had finally found.

"Wowza, this is cool," Schuyler said, reaching for a pair of skates. The leather straps were crumbly as she took them from the wall. The pitted metal was rusted, but the mechanisms were still intact. Someone had tied the skates together with twine. "Can you imagine these clamped to your shoes and skating on them? I couldn't balance on these things."

"Where would you use them?" Mathias asked. He carefully took them when she handed them over.

"Michigan has lots of lakes and ponds," Schuyler said. "I've read stories of how people cleared the snow from frozen lakes and creeks to have skating parties. Just think of it. A campfire on the riverbank, a pot of hot chocolate banked in the embers, and toasted marshmallows under a starry night sky. Sounds like fun. We should try it sometime."

Then she turned to Lucy and said, "You could probably clean and sell some of them. Rustic and Americana memorabilia is in enormous demand."

"People love to buy junk," Mathias snickered. He waggled the skates and shrugged. Schuyler poked him in the shoulder.

"They're antiques, thank you very much," she said, taking the skates back and returning them to the hook on the wall. "It's gives us a glimpse of life way back when." She struggled to get the skates back on the hook and inadvertently gave the hook a sharp tug. An entire section of the wall wobbled.

"Hold on. This portion is loose," Mathias said, examining the slatted wall. Though the thick board wall was loose, it didn't affect the rest of the structure. After investigating closer, he tugged at the boards. "Hey, there's a door back here," he said. With all the castoff junk, carriage parts, and horse equipment piled in front of it, the door was indistinguishable from the rest of the wall. "Let's dig it out and see what's behind it."

The group worked diligently for the next several minutes, moving the piled-up junk. It was obvious someone had boarded up the two barn doors deliberately.

Paul and Mathias pried the boards with their fingers. Lucy searched through an old dresser for a claw hammer and gave it to Paul. He pushed the claw under an edge and levered the tool back and forth. The long board cracked in half and fell off.

"Sorry, Luce. I didn't mean to break it." He broke the other piece off and gave the hammer to Mathias, who removed the remaining boards holding the door.

"It's okay. They will probably demolish it, anyway, when they finish the renovations on this side."

The boys got the creaky old doors open and peered into the dark interior. A secret room hid behind the structure. Lucy's hand searched for a light switch, but there wasn't one. She used the flashlight app on her phone, and the others did the same. The long, windowless room was only a few feet wide.

"Look over there." Lucy spied a large shadow in the corner of the secret room. She swept her beam over the object. As the others added their beams, a filthy, dilapidated canvas tarp came into view. It hung over the strange looming shape, obscuring most of the details except for one. A tall, wood wagon wheel. It stood straight and firm. It had to be attached to something.

Schuyler squealed, hands waving. "I know what it is!" she said, bouncing on the balls of her feet. Schuyler grinned and high-fived Lucy.

They had found a stagecoach.

Mathias lifted an end of the covering, and Paul grabbed another. Dust exploded into the air, filling the chamber with decades of dust and pollen as they pulled the tarp from the stagecoach. The cover slithered to the ground.

"Huh. Who would have thought that?" Mathias said. Several rounds of coughing and hacking echoed through the strange room.

The stagecoach was remarkable. The driver's box, baggage boot, and front boot trimmed in leather were in good condition, though the driver's padded seat cushion had rotted away to dusty remnants. A small oil lantern hung from a hook beside the driver's seat. The top rails were still intact, and the side curtains were stiff little rolls, their straps dangling.

"It must have sat in here for decades," Paul said, walking around the coach and waving his phone's light over it. "Why leave it behind?"

Schuyler gasped. "It may have been here longer than that," she said, consulting an app on her smartphone. "Listen to this—this article says the stagecoach line ran between Grand River Valley and Plankton from eighteen fifty-five to eighteen sixty-eight, and up to eight coaches a day made the fifty-mile trip. The coaches usually stopped every fifteen to forty miles, depending on terrain and weather, for fresh horses and tack. Stagecoach routes through the west covered up to one hundred twenty-five miles every twenty-four hours and stopped every twelve miles. Stagecoaches eventually shut down because of the railroad expansion."

"Were there sleeping establishments at each stop, I wonder?" Mathias said, stretching to peek inside the cabin. Though the tufted seats were dry, dirty, and cracked, they appeared comfortable.

"Oh my goodness," Schuyler said, slapping a hand over her mouth, her brows reaching skyward as she continued reading. "The article says the Concord coach weighed about twenty-five hundred pounds and was pulled by six or eight horses. No wonder they changed teams so often. The stable had to be large. It held dozens of horses and their tack."

"Holy cow," Lucy said, "those poor horses pulling so much weight." Squatting, she peered under the coach. A wooden trunk with metal straps nestled in the dirt. "I wonder if this is from the coach too," she said, lifting the rusty latch and slowly opening the lid, but the hinges resisted. She let it fall closed.

"What else does the article say?" Paul asked. "I love history." Lucy squinted her eyes at him. "What? I do now, thanks to you."

"Wowza," Schuyler said with reverence. "Look." Her phone light hovered on the dusty panel above the cabin door. The faint yellow lettering spelled Grand River Valley.

"I can't believe someone hid this in here," Lucy said, standing and brushing the dirt from her hands. "Why would someone do that? It's a wonderful piece of history."

"Oh no," Schuyler said, a hand on her cheek, eyes widening. "It couldn't be—you don't think this thing is haunted, do you? Why else they would hide it away?" She threw her hands up in frustration. "Aw, Luce, I don't want to fight another ghost." Neither of the other two Defenders responded. Schuyler looked questioningly at Lucy and Paul, then, realizing her gaff, slapped a hand to her mouth and stole a glance at Mathias. Thunderstruck, his mouth hung open, and he stared at her like she had suddenly grown two heads.

"You're joking, right? Nobody in their right mind believes in ghosts or spirits." He switched off the cell phone light and stuffed his hands into his jeans pockets.

"Well, actually—we do," Schuyler said.

Mathias huffed. "Then you're all nuts!" He twirled a finger at his temple. "Ghosts and spirits, magical armor, and a battle for the mind. It's all balderdash—you know, complete and utter nonsense! I can't believe I'm still standing here." He spun and stalked away. He kicked the false wall and knocked the ice skates off the hook. They clattered to the ground. Schuyler followed him out.

Lucy motioned to Paul, and they eased the doors shut, then replaced the castoff items to hide the room. The carriage was their secret for now. Lucy couldn't wait to tell her mom and the McGoos about the coach. They would know what to do next.

"Mathias!" Schuyler said, running to catch up with him. "It's true! We're not making this stuff up. The spiritual realm exists. You just can't see it unless the spirits want you to or you have special equipment like we do. Lucy, Paul, and I are ghost hunters. We've vanquished lots of ghosts. Last year, a spirit haunted Paul. It was scary."

"Seriously?" Mathias asked. "What do you do? Run around in the dark with your little ghost-detecting machines and electromagnetic meters and cameras? Do you squeal when you meet dead people?" His hands cupped his cheeks, and he feigned excitement. "Ooh! I think I've just seen a ghost!" he said, wiggling his fingers in the air. "Oh, wait! It's my dead great-uncle!" Dropping his hands, he gave her an icy stare.

"No, we don't see dead people," Schuyler said, hands on her hips. She returned his stare. "The spirits of dead people don't wander the earth. They have their eternal reward, and earth isn't an option."

"What do you think a ghost is? Maybe it's an alien from another planet?" Mathias snarled. Angry, he leaned against a stall door and crossed his arms.

"No, it's not an alien." She waggled her head. "Though it could explain some of the strange creatures we've met. But no. It is a fallen angel."

"Oh, c'mon!" he said crossly. "How dense do you think I am, anyway? I thought you were genuine, that maybe you all wanted to be my friends. I guess that's not true. Whatever your game is, I'm not playing." He kicked an old feed bag, then stomped through the stable and went out the door.

"That went well," Paul said. "I'll see if I can talk to him."

Conspiracies and Plots

"To say it didn't go well is an understatement." Lucy picked up the feed bag and dropped it in a bucket. She whirled and looked at Schuyler. "Wait a minute!" Heat raced up her face. "He was eavesdropping on our conversation this morning!" Her hands made a gripping motion. She turned and trudged toward the stable door.

"What are you talking about?" Schuyler followed her outside. The sunshine was overpowering after the dimness of the stables. She shielded her eyes with a cupped hand and stared at Lucy. "What made you think that?"

"'Magical armor, and a battle for the mind'?" Lucy's fingers quoted the air. "Remember what Haniel said about our magical armor? He quoted her just now when he was spouting off. He must have listened outside the viewing room this morning. Mathias shouldn't know about the magical armor. We've never told him, and he's never seen it before." Lucy stomped a foot, and clouds of dust wafted in the air. She placed her hands on her hips. "I am so mad—I don't even know what to do with that information."

"If he spied on us, he must know Iam and Haniel didn't leave the room with us. Where does he think they went?" Schuyler slipped her arm through Lucy's and tugged her toward the house. "We should go help Paul.

He might need an intervention about now. Together, maybe we can figure out how to help Mathias."

They slipped through the sliders on the sunporch. Lucy grabbed some bottled water and the bowl of strawberries from the refrigerator while Schuyler grabbed a bag of chips from the pantry. Then they bounded up the back stairs.

The staircase was windowless, but a skylight in the roof allowed for natural light. The white walls, step risers, and tiny light sconces kept the small space airy. The turquoise-blue treads added a pop of color.

Lucy and Schuyler had found the hidden room when the renovations began. It was the perfect opportunity to add a narrow back staircase for quick access to the upper levels, connecting the kitchen to the third floor. Since the viewing room was a public space, the hidden door remained, successfully hiding the steps that joined to the family level to the main floor.

As they exited through the viewing room, they heard raised voices coming from guest suite four. Lucy and Schuyler grimaced at each other. Mathias's rushed words sounded angry, and he kept cutting off Paul's attempts to explain. Lucy knocked on his door.

Mathias whipped open the door, startling her. "What do you want? Got more ghost stories to tell?"

"I thought maybe we could all watch a movie upstairs in the sitting room. We brought snacks." The water bottles were sweating. She handed one to him. "C'mon, it will be more fun upstairs. It's small and quiet. Maybe we can talk some more."

"Oh, yeah. I'd love to hear more ghost stories from the Ghost Writer here," he snarled, thumbing at Paul, who was shaking his head, a disgruntled expression furrowing his brow. "You can count me out, thanks."

"Well, okay then. We'll join you in your room," Lucy said, pushing by him and ignoring his chagrined expression. She tossed a water bottle to Paul and plunked into a chair by the window. Each guest suite had a small sitting area with a table and two chairs. Schuyler smiled, waggled her fingers at Mathias, and sat in the other chair.

"I guess I don't have any say in this. Since you're the proprietor's daughter, you can make yourself at home wherever you want, huh?" He shut the door and dropped on the bed, avoiding eye contact, and sulked.

"Mathias, we want to know what's happening to you," Schuyler said. "One minute you're fun and snarky, the next you're ready to bite our heads off. What gives?" She opened the bag of chips and offered it to him. He waved her off. Paul grabbed the bag, sat on the floor, and munched.

"Nothing gives. Just leave me alone."

"Mathias," Lucy said, "what's going on? You're with friends here. If you can't be comfortable among friends, you won't find comfort anywhere else." She waggled the bowl of strawberries at him. He shook his head. "Mathias?" she said in a singsong tone. When he looked up, she threw a strawberry at him. He caught it, stared at it, then popped it in his mouth. A smile tugged at his lips. She tossed another berry, and he ate it.

Schuyler joined in the game and threw a strawberry. He ate it with a smirk.

Paul grinned and jiggled the bag of chips.

"Don't even think about it, Matthews," Mathias said, ducking a handful of flying chips. "Hey, you're gonna mess up my bed." He gathered the pieces, flung them back at Paul, and grabbed the bag of chips.

"Food fight!" Schuyler said, munching a berry. "You're not getting any more of these. They're too yummy."

No one said a word for several minutes. A silent comradery permeated the room as they munched their snacks, the guys passing the chips between them. Schuyler pulled up her playlist on her cell phone featuring a blend of country, jazz, and classic rock. "What?" she asked, when three faces with raised brows turned toward her. "I like all kinds of music." They listened for a while, each lost in their own thoughts.

"I'm restless," Mathias said quietly, breaking into the thoughts of his companions. He picked at a thread in the bedspread.

"Me too. What would you like to do?" Paul stretched his legs out. He was sitting on a pillow on the floor. "I could do with a little activity. We could watch a movie, or we could go to the mall. I need a new pair of sneakers for basketball."

"It's not that kind of restless."

"Didn't you sleep well last night?" Schuyler said, prodding.

"Eh, I guess. I mean, I sleep, but it's just—I'm restless."

"Okay, are you anxious?" Lucy asked. "Or discontent? Are you sad about the move to Grand River Valley? It is a big deal when you think about it. You lived in a large city on the East Coast, had your own circle of friends, and then your dad moved the family to a small Midwest town that doesn't have a subway, tunnel, trolley, or tram."

"I don't want you guys to think I'm—never mind," he said, grabbing a pillow from the bed. He wrapped his arms around it. "It's nothing."

"But if it's bothering you," Schuyler said, "it is something. Can't you tell us? We won't laugh because we all know what it's like trying to solve a problem on our own. It's almost impossible without your buds."

"So, you're my buds now?"

"Well, we would like to be," Lucy said. "Even buds get on one another's nerves." Then she rolled her eyes. "Okay, I admit you get on my nerves a lot, but that doesn't mean we're not friends." She slouched in the chair and gave him an impish grin.

"Huh. Good to know, I guess." Mathias was quiet for a moment. His shoulders relaxed. Then he took a breath and sat up, seeming to brace himself for what he was about to say.

"Paul," Mathias said, "did you mean it when you told me about the hauntings you experienced? You weren't yanking my chain, were you?" His brown eyes clouded with concern.

"No way, dude. I would never joke about what happened to me; it was scary." Paul rolled up the empty chip bag, tossed it in the wastebasket, and brushed his hands on his jeans. He sat forward, an unsettled expression shadowing his eyes and creasing his brow. "What's going on?"

"I hear voices."

Three sets of eyebrows surged skyward, but no one laughed. Worry etched each face, and a tinge of fear glittered in Schuyler's eyes.

"What are they saying to you?" Lucy asked. She leaned forward and scrutinized his face and expressions. "Are you hearing them now?"

"I can't explain it. I don't hear them when I am in the B and B. They are everywhere else—at school, at the store—but not here. My head is blissfully quiet in this house. But my ears itch a lot." His gaze searched each face as if trying to gauge whether their concerned reactions were genuine.

"Okay, that's good!" Lucy stood, then paced the room. "The house received a blessing, and the blessing is protecting all of us. Whatever is happening, it can't affect you while you are in the house. But outside the house is when you are vulnerable."

"What should we do, Lucy?" Schuyler fidgeted with her bracelet, twirling it around her wrist. It was a nervous habit she'd developed since becoming a ghost hunter. Sometimes, she twirled a lock of her hair.

"Well, we are Defenders," she said, nodding at Schuyler's bracelet. "Maybe it's time we show Mathias what it means." Lucy dimpled her cheeks with a silly grin. She held up her arm and pushed her sleeve back, revealing her bracelet. Mathias gave her a wary sideways glance.

Paul stood and did the same, showing his leather wristband. Schuyler joined them and smiled sheepishly at Mathias.

"Mathias, this will shock you, but it is what we do," Lucy said. She felt like one of the Three Musketeers. She was pretty sure Alexandre Dumas, who wrote the French historical epic about three swashbuckling friends who fought for justice, had never considered the possibility of magical armor or a spiritual battle for the kingdom. She cleared her throat to smother a giggle.

"Defenders ready? Armor!" Lucy said.

Immediately, they were armor clad with helmets and breastplates. Shields bloomed from the bracelets, the metal sparkling in the light. Emblazoned on each shield was a white fox with a purple flag bearing a sword, a cross, and a crown. Mathias jumped to his feet, scrabbling for balance, and grabbing the bed's headboard. Groping to put as much distance as possible between himself and the apparitions in front of him, he kicked the pillows in their direction.

"This isn't real! This is some sadistic plot to drive me crazy," Mathias yelled. "Get out! Get out of my room." He picked up his schoolbook that was lying on the nightstand and threw it at Lucy. His breath came in ragged gulps, his chest heaving.

Dumbfounded, the Defenders exited the room before Mathias could throw the lamp he snatched from the table. He slammed the door behind them, clicking the lock. As they stood in the hallway, the armor and shields vanished.

"You were a little melodramatic, don't you think?" Schuyler snapped at Lucy.

Schuyler gave Lucy a hard stare. "I don't think we'll be able to explain things to him after this escapade." She sat on the couch in the private sitting room and dropped her head in her hands and heaved a sigh.

"Did you see his eyes?" Paul asked, sitting next to Schuyler. "He wasn't seeing us; he was seeing something else when our armor appeared. Yeah, okay, Lucy could have handled it better, but hey, that's just Lucy." He nudged Schuyler with his shoulder. She looked up, her eyes giving him a pugnacious squint.

The Ghost You Can't See

"Hey! I'm standing right here," Lucy said, throwing her hands up. "It would be melodramatic no matter what I did. We all squealed when our armor first appeared. Remember? Paul fainted, and you squealed, dancing around your room and screeching, 'Get it off! Get it off!'" Lucy said with finger quotes. Then she laughed. "Oh yeah, that was hysterical."

"Oh, hilarious, wise one," Schuyler said. "I doubt Mathias will ever trust us again. Got any more of those bright ideas?" With a huff, she scrunched into the couch, curled her legs under herself, and hugged a pillow.

"If Mathias is hearing voices," Lucy said, "it explains the weirdness with his ears. What if they have influenced him so he doesn't recognize what's real and what isn't?" She dropped into the desk chair and spun a pencil on the desk. "Iam said we have to protect our minds and our hearts." She filled Paul in on their adventure through the castle and the subsequent conversation with Iam and Haniel earlier that day.

"That's what I was trying to say," Paul said. He leaned forward, his elbows on his knees, and clasped his hands. "The voices are confusing him. He didn't say he had seen an entity, only that he could hear the voices in his ear, whispering. He said his ears itch."

"Wowza," Schuyler said. "No wonder Iam was so upset when we didn't wear our armor. Now I understand why." She pulled at the corner of the pillow, stretching it and kneading it. "Wowza, it's imperative we wear our armor."

"Schuyler," Lucy said, her eyes widening. She spun the chair around to stare at her companion. "Iam said we need to 'vanquish his immediate need' before we tell him about the King. Iam knew about the daemon influencing Mathias."

"What are we going to do about it?" Paul asked. "I don't think he will be receptive to anything we say. We need to tell him about the daemon. He should know, but he's going to see it as some horrendous conspiracy against him."

"Paul's right, Lucy. We should tell Mathias, but if we do, we risk driving him further away from us and the High King."

"But remember? Iam said the promise will help him determine what is true. Mathias already has an inherent truth. It's coded within the promise seal. But before he can understand, we need to vanquish that daemon."

"The questions are how and when." Paul shook his head, thinking. "He's holed up in his room. I wonder if he will even go to school tomorrow."

"If he does, he will ride the bus with me in the morning. I can scope him and the bus before we get to school."

"Then what?" Schuyler asked. "If we get anywhere near him with the Spectrescope or our magical armor, he's likely to bolt." She sat up and tossed the pillow on the couch. "Whatever this daemon is whispering, it has blinded Mathias to reality."

"I wasn't too sure I wasn't losing my mind either," Paul said, referring to his experience. "Confusing thoughts and images kept running through my head, and those hideous creature things visited me at night. At least Mathias has protection inside the house."

"True, but what about school tomorrow? Or if he goes outside—what then?" Schuyler got up and paced the room. When her companions didn't answer, she stared at the books on the shelves, seeming deep in thought.

A few of Great-Aunt Isabel's tchotchkes graced the shelves. The infamous porcelain cat sat next to a small potted artificial plant. On the top shelf was the Bob Ross Chia head Paul had given Lucy last year. When the chia plants died, Lucy had painted green hair on its terracotta head. It looked real from a distance. Schuyler snickered, glanced out the window, and gasped.

"Lucy! Mathias is outside—he could be in danger!" Schuyler clapped a shaky hand to her mouth and whimpered, watching him sauntering down the sidewalk, his hands in his pockets and his head downcast.

"You guys follow him. Don't let him get away. I'll grab the Spectrescope and Spectacles. I'll catch up with you! Take the back stairs. It will be quicker." She dashed to her room, snatched up the artifacts, and ran for the back stairs. Her sneakers gripped the blue stair treads, squeaking like a rubber duck in the confines with every step as she clomped down the stair well.

She swung around the doorjamb and exited into the kitchen, bounding through the sunroom and out the sliding doors. The others were standing with Mathias at the end of the street.

Mathias was flailing his hands and yelling at Paul and Schuyler as Lucy rushed to join them. Her lungs burned and her sides heaved as she struggled to pull enough air.

"What's . . . all the . . . commotion about? You're yelling loud . . . enough to wake . . . the dead in the cemetery on Maple . . . Street hill." She bent over, clutching the scope, and leaned on her knees, gasping.

"Can't you leave me alone?" Mathias snarled. "You tricked me. I thought you said we were friends, then I saw all three of you wearing creepy masks and medieval armor. It was a trick, wasn't it? What shenanigans are you up to, anyway?"

"Mathias, it's not us!" Schuyler declared. "Please believe us. We wouldn't do that to you. There is a spiritual realm that exists within our own—"

"Oh please!" he said. "You expect me to believe all that rubbish? Spirits and ghosts and daemons?" Mathias huffed and walked away from them. Then he spun around and glared at them. "Did the old man you were talking to this morning fill your head with nonsense? The woman too. What a nutcase, saying the battlefield is the mind. Where did you get those old fossils?" He turned, stalked down the sidewalk, and shoved his hands in his pockets.

"You're right, he was listening," Schuyler said as they all followed him from a distance. "Maybe it can work for our purpose. He's heard the others talking about the spiritual realm, so who knows? What do you think?" She was tugging at a lock of hair, winding it around her finger.

"Let's keep an eye on him." Lucy watched him through the Spectrescope. "He's okay for now. There's no spirit activity around him or on him, like there was with Paul. I don't think Mathias is cursed, but he is being influenced. That much we know."

"I think he's headed for the park," Paul said. "Maybe he needs to cool down a bit. He's so angry, he must feel we deliberately betrayed him. It's not us he's angry at, you know. He's angry at himself for not being able to fix this, whatever he thinks 'this' is."

"You're rather perceptive, did you know?" Lucy said, casting an admiring side glance at Paul. She blotted her sweaty forehead with the hanky she kept in her pocket. "Phew. I didn't know I could run so fast."

"Maybe you should go out for track," Paul said, grinning.

"Uh-huh. Not happening. I don't exercise well," Lucy said, still breathing hard. Paul chuckled. "I tried out for track once, missed a hurdle, and did a spectacular face-plant. Nope. Not happening."

"How about shot put? I hear you have a great throwing arm." He busted out laughing. "I'm surprised Bob the Chia head survived." He grinned at her chagrined expression.

"Lucy, I have an idea." Schuyler put a hand on her arm, stopping her. "Can the Spectrescope show Mathias the spirit attached to him? We did it for Paul. Otherwise, Mathias might never believe us." Tears welled in her eyes, threatening to spill over. "We must help him somehow." Paul nodded, encouraging her idea.

Lucy squeezed Schuyler's hand. "If we can get close enough to him, I think it's a great idea. I'd forgotten about it. Mathias won't be able to disbelieve the Spectrescope. C'mon. Let's catch up with him."

They found Mathias sitting on the park bench near the pond, slumped forward, his hands tugging at his hair and scratching at his ear. For all the anger and venom he had spouted earlier, Lucy's heart went out to him. Sitting alone, he looked like someone lost and forlorn. She understood his fear, not knowing who to trust or what to believe. Iam had explained the secret of the promise seal. It gave her hope they could help Mathias and vanquish his daemon.

He glanced up as they approached, his gaze flickering to each of them. Lucy was sure she saw a hint of hope in his brown eyes, imploring them to help him despite his actions. She sat crossed-legged on the ground in front of him. Schuyler and Paul sat on the bench, flanking him. No one said a word, the silence giving way to the chirp of birds and cricket song. The spot was restful, a good place to sit and talk without interruption. He didn't move. She tapped his knee.

"Mathias? Can I show you something?" she whispered, offering the Spectrescope to him. "Go ahead, take it." He raised his gaze and searched her clear gray eyes, then he took the scope. "This is a magical artifact. It is going to show you the spiritual realm. Once you see what is happening to you, it will be easier for you to understand." She tucked her straight brown hair behind her ears. Mathias met her gaze. "May I?"

He nodded.

"Okay, here we go," Lucy said. Schuyler scooted closer to Mathias, looped her arm through his, and gave it a squeeze. A brief smile tugged the corners of his lips. Lucy reached up and tapped a finger to the runes on the handle. "Spectrescope, please show us the daemon who is haunting Mathias."

The runes glowed, their golden light warm and otherworldly. Mathias stared in disbelief, his brows rocketing toward his hairline. The runes spun around the ring, fluid like mercury. Mathias's hands trembled as he held the scope, his head waggling back and forth. The lens clouded with a white mist, then cleared, but he closed his eyes and shoved the scope back at Lucy, shaking his head.

Lucy's heart plummeted. The Spectrescope returned to an inanimate object. The expression on Schuyler's face made Lucy want to cry, and Paul's shoulders slumped. Tonight, they had to be content to bring Mathias safely back to the house.

"Okay, no pressure. We're here when you are ready." She stood and held out her hand. "Come on, let's get you home."

A Lesson in Deviousness

"You fool! What were you thinking?" the Master yelled, pacing his office and shaking a fist at the daemon. "You nearly sucked his soul out before the Bachar and her friends showed up. You could have derailed the entire mission, you glutinous nincompoop!"

Darnathian glared at the cowering daemon in the chair. Berbatos was a highly respected philosopher, a thinker. Yet there he sat, nervously fingering a corner of his cloak. The entity should bide his time and gently lead the boy into bentness. Rushing only ever led to disaster. The boy had to retrieve the object. The jeweled artifact would aid in finding the cipher and decoding it to reveal the ancient magic.

"The boy almost confessed to the enemy," the Master growled. "Learn to curtail your hunger." He jabbed a finger into the rubbery belly of the daemon. "You will have his soul. Once he completes the task, you can feast on him all day long or gulp him down and fill your insatiable appetite." He leaned down, gripped the chair arms, and pushed his face next to the daemon's sweaty one. "But not until I have my artifact. Do you understand?" He stood, glaring down at the entity.

"I'm . . . I'm sorry, Master. It won't happen again," Berbatos whimpered, his belly jiggling. "My stomach keeps rumbling, and the boy tasted so delicious, his mind like pudding. I was getting impatient. I thought perhaps we could use one of his parents to accomplish the task. They're not as delectable, older and tougher, you know, virtually tasteless. Neither of the parents would tempt me. Couldn't you use a parent?" Berbatos tapped the tips of his fingers together and drooled, the slime oozing from his mouth and dribbling into his whiskers as he thought of the boy. "Please?"

"Stop it, you idiot," Darnathian warned. He held a sparkling energy ball in his hand. "Your babble doesn't work on me. Or did you forget who taught it to you? Do you need a correction to jog your memory?"

"No, no, Master. I was only hoping you might see it to your advantage to feed me now. It has been a while, and I'm so hungry." Berbatos smiled hopefully at the Master.

"Stop whimpering and listen to me, you dolt." Darnathian tossed the orb into the fireplace. Flames erupted and surged up the chimney. He sat in the desk chair, steepled his hands, and contemplated the cage hanging in the corner. The object gave him much pleasure. Its prisoner was currently pretending to be asleep, curled into a small, brown blob in the center of the cage floor. A smug smile creased the Master's face.

Darnathian stroked his chin thoughtfully, staring at the cage, then he glanced at the sniveling wimp in the chair. The daemon appeared sufficiently cowed. "What philosophy are you using to turn the boy? Tell me." Assuming a nonthreatening pose, he leaned back in the chair, one hand spinning the inkpot on the desk. The bright amber irises of his eyes reflected the flames in the vast fireplace. He knew once the daemon's mouth was engaged, he would blab all his secrets.

"The bad parent philosophy," Berbatos said gleefully, clapping his hands. "I've instructed him to disbelieve their love for him. After all, any loving parent would want his child to be happy. They should let him do whatever pleases him. Of course, I said, his parents don't understand him. They only want to control him with rules, taking away his dignity as an individual to make his own choices. They are not worth his time. He himself is so much more important. These are grievances he must hold against them." Berbatos's stomach rumbled, and he murmured under his breath.

"What did you say?" the Master asked, eyeing the daemon suspiciously. "Speak up, fool."

"Forgive me, Master," Berbatos said, patting his rotund stomach. "Unfortunately, this philosophy isn't penetrating the boy's mind as quickly as I had hoped. He has some resistance. I had to resort to the punishment philosophy, threatening harm to the boy if he doesn't do what I say. It seems to work. He's afraid of losing his soul, though he really doesn't understand what that is."

"I think you are using the wrong approach on the boy," Darnathian said, leaning forward and clasping his hands.

"What philosophy would you suggest, Master?" the daemon asked. "I would appreciate any suggestion. I do want to complete my task soon; I am so hungry." He leaned forward hopefully, his hands on the chair arms, and licked his lips.

"The boy is a descendant of the original family. Naturally, he has received tutelage in the old beliefs." Darnathian rose and mounted the stairs to the loft. He removed a book from its shelf and thumbed through the pages. He folded the corner of a page. "It may still take some time to obtain the object because of his resistance. We are looking for success, not speed. For that reason, I suggest a different approach." He stepped to the railing and tossed the book to the daemon. "Disillusion."

"Disillusion, master?" Berbatos said, studying the page. "Oh yes! I see what you mean. It says here that I must wear him down with little failures, emphasizing his life isn't as good as he believes it could be, that it's filled with only drabness and futility. This will build a growing resentment and disillusionment. Oh, Master, this is brilliant! His spirit will be mine before the end of the week. What a feast it will be!" The entity swiped a sleeve across the drool on his lips.

"Yes, it is brilliant," Darnathian said. "If you want to assure his parents' demise, I suggest using affluence. A promotion and influence will keep the parents focused on this world, not the world to come." He snickered. "It will keep their focus off the dreaded High King." He leaned on the balcony railing, watching the ghost eagerly scrutinize the pages. "Will three souls suffice for you, Berbatos?"

"Oh yes, Master. My belly will be quite full. Fullness is such a delicious feeling." He rubbed his round belly affectionately.

"Get me that jeweled artifact, and I'll give you more souls to fill your belly," Darnathian said, pointing at the door.

A Friend in Deed

Dispirited, the Defenders quietly sat in the private sitting room, each alone with their thoughts. They had left Mathias at his bedroom door and waited until he locked himself safely inside. Paul sat at the desk, absentmindedly twirling a pencil while Schuyler wound a lock of hair around her finger, huddled in a corner of the couch.

"Okay, should we look at the images in the Spectrescope?" Lucy asked, sitting cross-legged on the couch, holding the artifact and staring at it. "It feels like an invasion of privacy, but we need to know what we are up against. Thoughts, anyone?"

"I agree with you, Lucy," Paul said, puffing his cheeks and blowing out a deep breath. "I don't think it's an invasion of privacy since you asked and he agreed." He twirled the pencil between his fingers like a mini baton, his lake-blue eyes clouded with worry. "I say let's do it."

"Schuyler? What do you think?" Lucy gazed steadily at her friend, gauging the emotions flitting across Schuyler's face—fear, shock, sadness. "I'm trying to think before I rush in, and you and Paul are Defenders chosen by Iam, so your input is important."

Schuyler pulled her rolled lips into a tight smile and nodded. "I agree. We need to understand what is happening to him. Maybe Iam or the McGoos can tell us what to do next if we identify the daemon." She sat up and scooted next to Lucy and motioned for Paul to join them.

He sat next to Lucy and smiled. "I could get used to this, you know," he whispered. She dimpled her warm cheeks and poked him with her elbow.

"Okay, then. Spectrescope, we need to help Mathias. Will you please show us what is happening to him?" The Spectrescope vibrated, the runes glowing and morphing. The lens roiled with mist, and a golden-lettered message appeared in the glass. *Because he previously agreed, I can reveal the unknown to you.* Lucy nodded. "Thank you, Spectrescope."

The scenes appeared as they had begun earlier in the evening, only this time the Spectrescope beamed larger images on the carpet.

As the movie played out, they watched the image of Mathias arguing with his father in their old home, hands curled in fists, flailing in anger as he shouted at the man. His father's face paled as Mathias shouted and stomped away. Mr. Sasson blinked back tears.

"Do we need to hear this exchange?" Schuyler asked.

"I don't think so," Lucy said, shaking her head. "It's clear whatever was said deeply hurt his dad." Paul leaned his shoulder into hers and sent her an understanding glance.

The movie played on. In the next scene, Mathias sulked alone in his old bedroom, scrunching notepaper and lobbing the wads at a wastebasket. The floor was littered.

An inky-black shadow appeared in the room's corner.

As it approached the bed, the shadow changed shape, morphing into a wizened old man dressed like a duke in a velvet brown cloak with a fur collar. Beneath the cloak, he wore a thigh-length blue silk tunic embroidered with a crest, a leather belt below the rotund belly, tights, and knee-high leather boots.

He slung the cloak over his shoulder and leaned menacingly close to Mathias. Above his forehead, two little bony horns peeked amid a mass of ragged hair. His face twisted with a gaped, yellow-toothed grin made even more hideous by the scraggly gray beard and pink, forked tongue flicking in and out of his mouth.

The Defenders watched with fear and distress as the daemon eagerly wiggled his long, lumpy fingers as though he couldn't wait to attack his prey.

The daemon crawled onto the bed next to the boy, his cloak draping over the edge. Mathias, sullen and ill-tempered, was unaware of the malevolent ghost in his room. The entity put his face next to boy's and studied him. The movie wobbled slightly as the Spectrescope shuddered in Lucy's hand. Mathias lobbed another wad into the wastebasket.

A collective gasp of dismay and disgust emanated from the friends as the daemon stretched his neck, grinned manically, and sniffed the teen's ear. The daemon's eyes rolled in euphoria, and he licked his lips greedily. He sniffed again, breathing deeply, then blew a purple mist from his mouth.

Coalescing like a tendril of smoke from a snuffed candle, it writhed in the air and entered the boy's ear.

The ringlet of mist disappeared into the boy's head. Mathias flung a hand up and scratched, then rubbed his ear. His body quivered, then stilled as a dazed expression settled in his eyes, a stupefied smile on his face. He curled into a ball and went to sleep.

The movie revealed the daemon had visited Mathias at least once a week since arriving and always when he was beyond the protective confines of the Carriage House and its property. Each time, the stupefied smile appeared, followed by anger, hopelessness, and apathy. The playback ended, returning the scope to its inert form.

"Oh. My. Goodness." Schuyler was the first to speak, utterly astonished and repulsed, her eyes wide. She gasped. "My lunch is coming back for a visit!" She dashed for the bathroom down the hall.

"Wow." Paul leaned back against the couch cushions and stared, unseeing, out the window. "Grehssil was repugnant, and what I went through was bad. This is insidious and manipulative." His face flushed, and a bead of perspiration clung to his forehead. "I don't think we should leave Mathias alone tonight."

"He's safe enough in the house. Why? What are you thinking?"

"He slipped out earlier while we were discussing what to do. If he leaves the property, he's at risk of this spirit. Who knows how this evil has influenced him? No, we can't chance it, Lucy." Paul vehemently shook his head. "He needs our protection."

"What do you suggest?"

"I could sleep here tonight, watch his back." He leaned forward, elbows on knees, and clasped his hands, a furrow rutting his forehead. He tilted his head and shrugged.

"That's a great idea. You could sleep in the guest room across the hall. Or camp outside his door," she said with a sly grin. Paul's concern made her heart feel lighter. She knew she should tell him; perhaps she would later. "I have a better idea. I'll ask the Spectrescope to extend the Shimmer Shield around his room. Nothing can get through it, and he won't be able to get out. And we all can get a good night's sleep."

"It's a perfect solution," Paul said, standing and stretching. "I should go then. It's late."

"What's a perfection solution?" Schuyler asked, returning. Her face was pale, and her eyes were red rimmed and puffy above dark circles.

"The Shimmer Shield—it will protect Mathias during the night, and we can sleep with no worries. He will never know it's there. It will be up to us to keep him safe once we're at school. Schuyler and I will cover him on the bus ride and at lunch, then Paul can take Mathias duty the rest of the day." Paul flicked two thumbs up.

"Good. It sounds like a plan. Can we go to bed now?" Schuyler yawned and, not waiting for an answer, disappeared into Lucy's bedroom, shutting the door.

"Mathias!" Lucy yelled up the stairs. "What is taking him so long? He didn't come down for breakfast either." Sitting on the bottom step, she leaned backward, glancing up at the balcony railing that ran around the loft area. The chandelier chain snaked its way past the second-floor loft and anchored to the ceiling above. Staring at the monstrous chandelier upside down was disconcerting, the details of the bat and octopus in sharp relief.

Schuyler, anxiously waiting for the bus, kept watch out the window. "Did you cancel the Shimmer Shield, or is he still locked in his room?" She dropped the curtain, covering the sidelight.

"Drat!" Lucy hurtled up the stairs, spun around the balcony railing, and skidded to a halt in front of Mathias's door. The Spectrescope was in the waistband of her jeans under her shirt. "Spectrescope," she whispered, "cancel the Shimmer Shield, please!" Then she knocked lightly on the door and stepped back.

Grumbles came from inside the room. The doorknob wiggled, and the door opened suddenly. Mathias stood in the opening, surprise written across his face. "This stupid door wouldn't budge!" he said. "I've been trying to open it for like an hour. I texted you. Didn't you get my texts?"

"Huh, good morning to you too—and no, I didn't get any texts. C'mon! The bus will be here any minute."

"Fine," he grumbled and grabbed his backpack. He shut the door and followed Lucy down the main stairs. "What's for breakfast?"

"Lucy! The bus is here," Schuyler said, slinging her quilted book bag over a shoulder.

"You go stall them, and I'll grab Mathias something from the kitchen," she said, pushing Mathias toward the door. "I'll be right there."

Her mom and Mrs. Sasson waved to her from the breakfast salon. They were drinking coffee and chatting animatedly. Mr. Sasson was absent, having left earlier for work.

Lucy tossed several yogurt tubes in her backpack along with several pieces of fruit and grabbed some granola bars from the basket on the breakfast sideboard in the salon. Mrs. Williams had delivered her breakfast pastries, and Lucy wrapped one up for Mathias. Hurriedly, she kissed her mom on the cheek.

"Did Mathias come downstairs for school, Lucy?" Mrs. Sasson asked. "He didn't answer when I knocked on his door earlier. Perhaps he overslept."

"Yeah, that's probably what happened," Lucy said, her cheeks flaming. "These goodies are for him since he missed breakfast. Got to go, love you, Mom." She waved at a grinning Mrs. Sasson.

The school bus driver motioned to her to hurry as she rushed across the lawn and entered the bus. Schuyler and Mathias sat in the back. Already she could see his countenance was changing. His uncertain but grumbly demeanor in the house was growing sullen. He slouched next to Schuyler with his arms crossed.

Madison slipped her foot into the aisle, but Lucy saw the movement. Smiling, she leaned over and whispered to the mean girl.

"Don't even think about it," Lucy said, patting the girl's shoulder. "Have a nice day." The girl snarled at her and pulled her foot back.

She plunked into the seat by Mathias and put on the Spectacles. From the back seat, she could see nearly everyone on the bus. The Spectrescope was clear, and the Spectacles didn't reveal any anomalies either. Both went back into the backpack. She handed Mathias the pastry, a couple of yogurt tubes, and a banana. He nodded his thanks and split open the banana.

Schuyler smiled hopefully. Lucy rolled her eyes and handed her some snacks. While he munched, she noticed Mathias was nervously bouncing his knee, and his gaze shifted around the bus. When the school came into view, he sucked in a breath with a gulp. Whatever was happening to him, it was occurring at the school.

"Remember," she whispered to Mathias. "We will fight for you. You need only to trust us." Her breath hitched when he turned and looked at her. His pupils were huge, covering nearly every fleck of his golden-brown irises. He walked to the front of the bus before it stopped.

"What just happened?" Schuyler asked, getting to her feet and shuffling toward the exit. "He didn't even acknowledge you just now. It was like he didn't see you. He just walked away." Her gaze followed him as he got off the bus, then he got lost in the throng.

"His pupils were dilated," Lucy whispered. "Whatever the daemon is doing, it's already affecting him."

"What is it about this building?" Schuyler said softly, clearly frustrated. "Things happen at the old school."

"We have time before the first hour. Let's follow him and see what happens. Maybe we can vanquish this daemon quickly."

Lucy spotted Mathias as he retrieved his books from his locker and then slipped down the hallway and joined the throng on the turret stairs. At the second level, he strode toward the main auditorium. The room was empty at this time of morning. Lucy and Schuyler slipped unnoticed into a side entry. They tiptoed across the back aisle in the darkness, lit only by the exit signs above the door.

Once their eyesight adjusted to the low light, they spotted him. Mathias was alone, sitting two rows down in the center section. His head hung low, and he had his hands buried in his hair. His head swiveled side to side as though he struggled with his thoughts.

"Shouldn't we go to him?" Schuyler asked, inching her way toward their friend.

Lucy put a hand on Schuyler's arm and shook her head. "Not yet," she whispered, groaning inwardly. "This is so hard to watch, knowing he's in pain, but I don't think he's ready to accept our help."

Lucy raised the Spectrescope. The signature purple residue appeared in the lens, slowly transforming into a diaphanous, horned daemon in a brown velvet cloak. Schuyler grimaced. Her brow furrowed so deep, Lucy wondered if Schuyler would have a permanent indention.

The daemon grinned and approached Mathias. His tongue flicked from his mouth, the forked appendage waving like a pennant flag. He slithered up to the boy and repeated his previous actions. As he blew on Mathias's ear, the purple tendril of mist appeared and snaked its way toward the teenager. Lucy passed the scope to Schuyler and quickly put the Spectacles on and gasped. A chill ran down her spine, and her fingers turned to ice.

Hidden in the mist, groupings of bloodred runes floated in the air. The runes joined, twisted into small arrows, and pierced the ear. At each piercing, Mathias flinched. Lucy startled so violently, one of the articulating arms on the Spectacles' bow dropped in front of the lens. Immediately, she received clarity and understanding and the ability to read the unknown language.

You shall curse your father and mother and turn from the good that you would do. You shall hate your own life. It is dull, futile, and meaningless. You must serve the Master of Lies and retrieve the jeweled artifact. Misery will be yours until the day you give me your soul. Oh, give it to me now, for I am hungry. I am so very hungry.

The ghost grinned, fingers twitching as he reached for his victim, his tongue appearing greedily between his lips, stretching toward the boy's ear.

"No! Armor!" Lucy shouted, the armor enveloping her as she snatched the Spectrescope from Schuyler and charged forward. The lens disappeared, replaced by the blue metal of the Spirit Sword. "Reveal!"

Schuyler drew her sword, racing to flank the daemon, now visible and leaning over the unconscious boy. With a screech, the daemon straightened and stared in astonishment as the two armor-clad girls surged toward him.

He licked his lips and reached a piggy hand for the boy, but Lucy was almost upon him. His face twisted in rage, his pennant-like tongue flapping between his lips. He gathered his cloak about him and disappeared, leaving an odious stench of sulfur and decay behind.

"Drat!" Lucy slid to a stop. Only a moment sooner, and she would have skewered him with her sword. She stomped her foot. The sword retreated, and the magnifying lens took its place. "Ew," she said, waving a hand before her nose. She tapped her shield, and it disappeared, along with the rest of her armor. She slipped the scope and the Spectacles into the backpack.

Schuyler did the same, then blanched. "Lucy! What's wrong with him?" She kneeled in front of Mathias, who was slumped in the seat, unconscious. She gently patted his cheek. His eyes fluttered, but he didn't wake.

"I think he fainted."

"What should we do with him? We can't leave him here." Schuyler patted both his cheeks. He murmured but still didn't wake up. "He's not waking up." Her voice shook.

The side door opened. A shaft of light from the hallway backlit a tall, lanky form. He quickly slipped into the room and eased the door shut. The shape was familiar, but Lucy couldn't see much in the near darkness.

"You didn't seal the room?" Schuyler whispered, giving her a stern look. "Lucy, someone might have discovered us."

"I'm sorry—I forgot. Besides, I didn't think the daemon would show up again so soon. It's only been a few days since his last whispering."

Paul strode down the aisle toward them. "Hey, I saw you guys slip in here. What's going on?" He stared at Mathias slumped in the seat, his head dangling to the side. "That's gonna hurt when he wakes up. Why is he sleeping, anyway?" He toed the teenager's foot, eliciting a grumble.

"We tried to vanquish the daemon, but he got away. He whispered to Mathias again, and then Mathias passed out, and we can't wake him."

"I kept fainting, if you remember." Paul lightly jiggled the teen's shoulder but got no response. "Nope, he's out good."

"There's nothing else to do. We need to get him back to the Carriage House," Lucy said.

A Thief in the House

The first Saturday morning of October dawned gray, drizzly, and miserable, matching Lucy's mood. The week had remained uneventful, and though the Defenders had tried to keep Mathias protected as best they could, his mood was changing.

After the daemon attack, Mathias awoke in the auditorium that morning as the friends were discussing what to do. It made him so angry that they thought he needed an intervention. He yelled, told them to bug off, and stomped off to class.

If the daemon was still visiting him somehow, Lucy couldn't detect it. The Spectrescope didn't reveal any activity whenever she secretly scanned him. His ears remained a dark, red-tinged purple. At school, Mr. Bill watched over Mathias, much to Lucy's relief. When Mathias was alone in his room, Lucy had him covered with the Shimmer Shield. This worked until he pounded on his door and made a ruckus to get out.

Confused over the unbroken "broken" lock, her mom had one of the renovation carpenters check the lock. The poor man was befuddled. He found nothing broken with the lock mechanism, yet he couldn't explain why the lock would work most of the time but not at others. Lucy smiled, rolled her eyes, and kept her mouth shut.

The cursed words the daemon had whispered to Mathias in the school auditorium worried Lucy more than she let on. Since the daemon had not yet returned, she knew the words must have punctured deeper into Mathias's mind and heart. It was this thought that kept Lucy vigilant.

During today's morning session of orison, Iam told her to not worry and suggested she read the Chronicles of Ascalon. He said the history of Ascalon was powerful and enlightening, and it could help her stand against the devious and nefarious Dark Prince.

Curled up on opposite ends of the couch in the private sitting room, Lucy and Schuyler each read from the book. Lucy had found three extra copies in her trunk, just as Iam had promised, and now Schuyler and Paul each had a copy, but the third copy was unclaimed. Lucy hoped one day to give it to Mathias.

"Huh," Lucy said, the book propped against her raised knees. She poked Schuyler with her foot. "Did you read this part yet? Iam was trying to explain something to me this morning. It says, 'The King sets the lonely in families, and he leads out the prisoner with singing, but the rebellious will live in a sun-scorched land.'"

"It's beautiful prose. What do you think it means?" Schuyler asked, looking over the top of her book, her brows winging up.

"Iam knows Mathias is lonely, and he has sort of become part of our extended family. He's a prisoner of the daemon. But not for much longer if we can help it. I'm hanging on to the part that says there will be singing. I, for one, will be singing when we vanquish that daemon."

Schuyler nodded and gave Lucy a thumbs-up. "Listen to this, 'The good man out of the good treasures in his heart brings out good, but the evil man out of the evil treasures in his heart brings out evil. The mouth will speak what is in the heart," The book dropped in Schuyler's lap as she stared slack jawed at Lucy. "Explains a lot, doesn't it?"

"Iam and Haniel said the same thing. The daemon is speaking evil things to Mathias, messing with his head. And it's those things, the intangible, that are going to his heart—affecting his thoughts and his mood. No wonder Iam was so worried."

Schuyler sighed and clutched the book to her chest, staring out the window at the drizzle. "What are we going to do? This can't go on much longer," she said, her voice a whisper. "I need to do something, but I don't know what."

"We need to stay calm and wait this out, girlfriend." Lucy pointed her bare foot at Schuyler and wiggled her toes with an impish grin. Schuyler batted it away, rewarding Lucy with a small smile.

"The daemon wants his spirit," Lucy said with a shudder. "The nasty thing said he was hungry. Gross. I don't understand, though, what the 'jeweled artifact' means. I'm not sure what it is. The Spirit Sword has jewels, but it hides in the Spectrescope. We could consider each of our swords as jeweled artifacts. Zazriel, Ratha-nael, and even Paul's Briathos sword have jewels in their handles. They are part of our magical armor and are not readily available to just anyone."

"Could it be the Belt of Truth? It has jewels too."

"Eh, could be," Lucy said, lifting a shoulder. "It only has two types of jewels, blue and white diamonds. Darnathian must need the jewels to find the cipher and decode it. Any of these could be the artifact he is after. The Spirit Sword has the most jewels embedded in the metal."

"But Darnathian can't get to it because it must be freely given, remember? So, is he after one jewel or many jewels?"

"If we knew, it might be easier to figure out which artifact he's after. Don't forget, he is still after the Spectrescope because of the secrets it is supposed to hold." Her phone beeped. Checking the notification banner,

Lucy saw that she had a text from her mom asking her to come downstairs to the foyer. Lucy groaned.

"What's up?"

"Mom needs me downstairs. C'mon, we can grab a snack from the kitchen. Maybe Mrs. McGoo made more cookies. Or maybe there are still some of your mom's leftover breakfast pastries."

Lucy's mom and the Sassons had gathered in the foyer. Everyone wore raincoats and hats for the cool, drizzly weather. Mr. and Mrs. Sasson chatted while her mom, standing behind the registration desk, ticked off items on her to-do list. She glanced up as Lucy skipped down the steps, followed by Schuyler, who sat on the last step, waiting.

"Lucy," Mom said, "I need you to keep an eye on things while we're gone. We're meeting the McGoos to complete the offer on the house and furniture shopping afterward. Grandma is arriving later. She should be here for dinner, but we'll be back by then. Here's a list of items I need you to do this afternoon." She handed the list to Lucy.

"You've got to be kidding. Dust the books and bookshelves in the library?" Lucy stared in dismay at the list, her lips flattening. "This will take all day. Paul is coming over to study. He should be here soon."

"Lucy, I clean at least two rooms on each floor every day just so I can stay ahead of the work. By the end of the week, I start over. You can help by doing your share."

Lucy clamped her mouth shut as she noticed the dark circles under her mom's eyes and felt a stab of guilt. "I'm sorry, Mom. I never thought about how all the work was getting done," she said. She waggled the list. "Consider this done. Do you want me to do anything else?"

"Thanks, honey, but no. The library is enough for today," Mom said, cupping a hand to Lucy's cheek, a smile of admiration brightening her expression. "You should hurry if Paul is coming to study. Oh, there is a fresh batch of Mrs. McGoo's Chocolate Revel Bars in the pantry, too, in case all that studying works up an appetite." She bounced her brows. Lucy rolled her eyes, smirking.

"Where's Mathias?" Mr. Sasson said, glancing impatiently up the stairs. "He knows we're settling things with the McGoos today."

Mrs. Sasson texted Mathias. "I need him to choose a room today so I can measure for curtains," she said. "Jeannie, could we perhaps stop by the paint store? I would like to get some samples."

"No problem. I need to select colors for the antique shop," Mom said, nodding her head. "I'm so excited. It's almost ready for paint."

Moments later, everyone jumped at the raucous pounding emanating from the second floor. Mrs. Sasson sighed; her gaze raised to the ceiling.

"Oh dear," Mom said. "I honestly don't know what to do about that door!"

"No worries. I'll go get him." Lucy bounded up the stairs, rounding the balcony to Mathias's guest suite. She had the Spectrescope tucked under her shirt in the waistband of her jeans. She tapped it and whispered, "Release," and knocked on the door.

The door whipped open, and a startled Mathias stumbled backward. "Someone should fix this dumb door. It's so annoying." He brushed past Lucy and tromped down the steps.

"Good morning to you too!" Lucy grumbled, following him with a feeling of déjà vu. She hesitated in the middle of the stairs.

Mathias was already in a heated discussion with his father. The older Sasson's face piqued, his brows surging about on his forehead. Mrs. Sasson demurely held her handbag, her head shaking and eyes closed. Schuyler and Mom had retreated to the kitchen.

"I don't want to go. It's your house, your decision," Mathias said, crossing his arms and eyeing his father.

"It's important to all of us, Mathias," Mr. Sasson said. "I know it's been a tough move. This is a new start for the family. I have a good feeling about the job and this town. Besides, don't you want to choose your own room? It's important to your mother to help you make it your own. Won't you come?"

"No," he said, glancing down to avoid eye contact.

"Mathias, come with us, sweetheart," Mrs. Sasson cajoled. "We can swing by the paint store, and you can choose any paint color you want for your room."

"Within reason, of course," Mr. Sasson interjected. He grimaced as Mathias rolled his eyes. "I just don't understand you, Mathias. Fine, stay here. But you're not to go anywhere, understand? If you don't want to join your mother and me, then you are grounded."

"Fine," Mathias grumbled. "I have homework to finish, anyway."

"Oh, good. You can join us then," Lucy said, bounding down the stairs. She stood with her hand on the rail. "Paul will be here soon. We're going to study in the library. I've got snacks. You can't study without snacks, you know." She grinned at Mrs. Sasson. The lady steepled her hands and mouthed a silent, "Thank you."

Lucy's mom's shoes clacked on the floor as she entered the foyer. "Everything all set?" She dangled her car keys and grabbed her purse from the hall closet.

"Yes, thank you, Mrs. Hornberger." Mr. Sasson nodded, took his wife's arm, and followed through the kitchen to the back door and out to the car.

"C'mon, let's go find a snack." Lucy slipped past Mathias and down the hall. She found Schuyler perched on a chair at the big island counter, waiting.

"What's up, Buttercup?" Schuyler said as they entered the kitchen. "I'm hungry. Let's order pizza."

"Pizza? You just had breakfast like two hours ago."

"What can I say? I'm still hungry." Schuyler fluttered her eyelashes, grinning.

"Fine. What do you want on your pizza, Mathias?" Lucy retrieved the pizza menu from a drawer and spread it on the counter.

"Did somebody say pizza?" Paul asked, stepping through the back door, his blond hair plastered to his head. "I saw your mom in the driveway. She told me to come on in." Lucy pointed to the hall. Nodding, he stored his things in the hall closet, then sat at the counter with Schuyler. "What sounds good to you, Mathias?" He stole a glance at Lucy; she gave a minute shake of her head. Paul flashed a smile.

"Whatever." Mathias sat at the counter, his gaze averted.

"I vote for the Everything pizza; that way we don't have to decide on toppings. But we need an extra-extra-large," Schuyler said, leaning over the menu, her finger pointing to the selection.

Lucy snorted. "Are you sure it's big enough?" Schuyler gave her a scathing look. "I'm just asking," Lucy said, holding her palms up. Paul chuckled.

"Any other suggestions?" Lucy raised her brows and waggled the phone. "Okay, a loaded, supersized pizza it is." She dialed the pizzeria.

A few minutes later, the only sound in the kitchen was munching and chewing. Lucy plopped another slice on her plate and took the ranch dressing from the refrigerator and slathered it over the wedge. She offered the dressing to Mathias.

"Thanks," he said, popping the top open.

He met her gaze, and she smiled at him before his gaze dropped. He ate his pizza in silence, looking for all the world like a lost little boy. Lucy's heart squeezed, wishing there was something she could do or say to help. He gathered his plate and utensils and followed the others, putting them in the sink.

"Are you joining us in the library to study? I've got a fresh batch of Mrs. McGoo's Chocolate Revel Bars. C'mon, even you can't pass up on those," she said, smiling.

"Yeah, okay, maybe," he said, his eyes flicking to her and to the others as they disappeared down the hallway. "I'll go get my books and meet you in there."

"Great! I better clean up the kitchen first," Lucy said, putting the dishes in the dishwasher and throwing the paper remains in the trash bin.

Mathias turned to go, then glanced back and watched as she went about wiping down the counters. He gulped and hurried up the stairs.

He sat on the steps to the family level, listening to the banter and laughter coming from the library below. His fingers clutched handfuls of hair and tugged, but he couldn't reach the itch. It was deep in his ears and driving him crazy. For some strange reason, he had an overwhelming desire to sneak into Lucy's room. It would be so easy. Her room was at the top of the stairs behind him.

There was something he needed to find. If he found it, the itching would go away. But that made no sense. Stealing? To stop the itch? He had such an overwhelming desire to search her room. But it would be wrong; she was his friend. She was concerned about his welfare. No, he couldn't do it. He didn't want to do it.

He stood and leaned over the balcony railing, listening. They were engrossed in their banter, making wisecracks at one another. He yearned to join them. They were happy. He wanted to be happy, but he couldn't rid himself of this gloominess. He looked up the stairs, then glanced over the railing again to the foyer below. More laughter. They didn't miss him; didn't even know he hadn't returned to join them. He sprinted up the stairs into Lucy's room.

Mathias felt like a thief but entered and surveyed the room. The room held an antique brass bed with old-style quilt coverings, a dresser under the window, and the desk against the wall. Where would she keep the

The Ghost You Can't See

artifact? Artifact? Was that what he was looking for? He wondered how he knew that.

The wood trunk at the foot of her bed, carved with strange runes, had a brass doorknob on its lid. He knelt and opened it.

Inside, he found a strange metal-framed mirror, the glass milky and fluid, and a glass globe on a silver metallic base with a swirling mist inside. Each item displayed a fox, a flag, a sword, and a cross embellished with a crown. His hand shook as he held the items. He tossed them aside.

A large book nestled in the bottom in folds of fabric. His shaky hand caressed the leather cover. Its importance called to him. Lifting the cover, he fanned the pages and yelped. A pain shot through his ear, piercing and deep. Whimpering, he kneaded the ear with his fist. The itch was insatiable.

He plunged into the trunk again, pushing objects aside, probing its depths and ripping the fabric. There was another round brass doorknob in the bottom. He tugged, but it didn't budge. The knob was attached to the bottom. Frustrated, he flipped the trunk over. He shook the chest and more items tumbled out. A gray shadow streaked through the room with a whoosh. It startled him for a moment.

He harumphed. It was probably one of Lucy's imaginary ghosts who'd followed her home. He picked up an eyeglass case. Inside was an unusual pair of spectacles. They had the emblems but no jewels. He dropped the spectacles and picked up a small velvet box. His breath hitched. This must be it. He opened the cover.

The small belt-shaped ring glistened inside, the blue and white jewels sparking with an inner fire. He felt giddy holding the object. The itch in his ear lessened. His chest heaved, and it felt tight as he snapped the box closed. He gripped the box like a lifeline and got to his feet. He whirled at a noise behind him.

Lucy stood in the doorway.

"What are you doing? This is my room," she said and stepped into the room. Her gaze dropped to his clenched fist, then spied the items from the trunk spewed about the room. An icy chill gripped her, realizing he was searching for an artifact. She went to the trunk and peeked inside. He had rummaged through the contents, but she couldn't tell if the smaller items were missing. The ripped lining lay rumpled in the bottom.

"There's no harm in looking," he lied, stuffing both hands in his pockets. His face was flushed. "I was just curious." He moved toward the door.

"You didn't answer my question." She straightened her shoulders, confronting him. "Did you take something from the trunk?" The dark glint in his eyes was otherworldly. Mathias was no longer the sullen teen. He appeared aggressive, maybe even dangerous.

"Why do you think I took something?" Mathias stepped close, invading her space and staring down at her. His arms hung at his sides.

Lucy held her ground, her chin raised. He was looking at her, but it wasn't him. His dilated pupils had extinguished his gold-flecked brown irises. Something was controlling him.

"Give it to me." Swallowing hard, she thrust her open palm forward, waiting, hoping.

A smile spread across his face, but it didn't reach his eyes, mirthless and cold. "No, I don't think so," he said, grabbing her arms. With little effort, he lifted her and tossed her over the brass bed, her arms and legs flailing. She hit the wall and fell into the stack of bed pillows with a groan. Mathias darted from the room. She rolled off the bed and chased after him.

"Defenders! ARMOR!" she screamed, rushing down the steps. Her shield appeared on her arm. She missed a step and crumpled, landing in a heap at the bottom of the steps. Her helmet had dented. "Defenders! Mathias stole the Belt of Truth," she yelled, getting to her feet. Her head felt bruised. Straightening the breastplate, she took the Spectrescope from her waistband and ran down the steps to the foyer.

Mathias gripped the railing, swung himself from the last steps, and raced across the foyer to the clock. He grasped the latch on the door.

"Shimmer Shield! Seal the house!" Lucy grabbed his T-shirt. His arm swung up, knocking her hand away. She clobbered him with her elbow. He gripped the edge of her shield and shoved. Her feet slid over the plank flooring as she whacked him with the Spectrescope.

Schuyler and Paul charged from the library, skidding into the foyer where Lucy grappled with Mathias. Flanking them, Schuyler sheathed her sword and grabbed his arm; Paul dropped his weapons and gripped the teen's shoulders.

"Mathias, listen to us," Paul said. "This isn't you, dude. C'mon, wake up. We are your friends. We don't want to hurt you!" He jumped on his back and tried to pull Mathias down, pinning the teen's arms, but it was like wrestling a bull elephant to the ground.

Mathias whipped a powerful elbow into Paul's ribs, lifting his feet from the floor. Paul groaned and lost his grip. Mathias's foot slammed into Paul with a round-house kick and sent him sprawling across the foyer. Paul rolled to his feet and charged again.

Schuyler tugged Mathias's arm and pleaded. "Please, Mathias. Stop!" He shoved her roughly to the floor.

Impervious to the continued whacking from Lucy, Mathias seized her arm, grabbed the shield, and spun her. As her body rose in an arcing circle, he let go. She flew into Paul and Schuyler, knocking them to the floor. Lucy tumbled, crashing into the steps.

Mathias opened the clock, hesitated, and with one last look at his friends, he stepped inside.

Familiar Faces in Familiar Places

"He shouldn't have gotten away! Spectrescope, why didn't the Shimmer Shield seal the house?" Lucy asked. The lens clouded, then a message appeared. She groaned and showed them the message. It read, *The Shimmer Shield protects the house and everything in it, but the portal is in the clock, and it must be closed from within. Be careful, Defenders. The High King knows the path you must tread. You have his blessing to proceed. Be strong and courageous.*

"I lost my footing and fell down the stairs," Lucy said with a sad glance at her sneakers. "Spectrescope, we all need our magical shoes. Can you get them for us please?" As she watched, the sneakers transformed into sandals, the straps wrapping securely around her calves. Sandals appeared on Schuyler and Paul. They high-fived each other.

"Okay, here we go," she said, approaching the clock. "Wait! Spectrescope, should I take you with me or leave you behind?" The artifact vibrated and a message appeared. *By the power of his might I am protected. Take me with*

The Ghost You Can't See

you, Gatekeeper. Relief coursed through her, knowing the High King had provided a way. Smiling, she kissed the scope. "Thank you!"

Schuyler reached for Lucy and Paul. "Iam said orison is part of our armor."

"You're right." Lucy tucked the scope under her arm and clasped each of their hands. "Iam, please guide us. Mathias is in danger, and he's scared. We're scared. Help us be strong so we can help him and vanquish the daemons. Please be with us. Thank you, my King." Paul and Schuyler's determined faces told her it was time to go. She squeezed her eyes closed, surprised by the tears that wet her cheeks.

Taking a deep breath, she opened the door and stepped inside. The portal door was still active; she pushed it open and stepped out on the landing, followed closely by Schuyler and Paul.

Leaning over the railing, she could hear Mathias's footfalls in the passage below. He wasn't too far ahead of them. Tapping a finger to her lips, she tiptoed cautiously down the stairs. The Spirit Sword replaced the Spectrescope. The ethereal blue glow it emitted gave them a boost of confidence.

The torches in the passage were lit, tracing the way Mathias had gone. Ahead, they heard the striker drop on the bronze face, followed by a howl. Lucy glanced back at Paul. His eyes were wide, his brows arching skyward.

"It's a little unnerving, but it will be okay," she whispered. "I just hope we don't meet the other guy." Paul gave her a bewildered look. "I'll explain later." Schuyler grimaced and rubbed her forehead.

They heard a thump, a howl, and a click. "C'mon. He just went through the door. He's probably headed for Darnathian's office." Their sandals quietly gripped the rough-cut stone as they hurried along the passage to the door with the evil knocker.

The bronze face opened its eyes and immediately scrunched his face at them. "You again?"

"Yes, it's me again," Lucy said, reaching for the striker. "I know. Pain opens the door." She raised the striker.

"Heh, heh, heh. Yes, it does," the bronze man laughed, a devious smile curling his lips.

Lucy held the striker. "What do you mean? Will we feel the pain this time?" Behind her, Schuyler was shaking her head, her pinched lips down-turned in a severe grimace.

Paul stared in amazement at the talking door knocker. He swallowed and gripped his sword tighter.

"Only one way to find out," the bronze face said, leering at her.

Lucy squinted, glaring at the smirking face. Her eyes swiveled in their orbits. Then she smiled and pointed the Spirit Sword at the doorknob.

"How about this? I will give you two options. Option number one: open the door and let us pass." She bounced her brows.

"What's my second option, human?" the face spat. Its bronze eyes looked suspiciously at the sword.

"Option number two: I will blast your door to smithereens, which means it will probably destroy you along with it, and we'll go through any-way. I would prefer that you quietly open the door and let us pass. The choice is yours." She fluttered her eyelashes and smiled benignly at the evil door knocker.

"Well, maybe just this once," it growled. "Since you put it that way." The latch clicked, and the door popped open. "But don't expect me to do it again."

"Good choice. I could kiss you for your genteel manners," Lucy said, smiling but keeping the sword raised.

"You could?" the face said, a hopeful expression lifting his features. "Will you?"

"No," Lucy said. Schuyler and Paul hurried through the entry. She wig-gled her fingers at the face and slipped through the opening.

"Mean human girl," the face said, closing and locking the door.

They stood once again in the elegant hallway with the high ceilings and tall double french doors. The Zazriel sword quivered in Schuyler's hand. Paul gaped at the hideous illustrated tapestries with daemons hunting inhuman creatures. Lucy tapped his shoulder and nodded toward the end of the hall where Darnathian's office door was open. He blew out a breath and quietly approached with the others.

Voices issued from the Master's office. One voice was extremely gleeful. Lucy surmised it was the hungry daemon, which meant that Mathias was inside. Her heartbeat quickened, and her muscles tensed as they neared the open door.

Lucy could distinguish another voice too. She would recognize Darnathian's voice just about anywhere, with its timbre and eloquence. Coming from any other person, it would have had a calming, alluring effect. But this spirit was the enemy, the epitome of evil, and it chilled her bones.

She motioned to Paul and Schuyler to flank the door. She was going in first with the Spirit Sword.

"What's your plan?" Schuyler whispered, hugging the wall beside the door. Paul stood on the other side, his gaze swinging to her for instructions and then surveilling the hallway for danger. So far, their presence had gone undetected, no alarms raised.

"We go in, grab Mathias, and run?" she said, hunching her shoulders. "I'm not sure you can plan for these events. It's a battle, and anything can happen. I know we have the High King's blessing. I'm counting on that to keep us safe." Schuyler nodded; Paul flashed a brief, anxious smile.

She peeked around the doorframe. The office was dim, the curtains drawn, and the macabre lights on their arm poles created a myriad of shadows around the room. Besides Herman, the room held three occupants: Mathias, the hungry daemon, and Darnathian.

Mathias sat on the floor in front of the Master's desk, shaking, his hands clapped over his ears, eyes squeezed tight. Darnathian sat at the desk, and the hungry daemon sat in a chair near the fireplace. Closing her eyes, she leaned against the wall and mentally noted the location of each occupant. Another deep, cleansing breath; another quick orison to Iam for guidance. She held up three fingers, one by one. The others bobbed their heads in understanding.

Tapping her lips for silence, she peeked again and blanched. Only Mathias and the hungry daemon remained. The danger indicator in her head ramped up to DEFCON 1, alarms blaring.

Darnathian was gone.

Her rapid heartbeat thumped a staccato against her ribs. Flexing her shoulders and drawing a breath, she slipped unnoticed into the shadows at the edge of the room, the sword softly glowing behind the shield and lending her its strength. Schuyler and Paul waited a beat, then slipped inside and hid in the shadows near the door.

Lucy scanned the room. Darnathian was nowhere to be seen. His chair was empty, and he wasn't in the loft or reading from his book at the table. Lucy pointed two fingers at her eyes, then pointed at the desk. The Defenders nodded. They would keep watch for any sign of Darnathian's return.

The daemon sat on the edge of his chair, hungrily licking his lips and gleefully rubbing his hands together. He leaned forward and sniffed the boy, patting his rotund belly, his gaze glued to the teen. Mathias drew his legs up, wrapped his arms around his knees, and hid his face.

Herman sat quietly, observing the scene yet powerless to do anything from his gilded cage. His translucent face was strained, but his eyes didn't miss Lucy's movements. He slowly clasped his hands, one finger pointing toward the hidden passage behind the fireplace leading to the dungeons and the correction rooms.

Lucy gave a quick nod, a smile tugging her lips in gratitude for the old spirit.

Schuyler edged further into the room and slipped along the wall by the door. Paul followed, crouched, and carefully made his way forward to a large, tufted velvet armchair. He hid behind it.

Lucy didn't dare whisper this close to the daemon. Gripping the Spectrescope, she thought about her request: *Spectrescope, can you activate the Shimmer Shield around Mathias?* A message appeared. *With pleasure, Gatekeeper.* A clear, nearly indiscernible bubble appeared around the boy. Lucy could distinguish its slight variations, distorting the daemon as he rubbed his belly and mumbled. Even Mathias was unaware he was under it.

Lucy motioned Schuyler to follow and moved along the inside edges of the room where the shadows would obscure her movements. Paul was just ahead, behind the chair. Using the shadows behind the lights, she moved cautiously toward the desk. If the daemon glanced in her direction, the glare from the lights would hide her from his eyes. She gritted her teeth. There were two black velvet ring boxes sitting on the desk. Moving cautiously, she quietly opened each box and found identical rings inside. Hopefully, one of them contained the Belt of Truth. She hurriedly stuffed them in her pocket and then crouched in the shadows.

Berbatos was getting anxious. He toyed with the buckle on his belt. Lucy could hear his belly rumbling. He blotted drool from his mouth with the edge of his cloak and reached a lumpy hand for the boy sitting at arm's reach.

"Surely, Master won't be too mad if I take your soul now," he said, swaying impatiently back and forth. His fingers closed and opened several times, itching to consume the boy.

"Salt or pepper?" Herman asked, breaking the silence. He scratched the crown of his head above his tonsure.

The daemon flinched at the interruption, bemused by the old spirit's question. "What was that you said?" He got up and stood by the cage, his thumbs hooked on his belt.

"Well, I've heard those human boys are rather salty, not to mention stringy. I wonder, Berbatos, will you eat him whole, or consume only his soul?" Herman rose and moved to the rungs and waited, gazing innocently at the daemon. "Boiled, baked, or fried?"

Lucy rolled her lips and smothered a giggle. The wily old spirit had drawn the daemon's attention and given her the daemon's name so she could vanquish it. She knew Herman's fate could not change, but she secretly hoped one day the High King would remember how Herman had helped the Defenders.

The daemon leaned back and laughed uproariously. "Oh, you are amusing. No wonder the Dark Prince keeps you 'hanging' around," he said, using finger quotes. He snickered, his belly jiggling like gelatin.

Spectrescope, can you retrieve the real Belt of Truth for me? Lucy thought as she hid behind the desk. The belt appeared around her waist, its familiar weight comforting. Slowly rising, she raised the sword and approached the daemon. He laughed, his belly quivering like warm pork grease. It was revolting.

"Perhaps I could influence the Dark Prince to let you join me for dinner so you can observe the preparations," Berbatos said, waggling an annoying finger through the rungs at Herman. The old spirit smiled, and Berbatos looked befuddled.

"Perhaps you would like to meet my new friends?" Herman asked, pointing, a grin lighting his face. "My friends are worthy. They are strong and courageous. The High King chose well." He smiled approvingly at Lucy. She winked.

The Ghost You Can't See

The daemon whirled. Three armored teenagers holding pointy swords stood confidently behind him. He flung his cloak aside and grabbed a sword concealed under its folds. He chuckled, unsheathing the sword.

"Four souls! Oh, my feast is going to be scrumptious. My belly will burst with deliciousness," Berbatos said, a hand on his hip, holding back the cloak. He stood like a knight prepared for battle. "Who shall I slay first, I wonder?" The pennant tongue appeared, flapping eagerly. "Then, when I have finished feasting on you, I will go back and claim each of your parents!"

Without hesitation, Paul stepped forward, and his Briathos sword clanged against the daemon's. The blades flashed and screeched, metal clanging on metal as Paul swiftly blocked each of the daemon's strikes, flicking his wrist and easily deflecting the blade.

Berbatos cursed, his strikes whisked harmlessly aside. He lunged at Paul, who stepped aside, causing the daemon's strike to go wild. He stamped forward with his foot and twirled his blade.

Paul grinned and stepped back, and Schuyler stepped forward.

While the others kept the daemon occupied, Lucy quickly released Mathias from the Shimmer Shield. He didn't move or look up when she touched his shoulder.

"Mathias, look at me," she demanded. When he didn't respond, she gripped his chin and tilted his head up. His eyes were clouded, and his expression was blank, as though the daemon had already removed his soul. A chill coursed through her. The evil words were still infecting him.

"Iam! I need you! How can I help Mathias? He needs to wake up. Please send help."

"Hold out your hand," Iam's voice whispered in her ear. She opened her palm, and a leather wristband appeared with the boy's name on it. "Do as you did for Paul. The truth will purge his heart and set him free, revealing the promise. Soon, the band will become his armor."

Lucy grabbed the teen's arm, knelt, and placed the wristband on it. Mathias convulsed, thrashing violently, and ripped the wristband off. Lucy snatched it back and wrestled with him until she got the band on his wrist. As the magnetic clasp ends slapped together, tiny flames appeared and etched runes into the leather. Mathias screamed, flailed, and slumped forward, his forehead damp with perspiration, his breath coming in ragged gasps.

Schuyler and Paul took turns sparring with the daemon. Berbatos was tiring. Each time he lunged, his rotund belly shifted and threw his balance off. His dull blade had numerous nicks. The Defenders tattered his cloak and tunic with countless sword strikes. The Defenders were young and agile. He was a hungry, whispering philosopher. Weakened, he struggled to maintain his stance.

"Schuyler, come help Mathias. See if you can get him to his feet," Lucy said. "I'll deal with the daemon. We need to leave before Darnathian gets back." The Belt of Truth vibrated, and two blue stones popped into her hand. The messages glowed within their tranquil blue depths. It was comforting, and yet it was reality.

"Berbatos," Lucy said, "by the word of the High King, *The wicked have drawn out their sword to slay the innocent. But the arms of the wicked shall be broken.*" Lucy shattered the stone against the hearth. Roiling blue smoke erupted from the broken pieces and covered the daemon. Berbatos growled and cursed the High King and his Defenders.

The smoke dissipated. Berbatos was bound with blue coils, writhing on the carpet and cursing the intruders. His arms were broken and limp. "How dare you! Master made me a duke. You have no right to treat me this way," he shouted. He spied his sword laying next to the chair and squirmed to reach it, his lumpy fingers grasping. He grimaced painfully at the movement.

Lucy read the message inside the second stone and sighed. It gave her no satisfaction to vanquish the spirit. Even this ghost was once a mighty and noble spirit, serving and loving the High King until the Dark Prince beguiled him with a lie, causing him to love evil instead of good. She spoke this message aloud too.

"Their sword shall enter their own heart, and all their bones shall be broken. Berbatos, in the name of the King, I banish you to Shinar!" The stone shattered, and smoke covered the ghost. When it cleared, his lumpy body lay like a bowl of melting lard, his bones broken. Resolutely, Lucy reached for the daemon's sword, but Paul stayed her hand. He picked it up instead. Her eyes met his, and she saw determination in their blue depths. She nodded with a tremulous smile.

Paul leaned down and pushed the daemon's sword into its blubbery chest. Berbatos burst into sulfurous black grains, imploded to a pinpoint, and disappeared with a pop.

Schuyler stowed her weapons and helped Mathias stumble to his feet. Paul did the same and grasped Mathias around the waist, pulling the boy's arm over his shoulder.

"Thanks. I'll watch your back," Schuyler said as her weapons reappeared. Zazriel glimmered in the low light.

"No worries. I know you do." Paul hefted Mathias, setting him on his feet. "You know, after our battle with Merbas in the natatorium, Iam has been instructing me. My sword play has improved, don't you think?" Schuyler grinned at him and nodded.

"Well done, Defenders," Herman said, clasping his hands. "Your High King will be so proud, but now you must hurry. Darnathian approaches in the outer corridor. I recognize his stride." He pointed to the stairs spiraling up to the balcony. "Do you remember the way, Bachar?" He reached a thin translucent arm through the rungs, urging them to hurry. "I would hug you if I could, dear girl. How I wish I could have been like you are: strong and courageous. Remember me fondly, Lucy the Gatekeeper."

Schuyler and Paul were already mounting the steps with Mathias in tow. Lucy nodded and blew Herman a kiss, tears in her eyes. "Thank you, Herman. I—"

He shook his head. "Hurry!" He waved toward the steps. "You must go. Goodbye, Issachar Gatekeeper," he said, returning her kiss. At the top, she waved one more time, then closed the door.

"Goodbye, dear girl. You are a treasure," Herman whispered.

The door opened again as an arm snaked out, grabbed a book from a nearby shelf, and quickly disappeared. The door clicked shut. Herman chuckled and hid his smile as Darnathian strode into the office.

A Race to Freedom

Lucy stuffed the book in the door knocker's mouth before the woman's head could scream the alarm. "There's a good girl," Lucy said with a sharp nod. The bronze face glared at her.

Paul, his eyes wide, watched as the head thrashed about, mumbling and trying to dislodge the tome. He snorted, hefted Mathias higher, and hurried down the stone passage after Lucy. The torches flared to life as they went.

Schuyler followed behind, turning sporadically to check their flank. They were in the same tunnel, descending farther into the regions under the castle.

Mathias was still groggy, but his eyes appeared brighter. His legs and feet dragged like rocks bumping over the rough stone floor. Paul held him in a firm grip, with one hand clamped over Mathias's wrist and an arm around his waist.

"Thanks, Paul," he whispered, coming further awake.

They reached the end of the passage. The door had a bronze face on it. It opened its eyes and considered the four Defenders with their swords that glittered in the torchlight.

"Open the door!" Lucy said, circling her sword tip in front of his nose.

"Oh, so you're the nasty group my brother told me about. Threatened to blast him to smithereens, did you?" the face said. He laughed and grinned, a sinister gleam in his eyes. "The Master has tightened the security since your previous visit. I'd like to see you try to blast my door to smithereens." He met her gaze, a smug look on his face.

The Spirit Sword grew warm. The runes glowed briefly, changed, and settled into new characters. Lucy smiled at the cranky face. He eyed her suspiciously.

Lucy tapped the wristband on Mathias's arm, activating some of the armor. A helmet appeared. His eyes swiveled like roller balls in his face as he tried to see the armor. He flinched when the breastplate wrapped around his chest. His astonishment soon turned into a grin as he looked over his companions' similar armor.

"Does pain still open the door?" Lucy asked sweetly, with a simple smile.

The face slowly nodded, its expression puckered.

Glancing at the others, she jerked her head as she rolled her eyes, motioning them to stand back. The others stepped several paces away.

"Yes. Pain will open the door." Lucy raised her shield, lifted the striker to its full swing, and let it drop. It hit the face with a thump. The bronze face screamed, then melted like oozing wax and dribbled down the door. It coagulated in the wood grain. The latch clicked, and the door popped open.

"C'mon!" Lucy shoved it open and stepped aside as the others helped Mathias through. She followed behind and slammed the door. An energy beam blasted from the sword tip, melting the latch, too, and securing the door.

Torches flared down the passage lined with doors. Effigies, carved into their panels, depicted hideous creatures. Several doors stood ajar, their cell-like rooms empty. Lucy cautiously poked her head into an empty cell and felt immediate regret. Whatever creature occupied the room was overwhelmingly odoriferous.

"I hope this creature doesn't show up," she said, waving a hand under her nose. "Gross."

They sped along the corridor and through the door into the courtroom chamber. Across the gallery, an open door led to the next corridor. Angry shouts and heavy footsteps pounded behind them. Lucy shut the courtroom door and dropped the beam into the brackets.

"Wait for me there," Lucy said, pointing. "It's the passage leading to Ishi's silver door knocker. I hope it is still there. It will bring us to the clock portal. I'll be right behind you."

Schuyler nodded and raised a hand. "I'll make sure the passage is clear." She ran to the door and stood with her back to the wall. She clutched the Zazriel sword, the tip pointed at the ceiling.

Lucy pointed her sword, and energy blasted the hinges on the big wooden door until they were molten and sagged. The door would be impossible to open without Darnathian's spell work. A ruckus began with shouting and pounding. The beam bounced violently in its brackets.

Schuyler leaned into the passage and quickly scanned the corridor. She checked again, held up a thumb, and then waved, urging Paul and Mathias to get a move on. They were moving quicker now; Mathias was awake and alert and getting stronger. Paul kept a hand on his shoulder to guide him.

"I don't think it will hold much longer," Lucy said, joining them. The pounding stopped for a moment. Then a massive object slammed against the large wood door. The beam recoiled and nearly dropped to the floor before it settled in its brackets again. Another resounding crash splintered the wood. Lucy pulled the hall door shut, and the Spectrescope blasted the metal.

They sped down the passage, their footsteps slapping the stone and echoing. A door creaked open, and Stolas the herbologist stepped into the passage, chattering to himself and oblivious to the Defenders. He casually locked his door. In his hand, he carried a large vial filled with a green and sludgy fluid.

Mathias, shocked at the sight of the small daemon, tripped and lost his balance. Paul grabbed for him, and they both went down with a crash, Paul's shield and sword clanging loudly in the stone passage.

Stolas screeched and dropped the vial of elixir. It smashed on the ground. The sludge bubbled and frothed as it seeped into the stone. The small divo owl skittered around on his spindly legs, screeching, the noise shrill. His flapping arms shed feathers into the air. The tiny crown slid off and bounced into the sludge. It disappeared in a puff of smoke.

"Help! Intruders in the castle!" He twisted the key in the lock and scampered inside, followed quickly by Lucy and Schuyler. Shrieking, he ran to his worktable lined with beakers and containers of colored fluids. He grabbed the nearest container and hurled it at Lucy.

The beaker shattered against the magical shield, and the fluid vaporized. Stolas, his beak clacking, grabbed another container and aimed it at Schuyler. Her sword hissed through the air, slicing the container in half. The fluid vaporized; its mist hung in the air for a moment, then dissipated.

"There are no exits," Lucy whispered. "I'll seal the door hinges. It will keep him from going anywhere for a while." Schuyler nodded, and they backed toward the door, deflecting the noxious missiles the owl lobbed at them. Schuyler dove through the doorway first.

Stolas pelted Lucy's shield with more beakers, the fluids vaporizing, filling the air with an acrid stench. Scampering around the worktable, he launched another round of missiles as she ducked out the door and pulled it shut. The door shuddered. Containers and beakers smashed against it on the other side. The owl screeched and cursed.

"Charming little fellow," Lucy said. She glanced down and warily eyed the sludge.

Fluids oozed from under the door, combining and changing color. She skipped away from the muck and gasped. The door was disappearing—the cut stones and chinking expanded around it and consumed the entry. The herbologist was sealed in a tomb of his own making. His muffled screams were chilling.

"Lucy, look!" Schuyler backed away from the green sludge on the floor. The owl had dropped a beaker in the passage. The stone was turning to ash. The contamination grew, crumbling the stone floor and walls around them.

The courtroom chamber door exploded, shrapnel pelting them, pinging off their armor. Several daemons streamed through the opening, their gray, neoprene-like bodies glistening in the torchlight.

The portal was on the other side of the cursed floor. The daemons had them trapped. A giant sink hole opened in the floor.

Lucy glanced at Paul as he shoved Mathias behind him and covered him with his shield, holding it high. The long, kite-shaped shield protected them both. His sword flashed in the torchlight.

"Keep him covered. He's still in danger," Lucy said, tipping her head, indicating Mathias's wristband.

"Do you have an extra weapon? Mathias said. "I'm feeling much stronger. My head is clear, and the voices are gone. I can help." He swallowed hard. His face was pale, but his eyes were clear and unswerving.

Paul glanced at Lucy, and she gave an affirming nod. "We can use the help," he said. "May the High King be with us." He grasped Mathias's arm. "Ready?" Mathias nodded. Paul tapped the wristband. Mathias's eyes went wide as the wristband changed.

Immediately, it became a large kite shield. A sheath next to the handgrip held a sword. Its hilt glimmered. Mathias pulled it out and held it up. He had no time to admire the jeweled workmanship.

"Watch out!" Lucy yelled as a daemon launched itself at Mathias.

The daemon growled and lunged with its deadly claws. Mathias thrust forward with the sword, impaling the daemon. It shattered into thousands of tiny grains, imploded, and disappeared. "Whoa," he said. He swallowed again.

"Defenders! Watch your footing. The ground is sinking," Lucy yelled as she battled two daemons who were clawing and reaching around her shield. Their talons ripped the air. The narrow confines of the passage made it almost impossible to strike out.

"Ratha-nael! Shield down!" The sword appeared in her waiting hand as the shield retreated into the bracelet. Now she advanced on the daemons, her blades flashing, taking the two daemons in stride. The first spirit lost an arm and imploded. The second entity impaled itself on her sword and disappeared.

"Lucy! There are more daemons coming," Schuyler screamed, vanquishing another neoprene entity. "They are climbing the walls!" The daemons swarmed like spiders from the opposite end of the passage. The floor continued to crumble into a black hole.

Lucy maintained her attack, backing closer to the gaping hole in the floor. Her sword flashed and hissed as she dispatched more entities. Thrusting upward with both blades, she vanquished two more daemons scurrying over the ceiling to avoid the hole in the floor.

Paul and Mathias battled side by side, taking turns in the cramped space. They were barely holding back the daemons near the courtroom chamber. The spell continued to expand, advancing along the walls and floor, turning rock to ash.

The Belt of Truth vibrated. A blue stone popped into her hand. She read the glowing message.

"Defenders, huddle! Backs together!" she yelled. "Keep your shields up." She stood and pulled Schuyler close. Paul and Mathias edged backward till they had joined the girls. Standing together with their shields, they created a barrier.

"*The evil ones are like straw blown away by the wind.*" Lucy smashed the stone, releasing the familiar blue vapor. It billowed through the passage, obscuring everything, including the Defenders as they huddled together.

Screams and curses erupted, then suddenly, everything went silent. A wind rushed through the passage. They closed their eyes against the force as it whipped their faces and snapped their clothes. Then it was gone, taking with it the smoke and stench. They opened their eyes. The stone had vanquished the daemons; the ash had been blown away and the cursed elixir rendered inert.

Lucy surveyed the damage. She heaved a sigh. The tunnel had stopped crumbling, but the stones creaked eerily. The weight of the overhead structure might collapse the tunnel at any moment. They had to get out now, but there was a problem. *How are we going to get across the hole in the floor?* Lucy thought.

She looked around for another way through, but they were out of options. The portal was ahead. The belt vibrated. Another blue stone popped into her hand, its message reassuring. Relieved, she folded her fingers over it and breathed.

A deep chuckle echoed through the tunnel, reverberating off the walls. It was menacing. Lucy squeezed her eyes shut and turned to face Darnathian.

Clapping slowly, the Dark Prince stepped through the shattered courtroom door and stood in the passage. His eyes glowed like the embers of a dying campfire, his light-colored suit impeccable. Behind him, his pet manticore grinned manically. It twisted the ugly human face.

"Say nothing," she whispered. "We must not challenge him or rebuke him." Flanked by the others, she stepped in front of them and glanced at their determined faces. Even Mathias stood boldly, perhaps strengthened by the armor and the ordeal he had just survived.

"Once again, you walk so willingly into my home. What gives you the right to vanquish my spirits and destroy my home?"

Lucy smiled, though it didn't reach her eyes. The Defenders remained silent and steadfast behind her.

"Why do you want to serve that wretched High King?" Darnathian asked, his hands spread before him. His voice was melodious and pleasant, and his smile was gracious.

"I have great power. Soon, I will have the ancient power too," he said. "I can give you wealth beyond your imaginings. I can make you richer than old Midas. I can give you fame. People will fawn over you and hang on your every word. Renounce the King, and serve me instead." His eyes glittered dangerously.

"*The boastful and the arrogant will not stand in the High King's sight,*" Lucy said, reading the embedded message. The stone grew warm in her hand.

Darnathian's demeanor changed in a millisecond. His eyes blazed with hatred, and his face flushed with anger. He drew himself up to his full height, tall and imposing, his hands clenching.

Lucy smashed the stone. Billowing blue clouds filled the space and hid them. Another stone wiggled. Lucy caught it, read the message, and whispered. "*The children of the High King are guided and protected. Open your eyes and walk by faith.*" The spectacles materialized on her nose. She tossed the stone into the sinkhole.

Darnathian uttered an expletive. He raised his arms and murmured, calling forth a spell to counteract the stone's effect.

"Everyone, store your weapons and hold hands. Hang on tight and follow me." Lucy clasped their hands. Once they had chained together, she stepped toward the gaping hole in the ground. "I can see where to go. There is no need to be afraid, but don't look down. Follow me, keep your eyes up, and we will make it across. Okay?"

The friends murmured their consent, and she stepped forward. The Spectacles revealed a translucent bridge spanning the expanse. Her foot hovered over the hole. She took a breath and stepped out. It was like walking on a glass floor. Ahead, the smoke lessened with each step she took, and the Defenders followed her steps exactly, their eyes up.

Darnathian continued to murmur, but his spell had no effect. The blue vapor still filled the air, obscuring the Defenders. Cursing, he stroked the manticore's mane.

"My pet, you must do what I cannot," he said. "Find the intruders and kill them. Feast well." The manticore growled and scratched at the ground.

Lucy, who'd overheard Darnathian's instructions to the beast, picked up her pace. The Defenders crossed the hole and sped down the corridor. Torches sputtered and went out as they passed, plunging the passage behind into darkness. The last door was within reach. The manticore's growl echoed behind them, its claws clicking on the stone. Their weapons reappeared as they ran.

The last torch flared to life, and the door appeared at the end. It was a welcome sight. The stone landing and the portal through the clock and home were within reach. The silver knocker appeared. Lucy reached for the striker etched with the familiar message: *Knock, and I shall open it for you.*

The snarling manticore slid into view. The scorpion tail arced over its back, ready to strike. Schuyler squealed in terror but raised her sword. Mathias was stunned, unable to move. Paul brandished his sword, his shield blocking his body.

The human face creased with a lecherous grin, its fangs sharp behind the cruel lips. It wagged the venomous tail. The head tilted sideways as the beast spied the prey. Like a weird dance, it scurried from side to side, ready to attack.

Paul feinted with the sword, following it with a punch of the shield. The manticore whipped the deadly tail at him. Paul dropped and rolled away. The venomous point slammed against the stone. Paul regained his feet and swung as the creature struck again. His timing was perfect, and the sword sliced through the tail. It lay on the floor, the venom oozing from the wound.

The manticore screamed, its fangs bared. It lunged at Paul with its clawed hands. The scream stopped suddenly, then its head rolled down the passage. Mathias's sword was still arcing through the air like a baseball bat. The beast's crumpled body burst into flames, the pieces smoking, then everything imploded and disappeared.

Schuyler squealed and high-fived the unexpected hero.

Lucy dropped the striker, and the door opened. They scrambled through the entry, leaving behind the enraged curses as Darnathian realized they had vanquished his pet. The door vanished, leaving only a stone wall. They were in the corridor leading to the spiral staircase.

The Defenders sped down the passage. The staircase was just ahead. Lucy stopped and waved the others to go ahead of her. They charged up the stairs. She heard the bronze face utter expletives, and the door opened with a squeak, followed by rushing footsteps.

"Hurry! They are coming!" She took one last look down the passage, then ran up the stairs.

A hand grabbed her ankle and twisted it. Her scream tore through the passage. The hand yanked her leg, and she fell forward, her head smacking the steps. Her helmet dented again. Her sword and shield clattered on the stone as the daemon dragged her down the steps.

"Schuyler, get Mathias through the portal. I'll get Lucy," Paul shouted. He charged down the stairs after her.

Kicking and twisting, Lucy rolled onto her back and swung the sword. The daemon screeched and stared at his severed arm, its hand still gripping

Lucy's ankle. She smacked the daemon's head with the shield and thrust the sword tip into the spirit. He imploded with a pop. The hand grasping her ankle vanished too.

A second daemon leaped over Lucy. Paul quickly dispatched it. He grabbed Lucy's hand and yanked her up, wrapped an arm around her waist, and carried her up the stairs.

They hurried to the clock portal. Hands reached out and grasped her, lifting and pulling her through the entry. Then Paul rushed through the portal. It slammed shut and disappeared.

They collapsed to the foyer floor, gasping but breathing easily for the first time in hours. Lucy's painful ankle was rapidly swelling, and tears wet her cheeks. Weapons and shields clattered to the floor. Exuberant chatter followed.

Lucy sat up and massaged her sprained ankle with a whimper. A white stone tumbled from the Belt of Truth. White stones were special. It usually meant there was a blessing inside. The beautiful stone glimmered, the message clear and reassuring. She whistled, rousing the group from lounging on the floor.

"Listen to this! *In the name of the High King, be sealed forever and forever blessed!*" She tossed the stone into the clock. White mist shrouded the clock, swirling through its nooks and crevices and spiraling around the finial above the simple face. The others watched in awe.

The mist evaporated. The old wood shone with a glossy finish, and its brass gleamed in the light. The portal was closed and the clock blessed.

Then she collapsed on the floor again. Despite the pain, a big grin spread across her face. "Woo-hoo!" She punched a fist into the air.

Finally, Completed Renovations

The drizzle had turned to a drenching rain by the time the Defenders returned from the castle, the clouds low and gray. Lucy's mom and Mr. and Mrs. Sasson weren't home yet, so the friends gathered in the breakfast room to recap their adventures through the dungeons. Mathias bombarded them with questions about daemons, armor, and sword fighting techniques.

Lucy sat in a chair, her swollen foot resting on a small ottoman. Schuyler had brought the bandages and ice pack and wrapped her sprained ankle.

She smiled and watched as Schuyler took the milk from the refrigerator, filled the glasses, and passed the tray around. Only crumbs remained on the platter of Mrs. McGoo's Chocolate Revel Bars over on the sideboard. Fighting daemons could work up an appetite.

Lucy studied Mathias. He was a different boy now. The sullen teenager who had arrived at the house several weeks ago was gone, replaced by an animated and cheerful young man. His eyes were bright and playful, and he joined in the good-natured banter with Paul and Schuyler. *This is friendship,* Lucy thought. *When needed, we tease and lift one another up. And we come to their rescue when danger appears.*

She was relieved too; her spirit felt lighter. She took a bite of her cookie and washed it down with a gulp of milk, grateful that everyone had returned safely. It seemed like days since their return, but it had only been a few hours. Her gaze fell on the velvet box, and just like that, her appetite was gone. She pushed her dessert to the side.

The Spectrescope lay on the table next to the two velvet boxes. One contained the real Belt of Truth. The other held a replica. Her skin crawled, and her imagination fired up with scenarios and reasons for the existence of the duplicate ring. And all of them were evil. Suddenly, even her hands felt icy.

Her finger twirled the box on the table, her hand never far from the Spectrescope. She never knew when she might need to blast an evil entity into oblivion. Lucy couldn't wait to speak with Iam and give him the duplicate. He'd know what to do with it.

"Lucy?" Paul asked. "Did you hear what Mathias said?" He tipped his head toward the other boy and waggled his empty glass of milk at her with a grin.

"What? I'm sorry, Mathias. I zoned out for a moment," she said, struggling to sit up straighter in the chair. "I didn't mean to ignore you. I was thinking about what Darnathian had planned to do with this duplicate ring." She lifted her brows, her finger tapping the box. "Did you need something? More chocolate? Oh, wait, that would be Schuyler."

"Ha ha, you're so funny," Schuyler said. "Do we have more chocolate?" She waggled her brows. Lucy pointed to the kitchen. Schuyler got up and returned with a tin of chocolate chip cookies.

"Um . . . I wanted to say . . . thank you for coming to get me." He eyed her sheepishly and looked at each of them with a hesitant smile. "I was mean to all of you, and, well, I'm sorry." He was silent for a moment. "I'm not sure what to think. Spirits and daemons and creatures. Another spiritual realm. It's rather confusing."

"It is, at first. Me and Schuyler didn't understand everything at the beginning either. And we're still learning. I know the High King loves you just as much as he loves each of us. And when you truly stop to think about all of it," she spread her hands, "it makes sense."

"I'm sorry," he said, "for, you know . . . for stealing the ring from your room. I feel so ashamed for hurting you. I didn't want to do any of it, and yet I couldn't seem to help myself." He glanced down, then raised his gaze to hers. "Can you, maybe, forgive me?"

"Forgive you? Of course, I forgive you!" Lucy said. "You are my friend. You were being influenced by evil."

"What I've learned is this," Paul said, joining the conversation. "The spiritual realm is all around us, whether we believe in it or not. It has been there a long time." He slouched comfortably in the chair, his feet on the matching ottoman. He looked relaxed after the dangerous morning, especially his skirmish with the manticore.

"Who were the spirits in the passage?" Mathias asked, his finger tracing the patterns in the fabric on the arm of the chair.

"You mean the tall guy in the suit and Italian loafers?" Lucy said. "His name is Darnathian, and he was once the mightiest of angels. He became the Dark Prince when he turned evil and had to be banished from Ascalon." She saw his brows shoot up.

"Darnathian is our enemy," Schuyler said, adding to the explanation. "He turned many of the angels against the High King, and they became Darnathian's servants. Berbatos, the daemon who took you, was one of them. Then those fallen angels became the Irredaemon when they joined Darnathian."

"Whoa," Mathias said. His bewildered expression showed he had thoughts and questions running through his mind.

"There's a book called the Chronicles of Ascalon," Lucy said. "It talks about Darnathian and the Irredaemon. There is a lot of interesting stuff in it. I can give you a copy." He nodded gratefully.

"The daemon who took me called him Master. Darnathian was in the passage, too, but who were the others who fought on our side?" He glanced from Lucy to Schuyler, waiting. Schuyler hunched a shoulder, nibbled a cookie, and looked to Lucy.

"Who are you referring to?" Paul asked. His feet dropped to the floor, and he sat up.

"What did these others look like?" Lucy leaned forward in her chair, intrigued.

Schuyler's cookie hung suspended on its way to her mouth, her baffled gaze riveted on Mathias.

"Two spirits were inside the tunnel. They wore white and had large wings. The other two were difficult to see. One was an old guy with white hair and the second guy was younger."

"Huh. It sounds like Iam and Ishi." Lucy's hands gripped the edge of her seat. "They're father and son, and they are powerful spirits. Iam is the High King. I'm sure the two white-winged entities were probably my guardians. They always seem to know when we need help." Her brows puckered. "Did you see what they were doing?"

"The ones you called the guardians were holding back some dae-mons. The two guys were only there a short time. I didn't see them again. Somehow, it made me think they were in another dimension, watching over us."

"Wow, that's so cool," Schuyler said, finishing her cookie.

A flash of lightning filled the room. They blinked against the sudden brightness. Lucy pulled the curtain aside and peered into the gloom. It was raining hard, but it didn't appear to be storming, though it wasn't unusual to get lightning in October.

"Good afternoon," Iam said. He strolled through the kitchen into the breakfast room. Three voices shouted greetings as the King entered the room, followed closely by Ishi in his cardigan. Schuyler rushed to Iam and hugged him. Lucy hobbled over and hugged the King too. Paul stood, stepped forward, and shook his hand as the girls turned to hug Ishi. Excited chatter filled the room. Mathias stood, unsure what he should do. Iam grinned and shook the hesitant hand Mathias offered, then sat at the small dining table. Mathias slowly sank into the chair again.

Ishi waved to Paul, urging him to join him and the girls for a group hug, and Paul gladly accepted. As the group broke up, Ishi sat in the chair Paul had vacated and turned to Mathias with a grin.

Mathias's eyebrows hovered in the middle of his forehead, his eyes wide. A smile lit his face. "It was you. You were both in the passage today."

"Yes. Father and I watch over the chosen. The battle was well in hand, though we are always with you. The guardians did their part too."

"I feel like I know you. Why is that?" Mathias asked. Ishi smiled at him, his brown eyes twinkling mischievously. Mathias returned the smile. He marveled at the spirit.

Watching them, Lucy grinned. Ishi was so like his father, the King, and yet so different, and she loved them both immensely. She hobbled back to the table with Iam, sat, and toyed with the box.

Ishi stood and crooked a finger at Mathias. "Why don't we take a walk, and I'll answer all those questions bumbling around in your head. I'll tell you about the promise and the Triune seal." Mathias, completely at ease, followed Ishi from the room.

"Iam, I have a question," Lucy said, turning her attention to the King. "What should we do with this?" She pushed the duplicate box across the table to him. "I took it from Darnathian's office. I didn't know which one was real, so I grabbed them both."

The Ghost You Can't See

Inside the box was a ring with blue and white gemstones. It glittered in the half-light. Iam waved a hand. Lights popped on around the room. He held the ring to his eye, studying it closely. The real Belt of Truth appeared in his open palm, and he placed the duplicate next to it.

Lucy gasped. They were identical in every way. If the Spectrescope had not retrieved the genuine ring for her, she could easily have mistaken the fake ring as the magical artifact.

"Does this thing have any power?" she asked, chewing her lip. "I mean, like the Belt of Truth?" The deviousness of Darnathian was astounding, and it was always evil.

Schuyler and Paul gathered around them and gazed intently at the rings, amazed at the intricate details. The two rings twinkled competitively in the lamplight.

"Oh, it has power all right, but not the spoken word of the High King. Look closely," he said, pointing at the stones. "The stones in the Belt of Truth are rich in color and depth. That is because I saturated them with the authoritative word of the King. The duplicate contains the same stones, but without the King's authority, they are ever so slightly clouded. See?" He wiggled it with his finger. The stones catching the light were cloudy.

"They contain truth that is bent," he said. "And bentness always leads astray and to the final separation from the High King. Do you understand, my children?" He set the Belt of Truth aside, then closed his hand over the false ring and crushed it in his grip. The ring pulverized to colored dust and vanished.

"Holy cow! Darnathian makes me so freaking mad! His evil is destroying everything. He certainly has the—"

"Lucy," Schuyler interrupted, giving her the stink eye.

"*Audacity* to lead people away from the true King who loves them," she said, staring at Schuyler. "I wasn't going to swear, but I feel like it sometimes—I'm just being honest. Anyway, he makes me so mad. Look what happened to Herman."

"Oh, Lucy," Iam chuckled. "Herman was right about one thing. You are a treasure." Another chuckle shook his shoulders.

"Sir, how did the ring fit into Darnathian's plan?" Paul asked. "How would bending the truth keep Lucy from protecting the Issachar Gate or keeping the secrets of the Spectrescope?"

"Did you ever fly a plane?" Iam asked, glancing at them. Paul, bewildered at the random question, shook his head. Schuyler did the same.

"I did once with my uncle Bob. It was a blast. Why?" Lucy said.

"Did Uncle Bob explain how to use a compass?" he asked.

Lucy nodded. "It's used to determine your course."

"Correct. Let's say your destination city is due east of your current location," he said. "Your course is ninety degrees due east, but you fly a course of eighty-eight degrees east. What is the result?"

Paul nodded slowly. "Oh, I get it. The longer you maintain the wrong direction, the larger the course correction you would need to make to achieve your destination."

"But you are flying in a straight line, following the course. How can that be wrong?"

"It's wrong because your course was *bent* from the start," Paul said, using Iam's terminology. "And if you don't know it's bent, you don't make the correction to the true course."

"Exactly, dear boy. It is bent. It is the same if you are drawing a straight line and someone bumps your arm and deflects the line. It is no longer straight. It is bent."

"So, replacing your word with Darnathian's bends in it would lead me off course—"

"And you would lose your love for the King and your life would be rendered ineffective," Iam said. "Many will follow the half-truth and never realize they've gone astray."

"Can I swear now?"

"Lucy," Schuyler warned, squinting.

"What would you say if you could?" Iam asked, an amused expression on his face.

"Son of a buck snort!"

"That looks great, Schuyler, thanks." Lucy sat in the chair at the check-in desk with her leg on the counter and her ankle resting on an ice pack. She had a vibrant selection of colored wraps. Today, her ankle sported a bright pink bandage.

Saturday evening, when her mom and grandma had taken her to the emergency clinic, the doctor said a bad sprain like Lucy's could take up to three or four weeks to heal—sooner, perhaps, with the proper care. A crutch leaned against the wall. After nearly a week of navigating through the school with it, her arm and shoulders ached almost as much as her ankle.

Lucy didn't lie when she told her mom she had fallen down the stairs. She simply didn't elaborate which stairs she had tumbled down. While waiting for all the parents to arrive home that evening, Schuyler had swathed Lucy's leg with ice packs, and the boys had quickly finished her chores. Lucy smiled at the memory of Paul and Mathias scurrying to dust the books and shelves in the library.

Schuyler adjusted the artificial swag of fall flowers draped over the stair railing. The floral decoration contrasted nicely against the wood and white balustrades. She placed three different-sized potted plants at the base of the clock, and another at the bottom of the stairs. The pottery was from Great-Aunt Isabel's collection. Lucy had rescued the pottery from the antique store and hidden it away days before her injury. The yellow, gold, and burgundy colors added an autumn flair to the foyer. Paul and Mathias had brought them from the stables.

This afternoon, her mom had driven Mathias's parents to the bank just before they had gotten home from school. It was official. The Sassons had purchased Mr. and Mrs. McGoo's house. As a surprise, Lucy and her friends had decorated the B and B's foyer. Dinner was in the oven, and the house smelled like meatloaf and biscuits.

"This will surprise your mom. Think she will like it?" Schuyler said to Lucy, stepping aside to admire her work. "Thanks for inviting us. You go all out, girlfriend. Dinner and entertainment," she said, grinning. "Even if we're the entertainment." Paul and Mathias sat on the steps, munching from a bag of chips.

"Thanks for helping, guys. Mom planned to do it herself, but she hasn't had the time. She's been busy with the donation and setting up the antique store. At this rate, it will be Christmas before she gets any fall decorations put up." She adjusted the ice pack. One side of her leg was getting numb. "Grandma gets credit for the meatloaf. She made it before she left for Grand Traverse. It was in the freezer. And the biscuit recipe is your mom's. It's easy enough to make sitting down."

Lucy hobbled over, opened the clock door, pushed the pendulum aside, and scoped the inside. She knew the blessing had sealed the old clock, but it comforted her to see the sparkly residue the blessing stone had left behind. The lens revealed an iridescent dust embedded in the wood of the monastery clock, visible only through the Spectrescope. It permanently sealed the portal with the blessing. She placed a hand against the wood, thinking of Herman the kindly old ghost. The memory of him was bittersweet.

"Goodbye, Herman. I'll never forget you," she whispered. "You taught me how important our choices are in this life."

In memory of the monk, she had named the clock Herman. Her mom had thought it an odd name for the clock, but the Defenders knew the reason behind the naming.

She stood and let go of the big brass bob. It clicked and swung leisurely from its mounting, the mechanical rhythm smooth and measured. As it swung, the clock began ticking. "Oh. My. Goodness. Guys! It's ticking!" Lucy fist-punched the air. "The blessing must have canceled the curse. Woo-hoo!"

A car rumbled into the driveway, soon followed by animated chatter as Lucy's mom and Mathias's parents filed through the kitchen and down the hallway to the foyer. Lucy limped to the desk and sat, a sly grin on her face. The group on the steps waited quietly.

"Oh good! You're all here," Mom said, slipping off her coat and hanging it in the closet. She glanced around the foyer at the decorations. "This is lovely. You did all this? Thank you."

"Everyone helped since I'm kind of gimpy at the moment." Lucy grinned and pointed at her injury.

"Well, I can tell you now." Mom clasped her hands eagerly. "I heard from the museum!" The Grand River Valley Museum had gratefully accepted their donation of the eighteen-hundreds-era Concord carriage the teenagers had found sealed in the old stables. "They're sending a photographer to take our photos as a thank-you. They will inscribe the group photo with our names on the placard in front of the restored carriage in the Michigan History room. They've already written up a short story about the find for the newspapers."

The donation included the spare wheels and horse collars that were used for the horse teams. The restoration company would pick up the carriage sometime the following week. Until then, it proudly sat in the big room of the renovated stable, a reminder of an era gone by.

"Mom, that's so cool!" Lucy grinned. It was rare for her mother to be so animated and giddy. She was glad for the joy her mom was experiencing. The last couple of years had been difficult. Behind Schuyler, Mathias and Paul looked knowingly at each other and grinned.

"Jeannie, it's wonderful!" Mrs. Sasson passed some packages to her husband and gave Jeannie a hug. "I knew you were keeping a secret. Think of the free advertising for the bed-and-breakfast and the antique store." She grasped Jeannie's hand and patted it. "It's so exciting. I am happy for you."

"Miriam, speaking of antiques," Mom said. "You are going to love the grandmother clock. It will be perfect with the new living room furniture you purchased today."

"You've done so much to help us muddle through this, Jeannie," Mrs. Sasson said. "You and Lucy are just wonderful. You've welcomed our family and helped the transition go so much easier."

Mr. Sasson added his sentiments. "We love this house. It's been a great experience for all of us."

"And we've become such good friends! I couldn't have—" Mom paused, her mouth open and a frown forming. She held up a finger. "What is that sound?"

"What sound?" Lucy asked, barely containing a giggle. Her cheeks were quivering.

"It has a familiar rhythm to it," Mom said, one brow cocked. "Where is that noise coming from? It sounds like it's in the room somewhere."

"Beats me." Lucy lifted a shoulder. "What does it sound like, Mom?" She pulled out a drawer, lowered her leg on it and plopped the ice bag on top.

Schuyler smothered a giggle with her hand, but the liveliness in her eyes betrayed her.

Miriam Sasson glanced about questioningly, unsure what Jeannie was referring to. Mr. Sasson looked at Mathias and seemed to note the amused expression on his face. Mathias flashed his eyes at the big clock.

The sounds were ordinary. A neighborhood dog barked, a passing car honked its horn, and a train whistle wailed in the distance. Bewildered, Mrs. Sasson merely shook her head, and Mr. Sasson shrugged his shoulders, though his cheeks dimpled with a smile.

The relationship between Mathias and his parents had seemingly improved after he met the High King and his son, Ishi. Mathias was now officially a member of the Defenders and had received the Triune seal and his armor.

"Lucy, what is that ticking noise?" Mom asked, squinting suspiciously at her. "I haven't heard a tick in this room before. What did you do?" She crossed her arms and waited.

"I did nothing you didn't ask me to do," she replied innocently, with an insipid smile curling her lips.

"I asked if you could dust and polish the clock," Mom said. "Apparently, you did something else."

"My friends and I polished and buffed the old monastery clock," she said. "And I made dinner. With biscuits."

"Which smells amazing, by the way. And don't change the subject. Did you hide a wind-up clock somewhere in this room?" Mom huffed. "You did, didn't you? All right, where is it, young lady?" She glanced around the foyer, her head rubbernecking. "Did you put it in the clock?"

"I did nothing except clean the clock." Lucy crossed her arms. "It wasn't me."

"Um, Mrs. Hornberger?" Mr. Sasson said, pointing at the enormous clock. "The ticking is coming from the clock. Shouldn't it be?"

"No, no," Mom said. She waved a dismissive hand. "Lucy is playing tricks again. She's always up to some shenanigan. Trust me, she stashed a ticking wind-up clock around here somewhere, and I'm going to find it." She opened cabinet doors and searched the credenza and under the check-in desk. She even looked inside the dumbwaiter and the closet.

"Maybe you hear the mantel clock in the parlor. It's a wind-up clock," Lucy said. "It ticks." Schuyler dipped her head to hide a grin.

"Don't be silly. It's practically on the other side of the house. Give it up. Where did you put it?"

"But, Mrs. Hornberger, the giant clock is ticking. Really, it is," Mr. Sasson said, his head bobbing. Jeannie smiled patiently and rolled her lips.

"That's impossible, Mr. Sasson. The clock hasn't worked in centuries—*argh!*" Mom screamed. Mr. Sasson flinched. "Oh my goodness! It's . . . working!" She grabbed his arm to steady herself, a cupped hand to her cheek.

The clock whirred and clicked. The painfully thin minute hand clicked into position under the number twelve, and the clock began tolling the time. It gave three successful bongs. It wasn't the correct time, but at least the clock was working.

"What? How? I . . . I don't understand," Mom stuttered, the hand dropped to her chest. "Lucy, Aunt Isabel tried many times to have that clock fixed, and no one ever succeeded. Even Fergus couldn't make it work, and he repairs vintage clocks all the time." She went to the clock and ran her hand lovingly over the old wood, watching the gentle movement of the pendulum. "This is totally amazing!"

"See, told you it wasn't me." Lucy grinned and fist-punched the air. Her grin was infectious, and the Sasson's each returned it with one of their own. Mr. Sasson winked and turned away to smother his laughter. Mrs. Sasson, a wide smile firmly in place, silently clapped her hands.

"I'm absolutely stunned." Mom gripped the sides of the old clock, staring up at its simple face.

Lucy held up a fist and punched the air. "Boom!"

A Dance and a Surprise

"Ow! Why do you need to snarl my hair? It's fine the way it is," Lucy complained, fidgeting as her mom styled her hair. "Everyone is going to laugh. I never wear my hair like this." She waved a hand, fanning away the fumes of the hair spray. Her eyes widened at her reflection in the mirror. Her hair was twice the size of her head. "I look ridiculous!"

"Oh, hold still—I'm almost finished. Besides, you want to look your best in the photos. Grandma and I want pictures of everyone before you leave. After all, it is your first Sadie Hawkins dance. The dance is a rite of passage. It ushers in November and the romance of the holidays." Her mom added another burst of spray. "I'm so glad you asked Paul; he's such a nice boy." Lucy rolled her eyes. Mom gave Lucy's hair another pat. "Don't forget the lip gloss, and put some makeup on. You're looking a little pale."

"Yeah, okay," she said, studying her reflection in the long mirror. The dress was a simple, sleeveless sheath with a flirty overskirt and a high, round neckline. The royal blue was a lovely contrast to her gray eyes and nut-brown hair, which she was going to flatten as soon as her mother left the room. Schuyler saw the gleam in Lucy's eyes and pinched back a snarky remark, glancing out the window instead.

"Jeannie!" Grandma Elliot called. "Paul is here—his mother just pulled into the driveway. Mathias is already waiting in the front parlor." Grandma appeared in the doorway, a nervous flutter to her smile, as though she were hiding something. Lucy eyed her suspiciously.

"Now hurry up," Mom said, hurrying toward the stairs. "Remember to walk carefully down the stairs. You don't want to twist your other ankle in those pumps. You're not used to wearing them."

"One shoe! I'm wearing one shoe! I can't get the other on my swollen foot. And thanks for the reminder that I'm a klutz," Lucy said. Her nose scrunched; she waggled her head as her mom hurried from the room. Grandma scurried down the main stairs after her.

"You know she's proud of you, right?" Schuyler bumped her aside and checked her own reflection in the mirror. Her dark blond curls were upswept on one side with a sparkly barrette, her bangs feathered over her forehead. Her dark green A-line dress was also sleeveless and fitted; it had a high collar and lace insert. The belt was tied in a bow above the pleated skirt. The color made her hazel-green eyes appear even greener tonight. Because the night was cool, she had added her mom's imitation fur cape.

"Yeah, I know. And I love her for it. Sometimes I get claustrophobic with her hovering. I think it's more about keeping me from making mistakes she may have made. But we're two very different people." She leaned close to the mirror and applied a pink lip gloss.

"What did your Sadie Hawkins proposal say? Did Mathias like it?" Lucy sat on the daybed and slipped her shoe on. It felt tight after sandals and sneakers. And it looked ridiculous with the plastic boot the doctor gave her to wear until the swelling went down. She tugged a comb through her hair, reducing the big-hair look, and added a sparkly headband.

"I know he likes my mom's pastries, so I got her to make some of her sweet, jam-filled pastries with icing. The message inside the box read, 'Jelly is sweet, but you're sweeter. Let's jelly and roll at Sadie's.'" Schuyler pinched her lips in an impish grin. "I know, it's kind of derpy, but he said yes." She held two thumbs up and made a silly face.

"Derpy is good. He needs a little affirmation like that after the horrible time he's had with the ghosts." She brushed her hands down her waist, smoothing the material as she took one last look in the mirror.

"What did you write to Paul?"

Lucy's head dipped as she waggled it. "It was lame. I gave him a meat lover's pizza. The extra cheese on top was shaped like a ghost with pepperoni eyes. I sketched a shield and sword on the box with the proposal, 'I'm hunting for a date to Sadie's. Please don't ghost me.' It's all I could think of. I nearly died of embarrassment when he busted out laughing. When he finally stopped, he grinned and said yes." She looked at Schuyler, a sly smile forming on her face, and bounced her eyebrows. "Then he hugged me right in front of Madison and her groupies. It was great!"

"Lucy, you're naughty. Freaking funny, but naughty," Schuyler said, giggling. "It was creative, girlfriend. You used something you both have in common and gave him food. Food never fails."

"You know, I wanted to go to the dance, but wouldn't it be awesome if we could just stay here instead? We could order food in and watch a movie."

"What did I get all dressed up for?" Schuyler pouted.

"Well, we could watch a musical so you and Mathias can dance. Fun, huh?" She added a light swipe of blush to her cheeks and stared at her reflection in the compact. "Bleh." She slipped the compact in the desk drawer and ran a brush through her hair. She moved unsteadily to the stairs. "C'mon. The guys are waiting."

The walking boot clunked on the steps as they made their way down to the second floor. By the time they reached the top of the last flight of stairs, Lucy's ankle was throbbing. She wished she could go to her room, ice her ankle, and forget about the dance. But Paul stood at the bottom of the stairs, grinning. *Holy cow, he's so cute*, Lucy thought. Dressed in black

slacks, a vest, and a white shirt, the ensemble made him seem older somehow. Beside him, Mathias was dressed in tan slacks and a sport coat. His
blue shirt was open at the collar.

"Breathe," Lucy said, with a sideways glance. Schuyler stared at
Mathias as though she hadn't seen him before, her jaw slowly dropping.
Lucy grinned. "Sheesh, girlfriend. You've got it bad. Better close your
mouth before you start drooling." Schuyler jabbed her in the ribs. "You
go on ahead. Mathias is waiting. My ankle is hurting. It will take me a few
minutes to manage these stairs." With a tremulous smile, Schuyler proceeded down the steps.

Paul saw Lucy struggling with the boot and hurried up the steps.
"Would this help you?" he said, offering his arm.

"Yeah, I think it might," Lucy said. She grinned and wrapped her arm
through his, giving it a squeeze. A smile dimpled his flushed cheeks.

Flashes bounced around the foyer as the parents' snapped pictures of
the couples. Mr. Sasson slapped Mathias on the shoulder with a grin. Mr.
Bill and Vivian chatted excitedly and applauded the couples. Mr. and Mrs.
Williams beamed with delight. Grandma Elliot proudly held two wrist cor-
sages with pale pink flowers and tiny pearl beads.

"I had an idea. Wait right here," Paul said. He disappeared into the
library and returned with a knee scooter. He rolled it over to Lucy. "I
thought it might be more comfortable than your crutch, and it keeps your
ankle raised. I hope you don't mind."

"You got this for me? It's wonderful," Lucy said. "I think this night just
went from great to amazing. Thank you, Paul." She leaned over and kissed
his cheek while he held the scooter. More flashes bounced around the
room. "This could be fun," she whispered. "You might have trouble catching me," she said, an impish gleam in her eyes. He grinned.

"Um, Mathias and I had another idea," he said sheepishly. "With your
injury and all, it just seemed kind of appropriate somehow."

"Well," Mathias said, "once we shared the idea, all the parents helped pull it together, and I think you're both going to like it."

"What is going on?" Lucy said. She and Schuyler glanced at each other, totally befuddled.

"We're not going to the school to dance," Mathias said, a twinkle in his eye.

"What? Why not?" Schuyler said, looking at him with disappointment.

"It might be best if we just showed you," Paul said. "Care to join me?" He offered his arm again to Lucy. She hesitantly took it, and he led her through the kitchen to the sunroom's slider doors and pulled the curtains back.

Across the yard and the driveway, lights blazed in the renovated stables, and twinkle lights lined the windows and doors. Lucy and Schuyler gasped. It was beautiful with a fairytale charm.

Lucy navigated the scooter across the yard with Paul's help. Music was playing inside. A homemade banner fluttered above the door. It read, "The Carriage House Bed-and-Breakfast proudly presents: the Sadie Hawkins dance."

Lucy was speechless, her gaze taking in all the details. Paul stood quietly with his hands tucked nervously into his pants pockets. Schuyler squealed and tugged Mathias through the vestibule.

"You and Mathias did all this? Why?" Lucy was dumbfounded yet overcome with delight. She'd had mixed feelings about going to the dance since the injury. Dancing with one foot and a crutch was going to be a disaster ripe for laughter and snide remarks. This was an awesome turn of events.

"Well, you have a bad sprain and a crutch. Schuyler is looking forward to dancing with Mathias. And, well, I don't know how to dance, and Mathias is up for just about anything these days. It's kind of the best of both worlds. We can talk without anyone overhearing us or any interference. Your mom and grandma really got into the planning. Your grandma, Mrs. McGoo, and Mrs. Williams had food duty. Mathias and I helped your mom, and Mr. Bill set up the tables and decorations." He ushered her through the vestibule into the large, open retail space. "I hope you like it."

Lucy gaped at the room. The retail space was transformed. The display shelves were moved to make way for a dance floor. Balloons and crepe paper with the school colors floated everywhere, and another Sadie Hawkins banner was stretched above the buffet table loaded with drinks, food, and snacks. There was a table full of old games in the back. A bean toss game sat in one corner. Hidden speakers around the room played music from Lucy's favorite playlist. Schuyler and Mathias were already swaying on the dance floor, oblivious to her and Paul.

The antique sofas and chairs were placed in small vignettes for quiet conversation around the room. The dimmed chandeliers added a soft glow to the room. It was magical. Lucy's eyes misted over.

"Paul, this night went from amazing to fantastic—I love it!" She grasped Paul's hand, her eyes alight with mischief. "Thank you. This is so unexpected . . . and so freaking awesome!" With a grin, she scooted onto the dance floor, whirled around, and waved. "C'mon. It's time to learn to dance!"

Lucy lay awake reliving the magical night: the awkward dancing, the food and snacks, and the laughter as they played nearly every one of the old family games. The vintage View-Master with a selection of reels had turned out to be everyone's favorite as they passed it around. They had laughed at the old photos of faraway places like the Great Sphinx in Egypt, or the skiers on wooden skis somewhere in the Alps. It was a magical evening, and, with the parents in charge, it had ended much too soon.

Moonlight flooded the room through the window, casting shadows along the carpet. Over on the day bed, Schuyler softly snuffled and murmured in her sleep. Lucy slipped her feet into her slippers, padded across the hall to the kitchenette, and took water from the small refrigerator.

Settling on the couch in the sitting room, she curled her legs under herself and snuggled into the knitted afghan, then uncapped the water.

Across the yard, the moonlight bathed the stables in silvery light, bright against the white paint and glowing like an ethereal phantom perched among the trees. The twinkle lights were off, and the stable was locked up. Soon the carriage would be gone, and Grandma Elliot and Mr. Bill and Vivian would move into the loft apartments. Dale would be home for the holidays. Things were changing, but they were good. It would be awesome to have her loved ones so close.

She took a swig of water. As she sipped, a small shadowy figure sauntered across the floor and jumped up on the couch at her feet. She flinched. *A cat? How did a cat get in the house?* The cat's movement was familiar. She looked at the little figure, and it looked back at her as she replaced the bottle cap.

"Hello, Lucy. Don't you remember me?" the cat said, a twinkle in its eye. He casually licked a paw, then swiped his ear.

Gobsmacked, the bottle hung frozen in her hand with the cap in midturn. She leaned forward, wide-eyed, to get a closer look at the little gray cat. *I must be sleepwalking, and this is a dream. Cats can't talk, and this one just said hello,* Lucy thought. "Wait—Metrocom?" Her gray eyes riveted on the animal. "Metrocom!" she whispered, unable to pull air into her lungs. The Spectrescope was in her room. She scrambled past the cat, hobbled to her room, and snatched the scope from the nightstand. Schuyler snuffled and sat up.

"What's going on?" Schuyler said, blinking awake and pushing the hair away from her face.

"Metrocom is back!" she said, rushing from the room.

"What?" Schuyler bolted from the bed and hurried to the sitting room.

The cat was on the couch where Lucy had left him. She scoped him as he calmly waited, his big green eyes watching her intently. The image in the Spectrescope was simply that of a cat.

Schuyler slid to a halt and gaped at the cat on the couch, utterly astounded.

"Spectrescope, is it really my Metrocom? It can't be—he died in the fire. Who is this?" she said, her eyes wide and unbelieving. The lens sparkled as an invisible hand wrote the words across the glass. *It's really him, Gatekeeper. Maybe you should ask him where he's been.* "Don't you know, Spectrescope?" she asked. The scope vibrated. It felt like the artifact was laughing. *I do know, but you should hear the story from him.* She shoved the Spectrescope into Schuyler's hands and reached for the little gray cat. He leaped into her arms, purring.

"Metrocom, my little buddy! Where have you—wait. What? I should ask him?" Lucy said, looking at Schuyler who, apparently, was equally gobsmacked. She stroked the velvety spot between his ears, and the cat leaned into the caress. "I don't understand, little buddy. Where have you been all this time? I've missed you so." She buried her face in the cat's fur, his purr vibrating against her cheeks.

"I have been to another realm. It's called Ascalon, and all the animals there can speak. They taught me so I can tell you something that you need to know."

"This is amazing!" She cuddled him close, rubbing her face against his fur. "You can talk. I can hardly believe it." She kissed the top of his head.

Beside her, Schuyler smiled and shook her head in amazement. She softly stroked his neck, but her smile faded as he turned serious eyes toward her.

"Lucy, I've missed you. And you, too, Schuyler. But I must tell you something. It's urgent."

"What is it? Metrocom, you're scaring me."

The cat leaned close, his green eyes vibrant.

"Darnathian has a foundation stone."

A Note from the Author

Woo-hoo! I am thrilled you joined me for this adventure of The Issachar Gatekeeper. I enjoyed creating the story for you and hope you will come back for more.

In the meantime, there's something I want you to know: you were created in God's image, and you are an eternal spirit with free will—the freedom to choose. You have received an inherent knowledge to help you determine right from wrong and good from evil. Where did this knowledge come from? God gave it to you.

The spiritual realm does exist. God, our heavenly Father, is a spirit. We must worship him in spirit and with truth. This means that you must first believe he exists, and you must be truthful with him and with yourself. There are evil spirits who want to influence your decisions, especially your belief in our heavenly Father.

Just like Lucy and the Defenders, and each of their loved ones, have received a promise, you have received a promise of eternal life. It is only when you accept Jesus as Savior that you receive the seal of protection by the Holy Ghost for eternal life.

Choose wisely, dear reader. I love you, and so does your heavenly Father. These books are for you.

Acknowledgments

They say it takes a village to raise a child. How much more the publishing of a book! At the beginning of this adventure, I had no clue where to start. God brought together the right people at the right time to accomplish such an endeavor.

So, to each of the following, I'd like to offer my sincerest and heartfelt thank-you for joining me. God bless each one of you!

To my husband, Dann Nixon—thank you, sweetheart, for your love, support, and encouragement, without which these stories would still live in my head and my heart. And thanks for doing the laundry! You are the man.

To Wendy Mersman—you are an amazing artist, friend, and webmaster. Thank you for your creativity with the book covers, for the fun website, and for your friendship. I can't imagine this journey without you, girlfriend.

To Andy Sheneman—you are a one-of-a-kind videographer! You take my rough ideas and scripts and put them together with just the right soundtrack and animations to produce a great book trailer. So fun and imaginative!

To Whitney Bak—you have taught me so much about editing. I love your ideas, your fun and witty comments, and your creative and wise suggestions. You are a delight. I pray the Lord will continue to bless you in all that he puts before you.

To AnnaLisa Buol—thank you for your honest and straightforward editing of the Ascalon Chronicles. I love your ingenuity and willingness to ferret out my mistakes and your boldness to show them to me and to keep my doctrine straight! You are a breath of fresh air.

To Dan Wright—publisher and expert in all things book, writer, and author. Thank you for your encouragement, direction, and willingness to follow through. I value your knowledge, your experience, and your friendship.

To all my family and friends who have been so encouraging as I continue this journey—thank you! I love you all.

And to Jesus. Without you, none of this would be possible. I love you, Lord!

Think on These Things

1. Orison (prayer) is our secret weapon.

Philippians 4:6–7: "Do not be anxious about anything, but in every situation, by prayer and petition, with thanksgiving, present your request to God. And the peace of God, which transcends all understanding, will guard your hearts and your minds in Christ Jesus."

2. It's okay to ask why.

Jeremiah 33:3: "Call to me and I will answer you and tell you great and unsearchable things you do not know."

3. All good things are found in God and Jesus, his Son.

Philippians 4:8: "Finally, brothers and sisters, whatever is true, whatever is noble, whatever is right, whatever is pure, whatever is lovely, whatever is admirable—if anything is excellent or praiseworthy—think about such things."

4. Our brains and brawn are not enough.

Zechariah 4:6: "He said to me, 'This is the word of the LORD to Zerubbabel: "Not by might nor by power, but by my Spirit," says the LORD Almighty.'"

Just One More Thing

Scriptural references used in this story:

- Psalm 107:13–16: "Then they cried to the LORD in their trouble, and he saved them from their distress. He brought them out of darkness, the utter darkness, and broke away their chains. Let them give thanks to the LORD for his unfailing love and his wonderful deeds for mankind, for he breaks down gates of bronze and cuts through bars of iron."
- Proverbs 28:20: "A faithful man shall abound with blessings" (KJV).
- Ephesians 5:26: "That he might sanctify and cleanse it with the washing of water by the word" (KJV).
- 1 John 4:10: "This is love: not that we loved God, but that he loved us."
- Job 23:10: "He knows the way that I take."
- Psalm 91:11: "He shall give His angels charge over you, to keep you in all your ways" (NKJV).
- Proverbs 7:4: "Say unto wisdom, Thou art my sister; and call understanding thy kinswoman" (KJV).

Cast of Characters

Main Characters:

Lucy Hornberger—gatekeeper, Bachar, the chosen, Sho-are

Schuyler (sky-ler) Williams—ghost hunter and Lucy's BFF

Paul Matthews—friend, student, ghost hunter

Mathias Sasson (sah-son)—haunted, student, B and B guest, friend

Support Characters:

Iam Reynard (High King of Ascalon)—vendor from the flea market whose name means fox, mentor, adopted grandpa

Ishi—son of the High King of Ascalon, friend, rescuer

Bill McGoo—guardian angel, janitor, Lucy's adopted family

Vivian McGoo—guardian angel, mentor, Lucy's adopted family

Mrs. Leona Elliot—Lucy's maternal grandma

Mr. and Mrs. Sasson—Carriage House B and B guests, parents to Mathias

Madison—mean girl, influenced by evil, bully

Haniel (Ha-knee-el)—beautiful dryad who guards the Life Tree, an arch-angel, protector

Pheman (Fay-man)—dancing faun who accompanies Haniel, name means "trustworthy," directs choirs

Herman the Recluse—man in a gilded cage, formerly a monk

Evil Entity Characters:

Darnathian—the Dark Prince, adversary of the High King

Grehssil—weasel-like servant of the Dark Prince

Merbas—shape-shifter who causes confusion, discouragement, and loneliness

Stolas—herbologist in the employ of the Dark Prince, a conjurer who makes tonics, medicines, salves, and potent elixirs

Berbatos—servant of the Dark Prince, a philosopher who can change a person's thoughts, declares secret counsels, deceives the innocent, whisperer who teaches thievery

Glossary of Terms

Affluence—the state of having wealth, money, and influence

AnaPiel Rod—a tall staff containing power and knowledge

Augur Sphere—a crystal globe made from the pure sands beneath the Crystal Lake in Ascalon

Bachar—someone chosen for a purpose

Belt of Truth—bejeweled belt that contains power in the stone; binds evil

Briathos—Paul's sword; means "punisher of daemons"

Crystalline mirror—revealer of secrets; acts as a portal when needed

Daemons—fallen angels who followed evil; servants of the Dark Prince

Disillusion—to cause someone to believe something is false; to create insecurity

Ghost—a spirit, specter, wraith, soul, or shadow; appears as a purple mist

Irredaemon—the most brutal of the fallen; servants of the Dark Prince

Murmidones (mur-mi-dons)—followers of the Dark Prince who blindly carry out his commands as daemons murmur in their ears

Orison—a prayer, quiet reflection, and petition to the High King

Ormarrs—the lowest level of the fallen angels

Ratha-nael—Lucy's spare sword; means "thwarter of daemons"

Rogziel—Mathias's sword; means "wrath of the King"

Spectacles—eyeglasses that reveal hidden evil and wield the power of the spoken word

Spectrescope—an artifact that reveals hidden ghosts, spirits, or specters

Spirit Sword—sword of the High King; also named Puriel, "fire of the King"

Sho-are—a gatekeeper

Zazriel—Schuyler's sword; name means "strength of the King"

Sneak Peek
The Ghost in the Mirror
Book Four of The Issachar Gatekeeper

Prologue

The great doors slammed shut behind the Defenders with an echoing thud. The message carved into the wood doors was disconcerting. AnaPiel had translated the riddle that allowed the doors to open. The message left them in doubt and more than a little chilled as they proceeded into the mountain tunnel.

The subterranean passage continued to carve its way through the rock, low hanging, oppressive, and confined. It caused Lucy to feel claustrophobic and a little irrational. She kept imagining the rock was moving; the passage growing longer the deeper they traveled into the mountain. Theirs had already been a three-day journey through the mountain, and it seemed they were no closer to finding the Issachar Gate.

Beside Lucy, Schuyler's lips were compressed, her face pale and drawn, making her look older than her fifteen years. Following her, Paul and

Mathias were quiet, each alone with their thoughts, their eyes clouded and brows pinched. Lucy knew they, too, were worried about the imminent event that could decide the fate of two spiritual realms. The uncertainty added a heaviness to their steps.

The spirit went before them, the brightness of her being illuminating the passage as she led their group. Her quiet countenance was comforting and aggravating at the same time. The spirit exuded confidence without fear, yet she answered Lucy's every question the same. *"Follow through."*

The Defenders trudged on. Even this far into the mountain, AnaPiel's reading of the strange riddle carved into the entrance doors hung heavy in Lucy's thoughts.

My heart is stirred by a noble theme

As I recite my verses for the King.

Within the rhyme a warning, a curse,

Heed not those who are perverse.

Walk not the path that benders tread,

Trust him instead who lifts your head.

Consider not to stand in their way

Nor sit with the mocker and join their play.

Look and see—the wise man dies.

His wealth and gain to another lies.

They perish together, the fool and dolt,

In endless forever, time without hope.

Fools rush and come to destruction.

But Life to receive? Heed my instruction.

When you are disturbed, do not bend.

Ponder it, and begin again.

Lucy couldn't make any sense of the riddle, but the ominous warning was clear. Follow the right way, and maybe they would make it through to the meadow before Darnathian could reach it. If he reached the Life Tree before them, it would be game over—he would eat the fruit and gain immortality. She couldn't let that happen.

The passage ended at another set of giant wooden doors. Lucy knew the drill by now; she placed her hand on the door and waited. Slowly, the doors glowed, light beams seeping from their edges. Then they swung open of their own accord, spilling light from beyond into the tunnel and blinding their vision.

"Your journey starts here," the beautiful spirit said, stepping through the portal. She swept her hand toward the valley.

They exited the dim passage and stepped onto a precipice, squinting and blinking in the bright light. Below them, a beautiful valley stretched as far as they could see. The clear blue sky caressed the rugged, white-capped mountains, and verdant forests and grasses carpeted the foothills in shades of brilliant green, beckoning them to come lie and rest awhile.

Every kind of flower filled the bowl of the valley. The flowers had such rich hues that even the purest ordinary color would appear dim in comparison. The radiant and luminescent petals swayed gracefully.

The entire scene was a painter's dream, but there was no discernible source of the light. It was everywhere, but there was no sun visible in the clear blue sky.

Lucy smiled and lowered her shield, lost in wonder at the breathtaking beauty of the landscape. Her smile slowly faded, replaced by dismay, and then her eyes widened. A hand gripped her arm. Schuyler saw it too.

The flowers of the field were smoking.

Tendrils of translucent vapor gently rose from the petals and hovered over the flowers, never accumulating and never diminishing; perpetually burning but never consumed.

"What is this place?" Lucy whispered, the horror hitching her breath.

Mathias was speechless.

Paul stood next to her, holding the AnaPiel Rod. AnaPiel gazed sadly at the flowers, his head slowly shaking.

"These, dear girl," AnaPiel said, "are all those who had such beautiful potential but hardened their hearts and denied the High King, though he loved them so very much. This, now, is their eternity."

"Welcome to the Wilderness of Sin," the spirit said.

About the Author

L. G. Nixon grew up hoping to one day become a writer, and after a long career in office management, she began writing. She also grew up in a creaky old house where relatives told of ghostly visitations. Her joy as a writer comes from being able to share the stories God lays on her heart. She creates her otherworldly realms in Michigan, where she lives with her husband, a high-energy boxer dog named Cali, and a tailless cat named Pan. She enjoys motorcycling and skiing, landscape painting, and hopes someday to finish her pilot's license. (She wants to fly the Space Shuttle, if they relaunch it, which means she might need that pilot's license!)

If you are enjoying The Issachar Gatekeeper series, drop her a note. She would love to hear from you!

Visit her website at: www.lgnixon.com